TO WIN A WIDOW

Soldiers & Soulmates
Book 5

Alexa Aston

ARE YOU SIGNED UP FOR DRAGONBLADE'S BLOG?

You'll get the latest news and information on exclusive giveaways, exclusive excerpts, coming releases, sales, free books, cover reveals and more.

Check out our complete list of authors, too!

No spam, no junk. That's a promise!

Sign Up Here

www.dragonbladepublishing.com

Dearest Reader;

Thank you for your support of a small press. At Dragonblade Publishing, we strive to bring you the highest quality Historical Romance from the some of the best authors in the business. Without your support, there is no 'us', so we sincerely hope you adore these stories and find some new favorite authors along the way.

Happy Reading!

CEO, Dragonblade Publishing

Additional Dragonblade books by Author Alexa Aston

King's Cousins Series
The Pawn
The Heir
The Bastard

Knights of Honor Series
Word of Honor
Marked by Honor
Code of Honor
Journey to Honor
Heart of Honor
Bold in Honor
Love and Honor
Gift of Honor
Path to Honor
Return to Honor

The St. Clairs Series
Devoted to the Duke
Midnight with the Marquess
Embracing the Earl
Defending the Duke
Suddenly a St. Clair

Soldiers & Soulmates Series
To Heal an Earl
To Tame a Rogue
To Trust a Duke
To Save a Love
To Win a Widow

The Lyon's Den Connected World
The Lyon's Lady Love

CHAPTER ONE

London—May 1795

R HYS ARMISTEAD MOUNTED the horse and turned it in the direction of Hyde Park, which was only a few blocks away from Viscount Mowbray's London townhouse. The horse happily cantered along until they reached Rotten Row, where all the lords and ladies of Polite Society preferred to ride. Of course, the likes of them had only gone to bed an hour or two ago since the Season was in full swing. He had been awakened from where he slept in the stable's loft when the viscount's carriage returned from the previous night's ball. Rhys had risen and gone straight to the kitchens, where Cook had placed out bread and cold meat for his breakfast, and then he began his daily round of exercising the various horses in his employer's stables.

If he were the viscount, he would sell most of the animals off, leaving only the carriage horses and a mount for Lady Rebecca to ride. Viscount Mowbray suffered from gout, which flared up from time to time. He had given up riding several years ago but still kept horses to ride both at his country estate and here in London. Rhys exercised and groomed the viscount's horses and had even taught Lady Rebecca to ride two years ago. The daughter of the household had fallen from a horse when she was only six, breaking her leg, and she had never attempted to ride after that. As Lady Rebecca approached the age of her come-out, though, her father had insisted that she take up the sport again since riding apparently was one of the ways gentlemen courted ladies of the *ton* during the London Season.

Rhys was currently fifteen but he was known for his patience with both horses and people. He had made a good rider of Lady Rebecca within a few short weeks and she now sat a horse comfortably. She had enjoyed several outings to Rotten Row with various suitors during the past month. Once she married, as she undoubtedly was expected to do once the Season concluded, Rhys didn't see the point of keeping any horseflesh beyond those which would transport the viscount around London or back to his country estate. That was the difference between him and the rich, though. He had a pragmatic nature and would never be wasteful, as he saw so often in regard to the viscount. All the rich acted entitled. The laws of England certainly gave them advantages far beyond what they deserved, in his opinion.

As he reached Rotten Row, he heard the chime of a distant clock ring five times. Dawn would break in the next handful of minutes. For now, the park was deserted. He gave the horse its head and let it charge at full speed down the path, reveling in the wind blowing through his hair, exhilaration filling him. He reined in the horse, turning it and letting it gallop again back along the direction they had come before he eased into a canter and returned the horse to its stall. A sleepy stable lad rubbed his eyes and then took the reins.

"You know what to do," he told the young boy before going to a different stall and retrieving the next horse.

Rhys worked his way through the five horses over the next two hours and then personally rubbed down the final one he'd returned to the stables. He had just finished grooming the mount and feeding it when a voice called out to him. Rhys turned and anxiety filled him when he saw it was a footman from the house. He did everything he could to do his job to the best of his ability and not call attention to himself. A house servant calling his name did not bode well.

"You're needed at the house," the footman said abruptly, his eyes sweeping over Rhys' appearance and obviously finding it lacking.

"What for?" he asked, dread saturating him.

He needed this job, one he had held for three years. His mother couldn't work anymore. She had a weak heart and depended upon Rhys to pay the small monthly rent on her room, as well as the food she ate. The same weak heart had killed his sister when she was only eight and Rhys ten. By then, he'd already been the man of the house for two years, his father having been killed in an accident at the shipyard where he worked.

"Dunno," the footman said, shrugging his shoulders. "They just said to fetch you fast. Come along."

"Let me at least wash my hands."

"Be quick about it. They don't like being kept waiting."

Rhys assumed the footman meant the viscount. But why was the nobleman out of bed at this hour, having only come home shortly before? If Mowbray was going to fire a lowly groomsman, would he do it at this hour?

They exited the stables and he went to the pump, priming it and then washing his hands. He pulled his lone, tattered handkerchief from his pocket and wet it, running it along his face and neck and wringing it out before jamming it back inside his pocket. He combed his fingers through his hair, hoping the thick, unruly mess now looked somewhat tamed and presentable.

"Get moving!" the footman ordered, lording over him as only a house servant might do when speaking to another servant in a lower position.

They entered the kitchens, which now bustled with activity. Rhys nodded to Cook, who always treated him with kindness, as he followed the footman. They left the kitchens and went through a long corridor and up a staircase. He wished they could slow down so he could take in the grand surroundings. He had never been inside the main house before and was overwhelmed by the thick carpeting and elegant furnishings.

On the first floor, they continued down a long hallway and then arrived at a closed door.

"Wait," the footman commanded before knocking and entering the room. A moment later, he stuck his head back out and hissed, "Come in."

With trepidation, Rhys entered the most magnificent room he had ever seen. He clinched his jaw, else it might hang open like a dog's. Though he longed to study the art on the walls and take in the fine furniture, he knew he had been summoned for a reason and couldn't tarry.

He spotted Viscount Mowbray sitting in a chair across the room, his gray hair askew. He had some kind of robe on which shimmered in the light. Rhys approached him and saw another man, fully dressed, sitting in a nearby chair. He had never seen this gentleman, who studied him with keen eyes as Rhys came forward and then stopped before them.

"This is the boy?" the stranger asked.

"Yes, yes," the viscount said. "Rhys Armistead. He's the one."

He wondered why he had been singled out. Why this man wanted to know who he was. Why he had been sent for. Yet he knew it wasn't the place of a lowly groomsman to ask any questions. He was here to answer them, whatever they might be.

The man cleared his throat. "I am Mr. Goolsby, solicitor for the Earl of Sheffington. Have you heard of him?"

"No, Sir. Why would I have?"

Distaste crossed the man's face and Rhys realized he shouldn't have asked a question. He reminded himself to only answer what was asked of him so he could hopefully return to the stables and never be troubled again.

"The Earl of Sheffington is a very rich, powerful man," the solicitor said. "His country seat is in Surrey, several miles west of Addlestone."

He neither knew where Surrey was nor this Addlestone, which he assumed was a town. His education had only lasted for two years, where he had learned to read and write and do sums. Geography hadn't been a part of his lessons. He nodded but kept silent.

The solicitor's mouth tightened. "It has come to light that your mother is a distant cousin of the Earl of Sheffington. Which means you, as well, are very distantly related to his lordship."

This was certainly news to him. He knew his mother spoke very well and had a beautiful hand when it came to writing but he couldn't picture her as a part of the nobility.

"The chain of relations is complicated and too long to get into now," Mr. Goolsby continued. "Suffice it to say that you are related, however. Because of that, the earl wishes you to come to Sheffield Park."

"As a groom?"

Goolsby harrumphed. "No, lad. *Not* as a groom."

"Then what?" he challenged, disregarding his previous promise to himself to keep quiet. "I have a good job with Viscount Mowbray. I know horses well and love what I do. Why should I leave the viscount's employ?"

"Because Viscount Raleigh isn't in the best of health."

Now, Rhys was totally confused. "Who is this viscount? What does he have to do with me?"

His employer stood. "I am weary, Goolsby. See to things. I am off to bed." He glanced to Rhys. "Good luck to you, boy. You did well teaching my Rebecca to ride. I didn't think anyone would ever be able to get her back on a horse again. You did and she now enjoys riding tremendously."

The viscount trudged from the room, making it obvious his gout was paining him.

After he left, Goolsby said, "Sit."

Rhys glanced at the fine material on the chair and said, "I would rather stand, Sir," knowing the dirt and sweat from his clothes would ruin the chair's fabric.

"Very well. I will be as succinct and clear as possible since you obviously are not grasping the situation. Your mother is related to the Earl of Sheffington. The earl's son, Viscount Raleigh, is his only child and has been prone to be a sickly boy. No more children will be forthcoming in the marriage. The countess cannot have anymore. Because of that, the earl is looking to the future. He does not want to leave the estate in a precarious position nor does he wish to do harm to his tenants. If Viscount Raleigh does not live to adulthood and cannot succeed his father, *you* would become the heir apparent."

He stood there numbly, trying to take in the solicitor's words. "Are you telling me that I could one day become . . . an earl?"

The solicitor sniffed. "Yes, it is a possibility. Of course, the earl hopes that his son's unstable health will not be an issue. His lordship hopes as Viscount Raleigh matures, he will grow stronger."

"How old is the viscount?"

"Sixteen" Goolsby responded. "He is being tutored at home since his last bout of illness. You will share in that tutor."

"I . . . I will what?"

"You are to accompany me to Sheffield Park, Mr. Armistead. The earl was most insistent. In the event his son passes prematurely, Lord Sheffington needs you to be prepared to one day take on the earldom. You will be clothed. Educated, though not sent away to school. Your mother said you only had two years of schooling."

Surprise filled him. "You've spoken to my mother?"

"Yes. She was most agreeable. The earl doesn't believe a university education will be necessary. Instead, in three years' time, once you have reached your eighteenth birthday, Lord Sheffington will purchase a commission for you and you may enter the army. That way, you will earn an honorable living."

Rhys knew commissions in the army were costly. It would allow him to become an officer, something that he never would have imagined possible.

"In the event Viscount Raleigh does succeed to the earldom and becomes Lord Sheffington, his sons would naturally take precedence over your claim to the title," Mr. Goolsby said. "That is what the earl hopes for but he wants to be prepared just in case." The solicitor smiled brightly. "So, you will receive an education and become an officer in His Majesty's Army. You will continue with your career in the military unless the unfortunate happens and Viscount Raleigh meets with an untimely death before he can provide an heir himself."

Rhys' head reeled with the quick turn of events. "When am I to come to Sheffield Park?" he asked.

"Immediately. Lord Sheffington expects me to bring you back from London with me. First, we will stop at a tailor's shop, however, and see that you are suitable clothed for your new role in society, Mr. Armistead."

No one had ever addressed him in such a manner. He had been Rhys or Armistead. Suddenly, the magnitude of what was happening swept over him.

"Are you certain no mistake has been made?" he asked, thinking it must all be a dream.

Goolsby shook his head. "Every effort was made to find a male relative closer than you. You were all our investigations turned up," the solicitor revealed, his disdain obvious.

"What of my mother? Can she also come to live at Sheffield Park?"

Goolsby frowned. "Mr. Armistead, you are in no position to bargain. However, Lord Sheffington knows you have been sending money to her and she will be provided for. Do you understand?"

Rhys did. But it didn't mean that one day—*if* he became Lord Sheffington—that he couldn't bring his mother to the estate. For now, though, he would count his blessings. He would receive an education and be allowed to gain a profession. Even if he never became the earl, he would be an officer and be able to always provide for his mother.

"I understand perfectly well, Mr. Goolsby." Rhys smiled. "When do we leave?"

CHAPTER TWO

London—May 1798

D ALINDA BRETTON GAZED out the window, wondering if she would ever be allowed to leave her bedchamber. She had been forced to remain within it the past two weeks, all because of her role in *The Debacle*. Just thinking of that made her throat grow thick with unshed tears. She thought she had cried herself out, knowing Anna had been banished to the country and Dez sent away to the army. The two people she loved most were gone. Out of her life. And Dalinda had no idea when she might see either of them again.

She hated her father. Hated him. He had never liked her or Dez.

Probably because they had killed her mother.

No, she couldn't think like that. Women died in childbirth all the time. She couldn't help that her mother had given birth to twins and it had been too much for her. Of course, Ham had also blamed her and Dez for Mama's death. He was five years older than she and Dez and the biggest bully she knew. Ham had called the twins murderers for doing in their mother. As they grew up, Ham had played tricks on them. Mistreated them. Blamed them for things he did. Taunted them that he would be the earl one day and they would be no ones. Ham had said when their father died and he became the Earl of Torrington that he wouldn't even speak to her or Dez.

That would actually be a relief.

A bird landed on the windowsill and Dalinda held her breath, not moving so that it would remain in place. The bird pecked on the windowsill a few times and then warbled before flying away.

This was the most interesting thing that had happened to her in her two weeks of incarceration. She should be out enjoying herself. It was her first Season and in the month she had attended events, Dalinda had proven quite popular. A bevy of gentlemen had called upon her each afternoon. They vied to dance with her. Take her on carriage rides. Escort her through gardens and into supper.

Now, though, she languished in her bedchamber, wondering if she would ever be let out. She had nothing to read. Nothing to do. It was a wonder she hadn't gone mad.

At least she was still in London, though. Poor Anna had been sent back to Surrey, her brief Season coming to an abrupt end. Dalinda missed her best friend terribly. Anna was the closest thing Dalinda had to a sister. They had been friends throughout their entire childhood, thanks to the fact they lived on adjoining estates, and had eagerly looked forward to their first London Season. Dalinda had known, though, that her twin harbored feelings for Anna. She had come across them too many times in the last couple of years where they both wore guilty expressions, looking as if they'd just sprung apart. When she did catch them kissing last Christmas, she had eased from the room, not confronting either of them.

Dalinda thought Dez and Anna were perfect together but knew their fathers had other plans for the pair. When Anna's father had proclaimed his daughter was to wed a man old enough to be her grandfather, Dalinda knew she had to act. She had suggested to Dez and Anna that they elope to Gretna Green and the couple had eagerly taken her suggestion to heart. Unfortunately, someone betrayed them. Anna was sent home in disgrace without finishing her Season. Dalinda's father was going to choose a husband for her because of her meddling. And Dez, who was supposed to go to university in a few months before entering the army, had his education cut short. Their father had purchased his younger son's commission and now Dez, too, was gone.

"Your father is allowing you to attend tonight's ball at the Duke of Gilford's."

Dalinda whipped around and saw Aunt Mathilda had entered the room.

"What? I may?" she asked eagerly.

"Yes. I am to help you dress for the occasion."

She hadn't even known her aunt existed until a week ago. Aunt Mathilda had come to Dalinda's bedchamber and informed her of their relationship and that she would be taking her in hand in light of *The Debacle*. Dalinda had been too frightened to ask why she had never heard of this aunt, who revealed she was the sister of Torrington. Mathilda had visited her each day for a few, brief minutes but had revealed nothing else of her background.

"I think this gown will do nicely."

Dalinda didn't care if she wore a flour sack to the ball. She was itching to leave this room and the townhouse. Ready to be back with people. Hopefully, to find a gentleman who would suit her and offer for her. Only then could she escape this horrible house and her even more horrible father.

Her aunt helped her shed her current gown and undergarments and put on fresh ones for the ball. She tightened Dalinda's stays until she could hardly breathe but she wasn't going to complain and put a possible end to her newly-won freedom.

"Sit at your dressing table," her aunt instructed. "I will do your hair."

She hadn't bothered with her hair during her exile, merely combing and braiding her hair each day. Her aunt undid the single braid and brushed Dalinda's rich, brown hair until it gleamed. Then Mathilda began creating an elaborate hairstyle, better than Dalinda's own traitorous lady's maid had ever managed.

"Oh, I look quite pretty!" she exclaimed. "Thank you, Aunt Mathilda." Dalinda rose and embraced the woman, who stiffened at the show of affection.

"Before you leave, I must tell you something," her aunt declared, her expression grim. "I want you to be prepared."

She didn't like her aunt's ominous tone. "What's wrong?"

"Your father will announce your betrothal at tonight's ball."

"What?"

Immediately, she ran through a list of eligible gentlemen who might have offered for her during her absence from *ton* events. She had thought two or three of her suitors had potential and was delighted that hopefully one of them had spoken with her father. That must be why she was being released from her makeshift prison.

"Who, Aunt?" she pressed, naming a few names.

"None of them," Mathilda responded.

Her brows knitted together. "Then which gentleman could it be? I can't think of anyone else that has shown an interest in me this Season."

A dour expression crossed the older woman's face. "It is a choice your father has made for you, Child."

Dalinda's stomach tightened. "Who?" she insisted. "Who will he bind me to?"

Aunt Mathilda's mouth tightened. "I have sworn I would not say. However, I didn't want what was done to me repeated with you. I was unpleasantly taken by surprise when my betrothal was announced by my father in front of a ballroom full of guests." She grimaced. "Not a man of my choosing. I didn't handle it well and wanted you to be forewarned so you won't embarrass yourself as I did."

For a moment, Dalinda forgot about her own upcoming betrothal, thanks to the hurt she saw on her aunt's face.

Taking Mathilda's hands, she asked, "Was it so very awful?"

"It was worse than death." Her aunt swallowed. "He had debts.

Terrible ones. My dowry was quite large." She sighed. "Of course, I was not the first girl sold into marriage. My dowry covered his debts and I gained a fine title and my family those all-important connections. Unfortunately, my husband was a gambler. Before a year of marriage had passed, he was back in the mire, even worse than before. He sold off his unentailed estates. Then horses. Paintings. Furniture. All the while drinking himself to death."

She squeezed her aunt's hands. "That must have been awful for you."

"It was," Mathilda admitted. "He only touched me a few times. Though I longed for a child, I quickly understood one would not be forthcoming. And when he died, swamped in debt, I was cast aside. The new marquess couldn't even afford to keep the country estates open. Even today, he lives in a few rooms in London and subsists off the small income of his tenant farmers."

"Where were you all these years, Aunt?" Dalinda asked.

"I lived in a small cottage on the primary country estate. My father passed less than a year after my marriage, one which he thought would bring the Bretton family more prestige. My brother—your father—was so embarrassed by the turn of events that he refused to take me in, even as a poor relation. It was only after your brother's failed elopement that Torrington sent for me."

Mathilda's mouth turned down. "I am supposed to keep a careful watch over you. Curb your wild ways. Make sure you do nothing else reckless until you are safely wedded and gone from this household." She released Dalinda's hands. "I only want you to prepare yourself, Child. Tonight, your betrothal will be announced. You must accept your fate."

"Why? From what you are saying, I fear I will be charged with marrying a man I will despise."

Her aunt pulled away and began pacing the room. "I have told you all that I can, Dalinda. I did so not to have you try and prevent the outcome but to merely make you aware so you would not be taken by surprise in front of a ballroom full of Polite Society." She came to a halt. "Accept your fate, my dear girl. It's the only thing you can do."

With that, Mathilda left the room.

A sick feeling rose inside Dalinda. She was being married off so her father wouldn't have to worry about handling her anymore. Most likely, Ham was the one pushing for this decision. She hated that her father had turned his back on Mathilda when she was in such great need of family and comfort but it didn't surprise her. The Bretton men—Dez being the exception—seemed to be coldhearted and unfeeling.

How could she escape what her father had planned for her?

A knock sounded at the door. She answered it, finding her older brother standing in the corridor.

"Father says you are to come downstairs. We're leaving for the Gilford ball," he informed her, a look of glee upon his face.

"Are you the one who persuaded Father to keep me in my room so long, Ham?"

"Don't call me by that childish nickname," he said angrily. "My name is Hamilton."

"I will bloody well call you whatever I wish," she told him.

His eyes narrowed. "It's a good thing you will be gone soon." With that, he turned and strode away.

Dalinda slipped a shawl about her shoulders and retrieved her reticule before going downstairs. Her aunt was nowhere in sight. She didn't think Mathilda would be going to the ball. Polite Society—and her own family—had turned away from her long ago.

Her father awaited her in the foyer, his mouth set in grim determination.

"There you are. Come along," he ordered, quickly spinning away and going through the front door.

She followed the earl and Ham out to the carriage. A footman assisted her inside the vehicle and she sat opposite the two men. She didn't mention that she knew what would occur tonight. Until her father made the betrothal announcement, Dalinda would keep thinking on how to escape her fate.

Just before they arrived, the earl said, "I wish for you to dance with someone tonight. The Earl of Smothe."

Suppressing the shudder that ran through her, she asked, "Why?"

Her father played his cards close to the vest, however. "Do not question me. Ever. Dance the first number with Smothe."

"Yes, Father," Dalinda said meekly, wishing she could tear his eyes out.

The Earl of Smothe was at least sixty. Probably older. He was bald. Fat. Disagreeable. He would be the last person she would ever choose to wed.

Except she didn't have a choice. Women rarely did. Especially ones such as herself, who had done something the men in her family deemed terrible. Now, Dalinda was being punished for helping Dez and Anna, who were madly in love. She had only wanted to see the two people she cared for the most find lasting happiness. Now, all three of them were penalized. At least Dez wasn't being made to marry some old hag. Of course, being parted from Anna would seem like death to her twin. Dalinda assumed when Anna wed, it would also be to an older man, one who would be thought to be able to control her.

Well, she wasn't having any of it.

She went through the receiving line with her father and Ham. The Duke of Gilford and his son, the Marquess of Medford, welcomed them. The marquess looked to be close to her age. Both he and the duke had brown hair and brown eyes that looked like melted pools of chocolate. She heard Ham ask the marquess about school and the young man said that he would be off to university the next term. Once more, Dalinda thought men got to do all of the fun things in life. Go off to school and university and then a Grand Tour. Sow their wild oats. They were able to get out in the world and learn not only about it but who they were before they ever had to settle down. Meanwhile, women tried to look pretty and attract the right husband. It was wildly unfair.

Entering the ballroom, she accepted the programme from a footman, remembering her first dance was to be reserved for the Earl of Smothe. As if he had heard his name called, he suddenly appeared by her side.

"Ah, my dear Lady Dalinda, it is so good to see you. Your father said you have been rather ill."

So that was the story going around. Heaven forbid that the *ton* learn that she tried to help Dez and Anna elope and got caught up in the crossfire. Her father was always so concerned about the family name and wouldn't want it tainted by the knowledge that his young son had tried to run off to Gretna Green with his neighbor's eighteen-year-old daughter. Just look at how Torrington had abandoned his own sister for years. Until he needed Mathilda. Dalinda wondered if once her father washed his hands of his daughter he would do the same to his sister.

"Yes, my lord," she said, not wanting to bother with conversation.

The earl's eyes gleamed. "Well, I must say that you are looking better than ever." Then he licked his lips and she thought she might be ill.

"Would you do me the honor of dancing the opening number with me?"

"Yes," she responded succinctly and he signed his name to her card.

"Very well," he said, a satisfied smile crossing his face. "I will see you shortly."

As he turned to walk away, Dalinda was suddenly swarmed by a good number of bachelors, all vying for her attention and begging for a dance. She turned her dance card over to them, bile rising in her throat at the prospect of not being allowed to wed someone of her own choosing and close to her own age.

The musicians began tuning their instruments and Lord Smothe appeared again. He placed her hand on his sleeve and led her onto the dance floor. Her flesh crawled at his touch. They danced what had to be the longest Scottish reel imaginable. By the end, he was huffing loudly and his face was so red that she doubted he would last the evening. She didn't want to wish death upon anyone. But if the earl died, it would be ever so convenient for her.

"Your father wishes us to have supper with him," Smothe told her as he led her from the floor.

"I have already promised the supper dance to another," she said. "It is understood that I should dine with my partner."

The old man grabbed the dance card attached to her wrist with a ribbon and frowned. "Hmm. You'll simply have to tell him you are otherwise engaged." He chortled, amused by his play on words, thinking her unaware of the situation.

Lord Smothe captured her hand and kissed it, almost causing her to gag. "Until later, my lady."

Dalinda couldn't stand being in the ballroom anymore. The press of people. The swirl of colors. The heat from too many being in too small a space. She had to escape.

Turning, she fled the ballroom. She thought to go to the retiring room but couldn't bear the thought of being asked about her recent illness and recovery. Or where Anna might be. Everyone knew the two of them to be inseparable.

Instead, she rushed down the hall until she couldn't hear music anymore. She paused in front of a door and decided to go inside. She needed time alone to think.

Hurrying into the room, she closed the door behind her. A cheery fire burned in the grate at the far corner of the room. Moving toward it, Dalinda held out her hands, trying to warm herself from the cold dread which filled her.

"I won't do it," she said stubbornly. "I won't let him ruin my life."

Then the tears came, tears which had threatened to flow ever since Aunt Mathilda revealed what tonight held in store. Dropping to her knees, Dalinda wept copiously, her sobs racking her body.

"It's so bloody unfair," she said aloud.

A hand appeared before her face, holding a handkerchief. Though startled, she grabbed at it, mopping her eyes.

"Thank you," she murmured, afraid to look up and see who had caught her at such a weak moment.

"You are most welcome," a deep voice said.

Dalinda shot to her feet.

Standing beside her was the Duke of Gilford.

CHAPTER THREE

"**Y**OUR GRACE? I am so very sorry," she apologized. "I shouldn't be here."

"I know," the duke said, a twinkle in his eyes. "You should be dancing, Lady Dalinda."

"You . . . you know my name?"

He frowned. "Were we not introduced earlier this evening? Why, it couldn't have been an hour ago that you went through my receiving line."

"Yes, but . . . you're a duke," she sputtered.

"I am," he agreed pleasantly. "One who happens to possess an excellent memory for both names and faces and linking the two together." He tilted his head, studying her a moment. "I fear you are all out of sorts. Come, let us sit and you can tell me your troubles."

Dalinda wanted to protest but you simply didn't say no to a duke. Especially when he was the host of the event you attended and you held his handkerchief in your hand. She followed him to the settee and perched upon it, wiping her eyes again and then clutching the handkerchief in her lap, glad she had something to cling to in order to help still her hands.

"Now, I know you are making your come-out this Season. I learned that from the receiving line. Is it some young rake who has upset you in my household? If he has, I will box his ears for you."

She smiled at his sweet declaration. "No, Your Grace. Nothing like that."

"Then why is a beautiful young woman wearing a delightful gown so utterly sad? Sad enough to leave the ball and retreat to my library?"

She hiccupped. "Well, the library must have some appeal if you also have left your own ball," she said, hesitant to reveal why this powerful man had found her in tears.

He nodded knowingly, as if he knew she were reluctant to speak about her troubles and wished to put her more at ease.

"My wife and I used to host a ball every Season. It was my favorite night of the year, seeing my duchess in her finery, sparkling like no other woman present."

Dalinda hadn't met the duchess this evening and asked, "Is she no longer with us, Your Grace?"

A shadow crossed his face. "No. She passed away many years ago. When our boy, Reid, was but four years of age."

She remembered meeting the marquess and, for a moment, was sad that he had only been a little boy when his mother died. She supposed getting to spend a few years knowing his mother and then losing her hurt even more than her situation, where she had never known her mother at all.

"It sounds as if you were a love match," she ventured.

A smile lit his face. "Ah, we were, my lady. That we were."

He gazed off and she knew he was lost in happier times. Finally, his gaze returned to her.

"I continued hosting this ball to help keep my darling's memory alive. It has been more than a dozen years since she's been gone but I still miss her each day."

Dalinda smiled. "I would say you were lucky to have her for as long as you did and know love between you. You also have a beautiful reminder of your wife in your son," she added.

He nodded. "You're right, of course. But though the ball is in her memory, it makes me realize that she is never coming back. I watch the dancers. The women's skirts swishing. I hear the laughter. The music. And it only forces me to remember that she is gone." Shrugging, he said, "I find I leave my own event each year earlier and earlier. I retreat to the library and think upon happier times before I join my guests again at supper."

Pity filled her, seeing how the duke had loved his wife so.

"I am sorry to have interrupted your time to be alone and reflect on happier days, Your Grace. I will be going."

Dalinda started to rise but he stopped her. "No. Stay. Help me take my mind off my own troubles. Hopefully, you will share yours with me—and we will both feel better."

"I don't see that happening, Your Grace," she said frankly. "I find myself in the shoes that other women have. My father has chosen my husband for me."

"Has he?" the duke asked. "I am sure you have had a bevy of gentlemen calling upon you ever since the Season began, Lady Dalinda. Perhaps your father taking matters into hand will—"

"I was not hoping for a love match, as you had, Your Grace. I merely wanted to find a kind man who would provide me with children. And yes, I have had a good many young men show interest in me. However, my father wishes me to be tamed. He thinks my nature is reckless because I tried to help my brother and my best friend elope to Gretna Green."

She bit her lip, worried that she had shared too much, but the duke looked on with interest.

"Did they wed? And are they happy?"

"No. Father caught up to them, thanks to my traitorous maid. Poor Anna was banished to the country. Dez was hustled into the army and will miss out on going to university. As for me? I am to be managed by an older man who will bring me to heel."

His brows knit together. "Do you know the man Lord Torrington has chosen for you?"

She sighed. "I learned his identity tonight. And he is ancient."

The duke chuckled. "You might consider me ancient, my lady. I must be a good three decades older than you."

"Oh, no, Your Grace. You don't seem old at all. And you are quite kind and very nice to converse with." She paused. "Father will announce my engagement tonight to Lord Smothe."

Shock filled Gilford's face as he visibly shuddered. "No wonder you are in despair, my lady."

"I came here to collect my thoughts and try to find a solution to my problems," she said. "I am not a Catholic so becoming a nun is out of the question. I could run away but I have nowhere to go and no money to live upon." She paused. "I suppose I could become a governess or companion but I think I would be dreadful at either of those things."

He fell silent, as if lost in his own world.

Dalinda had imposed upon him enough and she quietly stood in order to leave the room. As she passed the duke, he caught her wrist, halting her movement.

"Your Grace?" she asked, uncertainty filling her.

"There is another option," he said quietly, his gaze penetrating her. "You could marry me."

"What?"

"You heard me. Marry *me*, Lady Dalinda."

Her legs wobbled, feeling as if they would give out. Gilford rose and placed his hands on her shoulders to steady her.

"Why would you wish to wed me, Your Grace?" she asked. "You have been a widower for many years."

"For my sister," he revealed. "Decades ago, our father forced her to wed a much older man. She was frightened of him. She begged not to have to go through with the ceremony. Father insisted she do so, claiming it was a good match." His face darkened. "She spent the next ten years in a living Hell before she escaped into death.

22

"One of her own making."

"She . . . died by her own hand?"

The duke nodded. "She used laudanum to dull the pain of her existence. The doctor told us that she had accidentally indulged in too much but I knew better. We had been close growing up and I knew the way she thought. She dropped enough hints to me so that I knew her actions had been deliberate."

Gilford squeezed her shoulders lightly. "I would not want to see you that unhappy, my lady." He paused. "I am free to wed. I cannot promise you love because my heart will forever belong to my beloved wife. I will, however, give you freedom from your father and this horrid match with Lord Smothe. A duchess is a powerful person among the *ton*. You could pursue your own interests and never be stifled."

Dalinda's heart pounded within her chest. "Would . . . this be . . . I mean . . . I know you are offering a marriage of convenience but . . ." Her voice faded. She swallowed, drawing on the courage within her and said, "Would it be a marriage in name only?"

"Is that what you would wish for?"

"No," she said quickly. "I told you of my desire to have children."

The duke smiled. "Then I will do my best to give you a few." He searched her face as if looking for her answer. "The choice is yours, my lady."

Hope sprang within her. She wouldn't be forced to wed and lie with the ancient Lord Smothe. She could wed this kind, generous man, a man who offered her a way out of the cage her father wished to place her inside.

She smiled, feeling warmth radiating within her. "I choose you, Your Grace."

"You are certain? I am old."

Grinning, she replied, "Not nearly as old as Old Smothe."

"I suppose not. My forty-eight years seem young compared to Smothe."

Dalinda giggled. "I will become a stepmamma."

The duke chuckled. "Reid doesn't need any mothering."

"Will he resent me taking his mother's place?"

Gilford's hand cupped her cheek. "I wouldn't worry about that, my lady. Reid is off to university soon and then has grand ideas of serving in His Majesty's Army."

"But he's a marquess," she protested. "He will be the future Duke of Gilford."

"I know. But the boy has a mind of his own. He will do as he wishes—and I will do the same by taking a new wife." His thumb stroked her cheek. "Though I cannot give you my love, I will treat you with the utmost respect. I will care for you and our children."

Tears filled her eyes. "That will be more than enough, Your Grace."

He released her. "Very well. I feel good about this decision. I hope you do, as well, Lady Dalinda. Stay here. I will return shortly."

She frowned. "Where are you going?"

"You'll see."

The duke left the room and Dalinda returned to the settee, his wrinkled handkerchief still in her hands. She smoothed it upon her lap, a bit dazed by the turn of events. She had come into this room filled with despondency, seeing no way out of her abysmal situation. Then, within a matter of minutes, the trajectory of her life had changed, taking her in a direction she would never have dreamed of going.

With a duke.

And she would be his duchess.

Dalinda understood how much Gilford had loved his wife. She knew she would never be a replacement for the first duchess. She would always remind herself of her husband's goodness and never wish for more. If he could give her children, she would be happy enough. She thought the life they would build together could be a good one. She hoped he wouldn't regret his hasty decision to offer marriage to her. Despite what he said, Dalinda knew the marquess might prove a bit hard to win over. Fortunately, Medford would be leaving for university in a few months. It saddened her that her new stepson would get a university education while that very thing had been denied to her brother.

The door opened and the duke entered, ushering in another man. Surprise filled her when she realized he had her father in tow.

The earl spied her, his brows knitting together. He asked, "What's this, Gilford? You said we needed to speak privately. What is my daughter doing here?"

"I have decided to take a wife again," the duke said. "I find I am rather lonely. Lady Dalinda is the catch of the Season. I want her—and I always get what I want. Always," he emphasized.

Her father's perplexed expression almost made Dalinda laugh aloud. Though he would never admit it, Lord Torrington was a bit afraid of those titled gentlemen that outranked him. As a duke, Gilford was one of the most powerful peers in the land.

When her father remained speechless, the duke pressed him. "I assume you will agree to the marriage, my lord."

"Agree? Yes, of course, Your Grace," the earl obsequiously replied. "I can think of no better man than you to wed my only daughter."

Gilford's eyes cut to her and she saw they were filled with mirth. She believed the duke was trying to refrain from asking if he were a better choice for her than Lord Smothe. He opened his mouth, a wicked glint in his eyes, and she shook her head furiously, hoping he would keep from doing so. He nodded deferentially to her and Dalinda now believed they were fully comrades-in-arms.

"Very well, Torrington. I will announce my betrothal to Lady Dalinda at supper this evening." He glanced to her. "You will dance the supper dance with me, my lady?"

"Of course, Your Grace," she said demurely.

"Then it's settled. I will call upon you tomorrow at ten, Torrington, along with my solicitor. We will finalize the contracts then."

"Yes, Your Grace," the earl said meekly. He glanced at her but she only had eyes for her soon-to-be fiancé.

"Shall we return to the ballroom, my lady?" the duke asked, offering her his arm.

"Certainly, Your Grace."

They left the library, her father trailing after them, and went to the ballroom. The duke had her stand by his side. She knew she was missing all the dances that had been claimed but no one approached them. It was as if they stood in a world of their own making, surveying their kingdom as they watched the dancers before them.

When the supper dance arrived, Gilford escorted her to the center of the room. He was a marvelous dancer, the best she had partnered with all Season. Dalinda gave herself over to the joy of the dance as he swept her gracefully around the ballroom.

The dance ended and he led her into supper, whispering something into a footman's ear. When the room had filled, he called for everyone's attention. She heard the buzzing and knew it was because she was on his arm and had remained there for some time. By now, footmen appeared with trays carrying champagne and she realized how quickly the duke's orders had been carried out.

"I would ask that my guests raise a glass tonight as we toast my betrothal to Lady Dalinda Bretton, daughter of the Earl of Torrington."

She felt the intense gaze of every eye in the room on her at the duke's announcement. A multitude of emotions swirled within her. Astonishment. Relief. Excitement.

The Duke of Gilford raised his glass and everyone in the room followed suit.

"To my fiancée, Lady Dalinda."

"Lady Dalinda," the guests echoed and drank.

Her betrothed looked down upon her. "Are you happy, my lady?"

"This may be the happiest moment of my life," she exclaimed.

"It gets better," he promised. "When you hold our first child in your arms. You'll see."

CHAPTER FOUR

Portugal—December 1810

"GOOD MORNING, COLONEL Armistead," the soldier said. "You may go in." He held open the flap of the tent for Rhys to enter.

Rhys was still getting used to being addressed as a colonel. The unexpected promotion had caught him by surprise but he was proud of the reputation he had built and grateful for the recognition. Selfishly, he knew it would mean writing fewer letters home to the families of his dead soldiers. That task mostly fell to officers of a lower rank. It had proven harder to do that than anything else the war demanded of him.

He glanced around as he joined the other officers gathered around a large rectangular table where a map was spread out. Every man present was capable, loyal, and had England's best interests at heart. The fact that he, a once-lowly groom in a viscount's stables, now stood among their midst was not lost on him. Each officer here had noble bloodlines and had been educated at the best schools. He was humbled to be among them and yet proud of the heights he had risen to in the last dozen years of military service.

As usual when colder weather occurred, a lull occurred in the fighting on the Peninsula. This assembled group would be talking of plans for the spring. The commander in charge called them to order.

"We are reaping the benefits of Wellington's far-reaching preparations," General Shepherd began. "Thanks to the Lines of Torres Vedras, the forts and other military defenses built to protect Lisbon have proven valuable beyond measure, stopping Marshal Masséna's recent offensive campaign."

Rhys had a grudging admiration for the French military commander. André Masséna, while one of the original eighteen Marshals of the Empire created by Bonaparte, had not been trained at the finest military academies as his fellow marshals had. Instead, he had soared to greatness without any formal education, rising from humble origins to become the man Bonaparte deemed the greatest name in the Little General's military empire. Though French, Rhys thought he and Masséna had more in common than Rhys did with the men gathered inside this tent.

"Marshal Masséna's last attempt to re-take Portugal three months ago failed, as you gentlemen know," Shepherd continued. "We are safe behind the Lines of Torres Vedras at this point. The French will be unable to break through them. We will remain deadlocked for the next few months. Masséna's troops will eventually find they are lacking in critical supplies. Coupled with the reinforcements we are guaranteed by the War Office in London come spring, our enemy will be forced to fall back."

Talk turned to future campaigns to be conducted once those reinforcements arrived, with discussion of fighting at Barrosa in early March, as well as plans for attacks and counterattacks at Fuentes de Oñoro by early May. Arguments were made for and against both locations and how troops could be moved and utilized to the best advantage. After two hours, General Shepherd said he would take all their suggestions under advisement and dismissed those in attendance.

Rhys returned to his tent. Today's strategy session was one of several he had partaken in during the last year but of those he had attended, none had worked on efforts so far into the future. He supposed the British had no choice but to hunker down behind the lines Wellington had the foresight to build and wait for fresh troops to arrive in warmer weather. Hopefully by then, the French supplies predicted to run low would cause their enemy to turn tail before new Redcoats even appeared in Portugal.

"Colonel Armistead?" a voice called and Rhys bid the soldier to enter.

"Mail for you, Colonel," the young private said, handing over a letter.

Rhys thanked him and then settled on his cot, breaking the seal of the Earl of Torrington and opening the letter.

Christmas greetings to you, Rhys. Or should I say Colonel Armistead? Congratulations on your promotion. It is well-deserved. You are a true leader and unflappable in battle. I take pride in having been your fellow officer and that I still call you my friend.

At least by the time you receive this, it will almost be Christmas. I know what you are going through now. Endless drills to keep the men busy and out of trouble with the fighting at a standstill. A few visits to the local village for wine and a woman. At least your weather is milder—and dryer—than England now experiences. We have been cold and damp, as usual.

Anna has grown quite large, her belly round with the babe growing inside her. Her arms and legs are still a tad too thin but both the doctor and midwife assure us that things are on schedule and she should deliver come mid-February. Her moods are mercurial, swaying wildly from feisty to sweet. She misses riding desperately and cannot wait to take it up again once the child comes.

I do long for the two of you to meet, Rhys. I have spoken of you fondly to my countess and we hope for the day this bloody war will come to an end. I have a feeling it will take Bonaparte's death for that to occur. The Frenchman is too canny to be caught and then give up, especially after all these years at war.

Know that I think of you daily and miss your company. Despite being at war, we had some good times, you and I. You are as a broth-

er to me and I hope the day will come when we will reunite in England. Until then, my dearest friend, I pray for your safety.

Wishing you well,

Dez

Rhys folded the letter and sighed aloud. There was but a ghost of a chance he would see Dez anytime soon. This idiotic conflict had dragged on this long and, at times, Rhys believed it might go on forever. Bonaparte was a fiend and a genius—and he would never willingly lay down his arms. If only some sane Frenchman would take the opportunity to assassinate the Little General, the soldiers from all sides might finally be able to go home.

Home. Where was home?

Even if the war ended tomorrow, Rhys had nowhere to go. His mother had died from her faulty heart two weeks before he entered military service. He still remembered the heat of the day and the smell of the flowers at her funeral. Additionally, he had only spent a day at Sheffield Park. Lady Sheffington had been appalled and outraged that her husband had thought to prepare for the future in case their son died prematurely before inheriting the title. Rhys had stood outside the drawing room in his new clothes as the two argued loudly, the countess hissing like an alley cat at the earl. In the end, Lord Sheffington had apologized to Rhys and sent him, along with Mr. Goolsby, back to London. Instead of sharing Viscount Raleigh's tutor, one was hired for Rhys.

It had probably been a blessing in disguise to be banished from Sheffield Park. Lady Sheffington would have made his life miserable if he had remained in the country. As it was, Eli Simpson had been hired to teach Rhys. They had spent long days together, studying Greek and Latin, mathematics, history, and economics. London had called to them and they had walked the streets and parks for hours, as well as visiting museums countless numbers of times. Eli had taught Rhys about architecture and taken him to buildings throughout the city to illustrate his lessons.

Most importantly, Eli had taught Rhys how to speak properly. They worked for hours in order for him to lose his thick, lower-class accent. He had mimicked Eli's public school speech and slowly the lessons had taken root. No one would know from hearing Rhys speak now that he had such humble origins. Despite the vast knowledge he had collected at Eli's hand and new accent, inside, Rhys felt vastly inferior to those officers around him. At least he had proven himself adept at war and the military had taught him skills that helped him be successful in his career.

The same private from earlier popped his head back inside the tent. "Sorry, Colonel. Another letter for you. Should've been placed with the first." He handed it to Rhys. "A good day to you, Colonel."

He wondered who the author of this second letter might be. With his mother dead and Rhys and Eli agreeing when they parted years ago not to write one another since neither man proved to be sentimental, he literally had no one beyond Dez who would wish to correspond with him.

Glancing at the spindly handwriting, his name barely legible, he turned it over and froze.

The seal of the Earl of Sheffington.

He knew it because the earl had written to him twice a year during the three years Eli tutored Rhys in London. Sheffington's last letter had been to wish Rhys well as he entered military service. After that—nothing.

With trepidation, Rhys broke the seal and unfolded the page, seeing only two lines scrawled upon it.

My son, Raleigh, is dead. I will be soon.

Come to London.

Sheffington

After all his time at war, Rhys didn't think he would ever be shocked by reading a few words on a page—but he was. He had pushed aside all ideas of becoming the Earl of Sheffington since he hadn't heard from the earl or any of his people in well over a decade. He assumed Viscount Raleigh's health had improved and had been grateful to be fortunate enough for his distant cousin to have purchased Rhys' army commission, enabling him to have a career in the military instead of being a servant in the stables.

All that would change now. He would need to leave immediately for London and eventually Sheffield Park, which was in Surrey, just under twenty miles outside the great city. He folded the letter and took it with him, returning to General Shepherd's tent. Rhys thought it best to speak directly with his commanding officer regarding the situation.

"Might I have a few minutes of the general's time?" he asked the soldier stationed outside the massive tent.

"One moment, Colonel."

The soldier returned quickly. "You may go in."

Rhys nodded and brushed past the guard. As he entered, he saw Shepherd at his desk, papers scattered across it. He crossed the tent and saluted.

Shepherd returned the salute and indicated for Rhys to take the chair in front of the desk. He did so.

"What is it, Colonel Armistead?" the general asked almost wearily. "Have you another idea to contribute to our spring campaign?"

"No, General Shepherd. I come to you to discuss selling out."

Angry spots of red immediately dotted the old man's cheeks. "Sell out? What the bloody hell would you want to do that for? We are in a war, man. We need every able-bodied soldier, along with officers to lead them on the battlefield."

He passed the letter to his commander. Shepherd opened it and, looking puzzled, asked, "I know Sheffington. What does this mean?"

"My mother was a distant cousin to Lord Sheffington. With the death of his only son, Viscount Raleigh, I am the earl's heir apparent. Since the earl writes of his imminent death, I will be needed in England. I know his estate is vast and I will have numerous tenants which I will be responsible for."

The old man's attitude changed completely. "Yes, of course, Colonel. I quite understand the need to sell your commission immediately. I had no idea you were related to Sheffington. We were at school and university together."

His words surprised Rhys because the general looked so much older than Lord Sheffington. He supposed the war had aged the man considerably. It also made Rhys hate the system. The *ton*. Shepherd had gone from outraged to contrite, now willing to do what it took to see Rhys got home safely because of a title he would soon hold. He really didn't want to be a part of Polite Society but at least by becoming the earl, he would be able to put the war behind him.

If he could put the war behind him.

Doubt filled him. Something told him memories of the past dozen years would haunt him the rest of his life.

"Certain steps are to be taken in the matter of resigning your commission," the general continued pleasantly, as if they were discussing the weather and not an end to Rhys' professional military career.

The commander elaborated on them and told Rhys he would help facilitate matters.

"We will get you home to England safely and as soon as possible," Shepherd said brightly, offering his hand.

"It has been a pleasure serving under you, Sir," he said, shaking the general's hand.

A day later, all matters had been resolved, including transportation to England, and Rhys packed a satchel with a few personal belongings. He left his trunk behind, telling his batman to take whatever he wanted from it and distribute the rest to those in need.

As he boarded the ship that would now sail to England, he knew he was walking away from a life he intimately knew and sometimes hated and into one he had no idea how to live. He wouldn't understand the people of the *ton* and would never fit into their company yet he knew he would provide the livelihood to huge numbers of tenants and servants. All he could ask of himself was to do right by his people.

Rhys vowed to be the best earl he could be and would do whatever it took to live up to the multitude of responsibilities now being thrust into his inexperienced hands.

CHAPTER FIVE

London

RHYS ACCOMPANIED MR. Goolsby from his office to the Sheffington townhouse. He hadn't wanted to go directly to the earl's residence when he arrived in London. From his war experience, he had learned reconnaissance could prove valuable in a situation and had gone to Goolsby to get the lay of the land first before walking in blindly to a meeting with Lord Sheffington.

Goolsby had recognized Rhys at once despite it being a dozen years since they had last seen one another. Goolsby greeted him warmly, probably because he wanted to continue as solicitor to the new Lord Sheffington after the current earl's death. From Goolsby, Rhys learned that Viscount Raleigh had remained in the country all these years, growing more ill with each passing day, his mother constantly by his side. Lord Sheffington had spent all of his time in town, having nothing to do with his wife or son for a good ten years. It stunned him to hear this and immediately he wondered how the estate had fared during the earl's long period of neglect. He might be walking into an impossible situation.

Rhys and Goolsby approached the door to a beautiful, classic townhouse in the Mayfair section of London. Rhys knew it well because of the many long walks he and Eli had taken through the area, admiring the elaborate architecture of the homes of members of Polite Society.

They were greeted by a somber-looking servant, whom Goolsby called by name.

"How is Lord Sheffington this morning, Wiggins?"

"He is near the end, Mr. Goolsby." The servant's eyes flicked to Rhys.

"I am Colonel Armistead," he said, using his military title. "My mother was a cousin to Lord Sheffington," he said.

"Wiggins is the family butler, Colonel," the solicitor told Rhys. To the servant, he said, "His lordship wished to see the colonel the moment he arrived in London."

The butler nodded deferentially to Rhys, no doubt recognizing he would soon be the new earl. "Follow me, gentlemen."

Wiggins led them up a wide staircase. As Sheffield Park had done, this residence housed a plethora of artwork on its walls and thick, plush carpeting on the stairs. He struggled to take in the grandeur of the place that he would soon call home.

They arrived at what he assumed to be the earl's rooms and went inside. The butler asked them to wait in what looked to be a sitting room. He returned moments later with another servant.

"This is Callow, Lord Sheffington's valet," Wiggins explained and nodded to the man, who was short and stout and reminded Rhys of Morrison, his former batman.

"Good morning, Colonel Armistead. Mr. Goolsby. The doctor said his lordship is too weak to receive any visitors but Lord Sheffington insisted he see his cousin. Alone," the valet added. "You may go in, Colonel."

"Thank you, Callow," he said and crossed to the closed door.

Opening it, he entered a chamber that smelled of death. He often encountered the scent on the battlefield and in hospital tents as he visited his dying men. His belly lurched as he walked to the bed.

Propped up with several pillows behind him lay the Earl of Sheffington. When he had met the nobleman years ago, the earl had been of average size, with a headful of dark hair and clear, brown eyes. This man, who lay atop the bedclothes, was painfully thin now except for his legs and feet. They were swollen twice their normal size and his bloated belly looked as if he carried a child within him. Dark bruising marked his limbs and bare chest, with his skin sallow and the whites of his eyes yellowed with what looked like jaundice.

"You came," rasped the earl.

"Yes, my lord. May I offer my condolence on the loss of your son? Mr. Goolsby told me Viscount Raleigh passed from the pneumonia."

"Help me stand."

Rhys took hold of the older man and aided him from the bed. He took a few steps to his chamber pot and relieved himself, the stream dark and vile-smelling. Returning the earl to the bed, Rhys helped prop him up again so they could converse.

"I am so weary." Sheffington sighed. "I cannot eat. I itch all over."

"What does the doctor say?" he asked.

"That I am dying," the earl spat out. He ran his fingers through the thin, greasy hair. "You want to know what is wrong with me?" He barked out a harsh laugh. "I have drunk myself to death."

Sheffington closed his eyes, his body sagging. Rhys remained where he was, unsure if the earl had fallen asleep or not.

Finally, the nobleman opened his eyes again, his fatigue obvious.

"I apologize for leaving things in such poor condition. It was selfish of me."

"The estate, you mean?"

"Yes. My father insisted I wed a woman who brought an immense dowry to the family coffers. I told him she was a shrew and I wanted no part of a union with her. Do you know what he said? That I should break her as Shakespeare's Petruchio tamed the shrewish Katharina." The earl shook his head. "He underestimated the tenacity of that termagant, as well as my ability to bring her to heel. She only produced the one, sickly child." He shook his head. "Worthless woman. A marriage of convenience that turned out to be most inconvenient if you ask me."

Rhys remained silent as the earl's breathing grew labored. Despite his struggles, Sheffington continued to speak.

"I grew tired of a perpetually ill boy and a nagging, angry countess and retreated to London for the last ten years. Washed my hands of them and enjoyed myself immensely. My wife died two years ago. I didn't even go to her funeral." He sighed. "I was too ill myself to attend Raleigh's last month. Now, no one is left—but you—to attend mine."

Again, the earl closed his eyes and was silent for several minutes. Rhys bided his time until the man's gaze suddenly bored into him.

"I have no idea what you will find when you go to Sheffield Park. You seem efficient. Confident. I am certain you will clean up any mess there and be a far better lord of the manor than I ever was. My father told me to grow up." He smiled malevolently. "I never did. The most responsible thing I ever did was locate your mother and you and prepare you for this day."

Despite the earl's words, Rhys felt more than inadequate. He was frightened. He wasn't raised to be an earl. He aped the manners of his fellow officers. He had heard stories from Dez about the *ton* and all of their insanely absurd rules. He wanted no part of this world. He never sought this man's fortune or title.

Yet it was being thrust upon him. Looking at Sheffington, he wouldn't be long for this world. And because Rhys would become the new earl, he would feel obligated to do far better than this bastard ever had. Rhys had come from nothing. Beyond this man purchasing him a commission, Rhys had worked hard for everything he had ever gained. He would work even harder to make things right at Sheffield Park again. Though he wasn't good with people after having been at war a dozen years and had little social skills to draw upon, he believed he could do a better job than the present Earl of Sheffington ever had.

It would also be imperative to wed and produce an heir to hold the title after him. This was an opportunity he had been granted and he would not let it go to waste. Rhys vowed to learn everything he could about estate management and make his land thrive for his offspring. Dez could help him. Although his friend had only been an earl himself for the past nine months, Dez was the most intelligent man of his acquaintance. If anyone could help Rhys learn what to do in order to get an estate back on its feet, it would be the new Earl of Torrington.

He determined once Sheffington had passed, he would go to Sheffield Park and inspect it thoroughly, learning all he could about its current state of affairs. Once he did, he would visit Dez, who resided only three hours away, and get his advice. He wouldn't be able to ask his friend to leave Torrington lands with Anna so near to giving birth but he could ask Dez questions and soak up everything he could and then put into practice successful methods at Sheffield Park.

"There will be bills to pay here in town," the earl said. "Who knows what needs to be done at the country estate?"

It amazed him that this man had let things go and Rhys asked, "Why did you not have a care for your property?"'

Sheffington snorted. "I wasn't passing it along to my direct blood."

Anger filled him. "Did you deliberately allow it to be run into the ground?"

The sick, old man shrugged. "I may have. At one point, I thought to keep things going and sought you out. After you left and I lost myself in drink, I frankly didn't care about anything." He paused. "When you become Sheffington, simply do what all gentlemen of the *ton* do when they find themselves in trouble—marry well. It's likely you'll need a huge dowry to bolster the family fortune."

Rage boiled within him for this man's carelessness with the wealth he had inherited. Instead of caring for his lands and people, he had indulged in a selfish lifestyle, drinking himself to death, abandoning his family and neglecting those he should have supported.

Rhys shook his head in disgust, wondering who would want to wed him. He had no polish and no social skills. No formal education—just the streets smarts and savviness learned in the army. Emotions overwhelmed him as he quickly filled with worry. Regret. Anger. It was the anger that took possession of him now as he glared at Sheffington.

"I don't care when you die. I won't be attending your funeral, my lord. You have wasted every gift given to you. You deserve to die alone and be buried and forgotten."

The earl's mouth dropped in amazement. He sat up to argue, fury in his eyes. "You baseborn fool. I will see that you . . ." His voice trailed off and he fell back against the pillows, his eyes wide, staring out into nothingness.

Rhys took a step forward and saw the man had died. He took a calming breath and then crossed the bedchamber. Opening the door, the trio of waiting men looked at him expectantly.

"Lord Sheffington is dead," he said brusquely. "Callow, prepare him. Mr. Goolsby, you may plan his funeral."

"I, my lord?" the solicitor asked and Rhys was aware the man had not referred to him as a colonel.

"Yes," he commanded in a voice he used when giving orders to his troops. "Do with him as you see fit. Take him back to Sheffield Park and see he is buried there or in the local churchyard, preferably next to his wife and son. See to it at once, Goolsby. I leave you in full charge of all the arrangements."

The solicitor nodded and hurried away as the valet entered the bedchamber, leaving Rhys with his disapproving butler.

"Can you blame me?" he asked softly. "I was a servant myself until age fifteen, Wiggins. A groom, plucked from anonymity and briefly educated by a tutor the earl provided. Sheffington refused to fight for me when his countess said she didn't want me at Sheffield Park. I could have stayed in the country and learned about the estate. Instead,

I will go into things blindly."

He looked the butler squarely in the eye. "I will need people like you. People to guide me in my new role. I was one of you once and now find myself one of them." He gave a tight smile. "I am not sure I will even like being on this side."

Surprisingly, the butler's features relaxed and he smiled. "You are a breath of fresh air, my lord. I would be most happy to help you. You seem to be an intelligent man so heed my advice. You and Mr. Goolsby should accompany the former earl's body back to Sheffield Park. Whether you choose to attend his funeral or not is for you to decide but I would strongly suggest that you do so. Your servants and the locals will look poorly upon you if you don't and as you said, you will need all the help you can get. No sense in alienating them and getting off on the wrong foot at the start."

Rhys nodded slowly. "That is excellent advice, Wiggins." He thrust out his hand and they shook. "Why don't you come along with us? You can help me assess things once we reach Sheffield Park. You can decide if you would rather stay in London or come and be my country butler. I have a feeling I will spend far more time at Sheffield Park than in the city."

Wiggins looked thoughtful a moment and then said, "There is certainly more prestige in being a town butler but more power in the country."

"Lord Sheffington informed me that things might be quite the mess at Sheffield Park, due to his lack of interest in the estate. Since he led me to believe thus, I could use someone I can rely on."

"I will think upon it, my lord," Wiggins replied. "In the meantime, I will have the body removed from your chambers. It will be washed, dressed, and laid out downstairs in the parlor. For now, I am happy to show you to the former countess' rooms while yours are being cleaned and aired and all clothing and personal items of the previous earl removed."

"Thank you, Wiggins. You are already proving to me that you are resourceful and reliable. For now, I would prefer to go to the study and see what I can sort out among the former earl's papers."

"Very good, my lord. If you will follow me?"

The butler led him downstairs and showed him the location of the study. Rhys entered and took a seat at what was now his desk. Sitting there, he felt the power—and the burden—of the title he would now assume.

Withdrawing a piece of parchment from a drawer, he decided to compose of list of all the things he wanted to see once he arrived at Sheffield Park and the questions he might have for the different people who worked for him in various capacities. He thought a moment, cracked his knuckles for good measure, and then dipped the pen into the inkwell and began.

CHAPTER SIX

March—Torville Manor

DALINDA, DUCHESS OF Gilford, gazed out the window as the carriage rumbled along the Surrey road. She watched the passing countryside, not truly seeing it with so much on her mind.

She hadn't been back to Torville Manor since before her come-out Season years ago. Once Gilford offered for her, she married him and never looked back. He understood her feelings toward both her father and Ham and had supported her when she cut all ties with them. Instead, she had looked to her new husband and found a satisfying life. They didn't love one another but they liked each other a great deal. Gilford had taught her about art, politics, and farming. They had ridden the estate together frequently and she had enjoyed getting to know their tenants.

More importantly, she had been blessed with two healthy boys, Arthur and Harry. They, along with her husband, had been her world. Motherhood had felt so right to her and she and Gilford had taught the boys together, with them learning to ride, swim, fish, and hunt. Unfortunately, the duke's health had begun to wane and the last two years he had gone steadily downhill, experiencing two heart attacks which severely limited his mobility and a final one which killed him.

A lump formed in her throat at the thought of never seeing him again. He had encouraged her not to wear widow's weeds and mourn him, telling her she was still young and that she needed to think of marrying again. He reminded her how delightful his own life had been when he remarried late in life and got a second chance to father more children. He urged Dalinda to keep an open mind and the right man would come along—one of her own choosing.

She wiped a tear away at the thought. Gilford had been so good to her, rescuing her from a fate she didn't dare think upon even all these years later. At least Reid had returned from the Peninsular War and taken up his father's title. Though her boys had initially resented their much older half-brother, Dalinda knew Reid already proved to be a good influence on them. He had a firm, steady hand, which she appreciated, since she had spent too much time in the sickroom to pay her sons much attention. Consequently, the boys had acted out and been tossed from several schools. Now, though, they were settled at the nearby Dunwood Academy, run by the very capable Lady Dunwood. Already, both Arthur and Harry were making friends and behaving beautifully.

With her boys safely in hand, she had asked Reid for permission to visit her brother, which he readily granted, telling her that she was her own person and had no need to seek his approval. Though Dalinda knew exactly how Gilford had generously provided for her, Reid had also gone over with her what had been left to her. Her husband had made sure she had a large fortune, as well as an estate of her own in Surrey. Both Arthur and Harry also received ample compensation, enough to pay for their schooling and provide them with an income once they reached the age of twenty-five.

The landscape began to look familiar to her as she began studying her surroundings and she knew within a quarter-hour she would arrive at Torville Manor. It would be so good to see Dez and Anna again. They had come to Gillingham shortly after their wedding last June since she had been unable to attend with Gilford so ill. Reuniting with them had been like a dream come true after so many years apart. Dalinda was now ready to celebrate the birth of their first child and get to know her tiny nephew, who was all of a month old.

Anticipation filled her as the carriage turned and headed up the lane. She had always loved living at Torville Manor. Her father spent a majority of his time in London, usually keeping Ham with him. That left her and Dez to freely roam the country estate. She was happy Dez had gained the title and been able to return from the war. Learning Anna had been committed to a madhouse by her father after their failed elopement, her twin had rescued his childhood sweetheart from the asylum and patiently helped her assimilate back into the world. Their love had been the bond which had seen them through their awful years of separation and Dalinda knew the pair would spend the rest of their lives in happiness, hopefully filling Torville Manor with a large brood of children.

She spied Anna and began calling her friend's name, both of them waving frantically as the carriage came to a halt. The moment the door opened, Dalinda raced down the steps and threw herself into Anna's arms. Tears of joy flowed freely as they embraced. She grasped Anna's hands and smiled.

"You are glowing. Motherhood certainly suits you."

Anna returned the smile. "You had told me how much love burst within you when Arthur was born."

"And it only magnified with Harry's arrival," Dalinda added. "It is fierce and all-consuming, isn't it?"

"Very much so," Anna agreed. "I love Dez madly but Charlie makes my heart swell with joy."

"I am ready to meet my little nephew." She linked arms with Anna.

"What? You haven't even asked about Dez," Anna teased.

"I will see my twin afterward. Babies trump brothers."

The two women entered the household and ascended the stairs to go to the nursery.

"You are not our only visitor," Anna informed her.

Curiosity filled her. "Who else might be here?"

"The former Colonel Armistead, now the Earl of Sheffington, arrived this morning."

"Rhys? Rhys Armistead? Dez's army friend? Dez mentioned him so many times over the years in his letters to me. But . . . an earl? I had no idea the colonel was an heir apparent."

"Neither did Sheffington," Anna said. "It seems he was a distant cousin to the previous earl and never really expected to claim the title."

"When did this happen?"

"A few months ago. Sheffington thought he would spend his entire life in the army, much as Dez believed he was destined to do the same. Lord Sheffington has admitted that he is totally unsuited to be an earl and terrified of his new responsibilities." Anna frowned. "It seems the former earl sorely neglected the estate and spent all of his time in town, carousing with friends and drinking himself to death."

Dalinda felt fortunate to have had a husband who was attentive not only to her and their sons but his estate and their people. The duke had taught her much about estate management, which proved complicated at times, but something she enjoyed being involved with.

"I am sorry Dez's friend is faced with such an uphill battle."

Anna shrugged. "Sheffington scoped out his estate and has gotten a tentative grasp on his holdings. He arrived yesterday in hopes of Dez being able to help him understand all that he doesn't. They have been out all day, riding the estate, so Dez could point out what he has done since coming to Torville and assuming the title."

They reached the nursery and Anna quietly pushed open the door without knocking. A nursemaid held the baby, swaying slightly.

"Good afternoon, my lady. Lord Charles just awoke from his nap. Would you care to hold him?"

Anna glanced at Dalinda, who nodded eagerly.

"Give him to Her Grace," she said and the nursemaid handed over the infant.

As she looked at her nephew's chubby cheeks and deep, blue eyes, love filled Dalinda, seeing this new family member, the physical manifestation of Dez and Anna's love. A deep yearning filled her instantly and she knew Gilford had known all along that she would want to bear more children. Her boys had brought her the greatest joy of her life and she knew now, without a doubt, that she would wed again in order to have another baby.

"You are most handsome, Charlie," she told the wide-eyed infant. "I am your aunt, Dalinda, and I already love you so very, very much."

She went to the rocker and sat, rocking the baby and singing to him as Anna and the nursemaid looked on with smiles. Finally, she rose and gave Charlie to his mother.

"I better let you hold him now—else I might make a dash for the carriage with him," she teased.

They spent another half-hour in the nursery and then left, both her and Anna covering the baby's face in kisses.

Retiring to the drawing room, Anna rang for tea and said, "I had forgotten what a beautiful voice you have, Dalinda. I am afraid my feeble attempts at warbling hurt Charlie's ears."

"He will love it because it is his mama who sings to him. You will always be first in his heart." She sighed. "I haven't sung or played in some time. I used to do so often for Gilford, even after his first heart attack. He enjoyed sitting and listening to me play for hours."

Tears pricked her eyes and she blinked them away.

"You cared for him a great deal," Anna observed.

"I did. Very much. He rescued me, as you know. Gave me time and attention and did the same with our boys. He was a remarkable man."

"Who was remarkable?"

Dalinda glanced up and saw her twin rushing to her. He snatched her up and twirled her around, soundly kissing her cheek.

"I am so glad you are here," Dez said. "I hope you can stay a good while."

"With Arthur and Harry settled at Dunwood Academy and Reid now back from the Peninsular Wars, my time is my own for now."

Dez kissed her cheek again and then said, "You must meet my friend." He released her and stepped to her side.

Dalinda looked up, a pleasant smile on her face as she waited to greet Lord Sheffington.

And then the air seemed be sucked from the room.

The new earl was just over six feet, with an athletic frame. His dark, thick hair was worn a little too long for the current fashion and a bit unruly. His vivid, green eyes bored into her. His cheekbones could have cut glass. His nose, slightly crooked, must have been broken at some point, but the overall effect only added to his handsomeness. She had never been struck physically by a man's presence—until now.

Then he smiled, a dimple showing in his right cheek, and her knees wobbled.

"This could be none other than Her Grace," he said, his voice low, rumbling in his chest. "You favor your twin in looks, Your Grace. I am Lord Sheffington and most happy to make your acquaintance."

The earl took her hand and brought it to his lips, pressing a soft—and searing—kiss against her knuckles. Dalinda, who had never fainted in her life, became quite lightheaded. He seemed to understand this and held on to her hand for a moment to steady her as they gazed at one another. Then Sheffington released her hand and she finally remembered to take a breath.

A maid arrived with the teacart and Dalinda took the chance to take a step back. She broke the gaze and looked to Anna.

"Do you still have a sweet tooth?" she asked lightly, trying to calm her racing heart.

Her friend laughed. "It started the moment Charlie began to grow within me and it hasn't left. Come, everyone. Please make yourselves comfortable. Dalinda, come sit here."

She did as asked, perching on a settee, trying to take calming breaths in order to still her racing heart.

Until Lord Sheffington took the place beside her.

Again, her heart began thumping wildly. She clutched her hands in her lap, trying to still them as they trembled. She couldn't understand her body's reaction. Confusion filled her as she inhaled the bergamot and musk scent rising from the man seated next to her. Her cheeks heated and she looked away, taking the cup and saucer that Anna offered her and willing her fingers to be still as she brought the cup to her lips.

"No cream or sugar for you, Dalinda?" Anna asked.

She hadn't even realized she'd accepted the cup and not sweetened her tea.

"I take it this way sometimes," she said meekly and took another sip, aware now how unpleasant the taste was without the additions she loved.

Anna handed the next cup to Lord Sheffington, who leaned across her to receive it. It caused her to inhale another deep breath of his shaving soap. And that made her heart race even faster. Good heavens, it might burst from her chest!

She closed her eyes. This was ridiculous. She had never been attracted to a man in such a way, much less upon first sight. Yes, the earl was quite virile and handsome. Sinfully handsome. No, she was not going to act like some silly young girl making her come-out. She was a duchess. Gilford had taught her to behave with poise and charm. She would do so now and make him proud.

Turning to her right, she asked, "What is your country estate like, Lord Sheffington? I gather from Anna that you find yourself in my brother's position and have become an earl with little training."

Those emerald eyes held her spellbound as he replied, "Though my London property seems to run like a finely crafted Swiss watch,

Your Grace, I discovered upon arrival at Sheffield Park that things there are in shambles."

"I am sorry to hear that," she murmured, taking a sip of her tea.

"It didn't surprise me," he continued. "The former earl had sadly neglected the property, favoring town over the country. He had left behind his wife and ailing son and lived a dissolute life apart from them for many years."

Dalinda sniffed. "He sounds like our older brother, Ham, who is deceased. He, too, indulged in drink—and far worse."

The earl nodded solemnly. "Yes, Dez shared that with me." Then his lips twitched in amusement. "He also shared a good number of things about you, Your Grace."

Dalinda felt her cheeks burn. "Did he, now?"

Sheffington laughed. "He did, indeed. Between trying to kill or be killed, there is quite a bit of down time in the army. Campaigns are waged in more favorable weather. When your brother and I found ourselves bored, he would tell me stories of your shared childhood."

Her eyes flew to Dez, who shrugged, mirth about to explode from him. Looking back at her companion, she asked, "Were *any* of them flattering, my lord?"

"If you have a fondness for hellions, then yes, they were most flattering," he said, his eyes twinkling in mischief.

She couldn't help but laugh. "If I were sitting closer to my brother—and not in the company of a gentleman that I have just met—I would soundly box Dez's ears."

"That's the spirit!" Sheffington cried, his eyes now warm with approval. "Dez did make you out to be vivacious and energetic. That whatever devilry you led him in to, it was done with enthusiasm and boldness."

Dalinda chuckled and then regally said, "I was a mere child during those escapades."

He smiled at her. "And as a duchess, you are above reproach. Tell me, Your Grace—do you still find yourself getting in trouble?"

CHAPTER SEVEN

R HYS HAD NEVER wanted a woman as much as he did the Duchess of Gilford.

Which was absolutely ridiculous.

She was a married woman. His closest friend's sister. So far above him socially that he probably shouldn't even be in her presence, much less flirting with her the way he was. Yet he couldn't help himself. He wanted to run his fingers through her chocolate brown locks. Skim his fingers along the silk of her skin. Kiss the rosebud lips that beckoned to him.

He saw the blush spill across her porcelain cheeks and wondered what it would be like to bed her. She was a woman who would deserve hours of attention to do her justice. He thought of exploring every lush curve and quickly took a sip of tea, trying to distract himself.

"I believe I have curbed my tendency to seek out trouble," she replied. "Fortunately, it does not find me. However, I must have passed down the ability to my boys, Arthur and Harry. They seem to constantly find themselves on the wrong side of the rules." She paused. "They are good boys. Merely high spirited. And they are at a new school, Dunwood Academy, which is only three miles from Gilling-ham. I believe Lady Dunwood, the headmistress of the school, understands troubled boys and has them well in hand."

He wondered why the boys might be troubled and decided it was because their father had been so ill. Rhys remembered Dez sharing that the duke had suffered not one but two heart attacks, the second severely curtailing his activities.

Dez placed his saucer down. "It's time for Anna and me to visit Charlie. We do so after tea each day." He looked to Rhys. "Would you be so good as to entertain my sister during our absence?"

"I'd be happy to." Looking to the duchess he said, "Of course, if you are tired from your journey to Torville Manor, perhaps you would prefer to rest."

Those bewitching brown eyes sparkled as she said, "Not at all. I hate being cooped up in a carriage. I would prefer walking the gardens if you are amenable to that, my lord."

He rose. "I would be happy to escort you there, Your Grace."

She asked her brother, "Country hours for dinner?"

"Of course," Dez replied easily and led his wife from the drawing room.

Once again, Rhys experienced that pinch of anxiety, feeling totally inadequate. He had no idea what country hours might mean. It was just one of many things that made him feel as if he would never be part of the world of Polite Society. Though Dez had been an army officer alongside Rhys, Dez had come from this lifestyle and innately understood it. Rhys doubted he ever would.

The duchess came to her feet and he had enough sense to know he should offer her his arm.

"Shall we?" he asked.

She placed her fingers on his forearm and something sparked between them. She drew in a quick breath. He was gentleman enough not to look at her or refer to it. But it did increase the growing desire he had for her. Rhys tamped it down. Dalinda Baker may have been a hellion as a child but she was a mature, married woman now and didn't seem the type who would take her marriage vows lightly and indulge in a casual affair.

They came to the gardens and she removed her hand from his arm as they strolled side-by-side along the path.

"I always did love these gardens," she confided. "I used to follow our gardener around and help him with the flowers and plants."

"Physical labor was allowed?" he asked.

She laughed, a deep, throaty laugh which made his spine tingle pleasantly.

"I'm sure it wasn't in other families but Torrington didn't really care about Dez or me. We were afterthoughts. The twins who killed his wife. He and Ham spent most of their time in town. Dez and I did pretty much whatever we wanted to do."

The duchess laughed again as she remembered the past. "Those were good times. And Anna was always a part of them."

"She seems well," Rhys said. "Dez has shared some of what she went through at the asylum."

"Anna is the sweetest person you shall ever meet—but her core is made of steel. I could never have survived what she did. Or even being in the military and fighting in battles, as you and Dez have."

"I believe you underestimate yourself, Your Grace."

She grew thoughtful. "No, I don't believe I do. I was the lucky one of the three of us. Fortunately, Gilford offered for me—and saved me from wedding a fat, old stranger. He gave me two lovely sons and taught me quite a bit."

That intrigued him. "What did he teach you?"

"Everything," she said simply. "I knew nothing about world affairs. We would read the newspaper together and he would explain politics and economics to me. He was quite fond of art and architecture and shared his knowledge of those subjects freely. He thought it important for me to know about our estates and so I learned about farming and horse breeding."

Rhys frowned. The way she spoke of Gilford, it was as if he were deceased.

"Forgive me, Your Grace, but I must ask about your husband."

"What do you wish to know?"

"Is he . . . alive?"

A shadow crossed her face. "No, Gilford is no longer with us. He passed away a month ago."

Stunned, he looked at her and she quickly said, "I know I am not wearing widow's weeds. I hope you won't judge me too harshly, Lord Sheffington. My husband was in the sickroom for the last couple of years and he told me I had mourned for him enough during his ill health. He wanted me not to bury myself, as well, but to celebrate that I still had life and our sons. He begged me to forgo the mourning period."

A sweet smile crossed her lips. "Gilford insisted that I wed again. He knows how fond I am of children and how I had hoped for more." She chuckled. "Not that I will rush out and find a husband tomorrow, but he was the wisest man I know and I respected him above all others. If he wants me to move on, I will do so, content with the memories of our time together."

Rhys decided she must have loved the duke a great deal and that love was returned, especially since he encouraged her to proceed with her life after he was gone. She would never do so with the likes him, though. He had to put all thoughts of this irresistible woman from his head.

Instead, he said, "Tell me about your children," thinking that a safe topic.

Her face lit up as if she were a flower kissed by the morning sun and Rhys could tell how much she loved them.

"I have two boys. Arthur is my oldest and quite a bit like his father in looks and personality. He enjoys working with numbers. I believe he has leadership skills within him that may thrive at the new school he has begun to attend. He takes being an older brother very seriously and is quite protective of me. Especially with Gilford now gone."

She fingered the petals of a flower and then said, "Harry is ten, Arthur's junior by two years, and full of promise. He is my baby and still very affectionate, whereas Arthur is of a mind that he's too old to give me kisses anymore. Harry is more of a follower and takes his lead from his older brother. I am hoping at their new school that he will learn to stand more on his own two feet and become his own person."

"They sound like lovely boys."

She laughed and the delightful sound made his chest grow tight. "I am not sure the headmasters at their previous schools would agree with you, my lord. I am a bit embarrassed to admit that my two haven't been on their best behavior in recent months." The duchess grew solemn. "With their father so ill, they didn't spend much time with him. I was constantly in the sickroom and when I wasn't, I was busy with estate business. I am afraid my boys have been a bit neglected but I aim to remedy that now."

They began walking again and she asked, "Has Dez begun advising you? You mentioned coming to him to help you with your estate."

"I only arrived yesterday," he shared. "Today, we rode Torville lands and he pointed out various aspects to me. We spoke to a good number of his tenants. Tomorrow morning, we are going to go over the ledgers with his estate manager. I fear I have a great deal to learn in a short amount of time."

"We learn all our lives, my lord. At least, that is what I have found to be true." She paused. "I know this sounds forward of me but perhaps I could offer a few suggestions to you. I have done so with Dez since he is rather new to his responsibilities as an earl, while I have been a part of helping to run Gillingham for well over a decade."

Her offer surprised—and touched—him. "That would be very kind of you, Your Grace."

"How do you find your household at Sheffield Park?" she inquired.

Rhys laughed aloud., thinking of the disaster he had come upon when he arrived at the estate.

"I must confess that it is in a terrible state. My London townhouse is impeccably run by Wiggins, my butler. I tried to convince him to come with me to the country—and that was even before I saw the sad way things had deteriorated—but we eventually decided, together, that it might be best for him to stay in London and keep that household running efficiently. I have written to him for advice, though, regarding what I should do at my country house to bring it up to snuff."

The duchess looked intrigued. "You discussed this with your butler—and even wrote to him? How unusual."

Knowing he would never have a chance with this woman, Rhys chose to place his cards upon the table.

"Your Grace, I am not what I seem," he began.

She looked puzzled. "And what might that be, Lord Sheffington?"

"I am a fraud," he said flatly.

The duchess frowned. "I beg your pardon?"

"Oh, I am an earl. But the way that came about is a long story."

Curiosity filled her eyes. "I do enjoy a good story." She glanced around. "There. That bench. Come sit with me and tell me everything."

She made her way to the stone bench nearby and settled herself. Not wanting to seem churlish, Rhys followed and sat beside her. The faint scent of roses wafted over him, coming from her and not the garden. Her cheeks even bloomed as a rose might and he itched to cradle it and caress it with his thumb.

"Well?" she asked expectantly.

He sighed. "I was born to a man who helped in the building of ships. He died when I was eight and I became the breadwinner for my family. My mother had a weak heart and passed that condition along to my sister, who died when she was eight and I was ten. Mum was too ill to work by then. I eventually found work as a groom, working in a viscount's stables."

Her hand covered his in a gesture of comfort.

"I am so sorry, my lord. I had no idea."

"It's not a story I share," he said brusquely, wondering why he was opening up and telling it to her.

"You had to grow up very fast," she said softly.

"I did. It made me the man I am today. At fifteen, though, I was plucked from obscurity by Lord Sheffington, who was a distant cousin of my mother's. His only son was sickly and the earl discovered I would be next in line for the title. I was given new clothes to wear and a tutor, who spent the next three years giving me an education and spending tireless hours helping me try to lose my thick accent."

Rhys met her gaze and saw nothing but admiration, putting him off-balance.

"How remarkable. A self-made man."

"Sheffington purchased my army commission and I never heard from him until shortly before this past Christmas. I had assumed Viscount Raleigh had recovered and would one day assume the earldom if he hadn't already."

"Instead, you were called home and became the new earl."

He nodded. "My mother's cousin may have held the title of gentleman but he had behaved abominably. He'd grown tired of his nagging wife and feeble son and walked away from them, living a separate life in London for a good decade. When I arrived in London at his urgent request, I learned Viscount Raleigh had died from pneumonia and that Lord Sheffington himself was on his deathbed."

He pulled his hand from under hers, self-conscious about it, and looked her directly in the eyes. "So you see, Your Grace, I feel like an imposter. My mother, who was a gentleman's daughter, fell in love with a common laborer. I was raised in poverty but had the good fortune to become an officer in His Majesty's Army. As a former groom, I suppose I relate more to my butler than I do members of Polite Society, which is why I consulted Wiggins."

Rhys stood, uncomfortable sitting next to her, linking his fingers behind his back.

The duchess sprang to her feet, her smile wide. "Oh, I quite admire you, my lord. I think it brilliant to have consulted your Mr. Wiggins. Who better than a butler to know how to run a household? I am just sorry that he did not accompany you from town. It would have made things easier on you."

He shook his head. "You are very understanding, Your Grace. Yes, I have my work cut out for me at Sheffield Park. I have much to learn about the land and my tenants. The household itself is in a state of disarray. The housekeeper quit soon after the former countess' death. Several of the servants left around the same time. When I arrived, I found both the steward and butler to be too old and infirmed to manage much of anything and pensioned them off. Right now, I am only using two rooms in the house since there is only one maid and a cook. My valet, Callow, is trying to put things in order but the house is in great need of several repairs."

She smiled. "Then I insist upon helping you, Lord Sheffington. My late husband gifted me with one of his unentailed estates upon his death. It was one of my favorites to visit, thanks to Mr. and Mrs. Marsh, the dear couple who runs the establishment. I will write to them to come to Sheffield Park and they will put things to right. They can organize everything and help hire a new staff for you." She paused. "In fact, I know this sounds rather forward but I would like to come, as well, and help you establish your household. I would love to see your country seat firsthand and help you get on your feet. Would you allow me to do so?"

Rhys stared at the beautiful woman before him. "Why would you do something like that?" he demanded. "I am a stranger to you."

She placed a hand upon his sleeve, sending a jolt through him. "Because you are my brother's dear friend. Dez would not have survived the war if not for you. You stood by him during battle and in times of trouble. You were—and are—a wonderful comrade." She squeezed his arm. "Please, let me help you. I enjoy arranging domestic duties and can make sure you have the proper staff in place and see that things are up to snuff.

"Will you let me help you?" she implored. "I have felt a bit useless ever since my stepson returned from the war and assumed the dukedom." Her eyes pleaded with him.

Against his better judgment, Rhys heard himself saying, "Of course, Your Grace. I will gladly accept any and all help you can provide me."

CHAPTER EIGHT

*W*HAT ON EARTH *had she done?*

Dalinda shook her head as she left her guest bedchamber and made her way to the drawing room. She chastised herself for boldly proclaiming to Lord Sheffington that she would give him advice on how to run his estate. The poor man had probably been shocked into accepting her offer. He had already told her how inadequate he felt coming into his title and being overwhelmed by the disarray he had discovered. She had only added to his chaos and feelings of incompetence by insisting she come and take over his household. The earl had indulged her proposal, which she knew would be disastrous. Not only did she have no business taking over the life of a stranger, she would probably be distracted entirely by the man himself and her wild, schoolgirl crush on him.

She would speak to him at the earliest time in which she could draw him away for a private conversation and apologize for her brash behavior. Sheffington had Dez to offer guidance and support. It was the very reason he had come to Torville Manor. She would make certain he understood he had done nothing wrong; rather, it was she who had behaved atrociously. What man in his right mind—even one desperately seeking help—would want a woman's advice on any matter?

She supposed it was because she now was in limbo. Her boys would be at school the majority of the year. With Reid home and assuming full control of Gillingham, he would most likely seek a bride in order to provide an heir to the dukedom since he was now thirty. The new duchess might be anything from resentful to indifferent regarding Dalinda's presence at the estate. Perhaps she would retire to Laurelwood, the estate her husband had left her. The Surrey property was the perfect size and would help keep her occupied, giving her a purpose she sorely lacked nowadays. She would still send the letter she had written to the Marshes, asking them to come to Sheffield Park and aid the earl in getting his household up and running in a proper fashion.

Reaching the drawing room, she entered and found Dez and Anna sipping a glass of sherry. A footman offered her one and she accepted it from him before joining the pair.

"How was your time in the nursery?" she asked, watching her brother's face light up in a way she had never seen before, which brought a thrill to her.

As Dez waxed almost poetic about all that Charlie could do at only one month, she hid her smile.

"It seems you have taken to fatherhood. Much more than our own father did."

Dez sighed. "How could Torrington have not thought you and I were the most incredible people on earth? I can gaze upon Charlie for hours. I live to see one of his smiles. The nursemaid tells me it is only gas but I don't believe that for a moment. My son knows my voice and he does smile at me."

Dez launched into another story enthusiastically. As she listened, a subtle shift in the air occurred and Dalinda knew Lord Sheffington had arrived. He joined them, nodding deferentially to her.

"I am happy you are enjoying your son so much," she told her twin. "I cannot wait for Arthur and Harry to meet their cousin."

Her brother's eyes twinkled. "Remember when we discussed the boys coming to visit Torville Manor? Anna and I would still enjoy hosting them for a few weeks this summer during their school holidays."

Anna added, "Of course, you would be invited to accompany them, Dalinda."

Before she could reply, Lord Sheffington said, "Her Grace may be occupied with helping me at Sheffield Park."

She saw Dez and Anna exchange one of those glances only a married couple who knew each other well did and wondered what it was about.

Dez asked, "How so, Rhys?"

"Her Grace graciously offered to help me in hiring a staff and making recommendations regarding the various repairs that need to occur to the house. She also has more experience than you, Dez, as far as running a large estate goes. I appreciate her offer, given in goodwill to a stranger."

"It's not as if you are a complete stranger," Dez chided. "Dalinda knows about you from the many letters I wrote to her over the years—just as you know her from what I shared with you." He beamed. "I think it a marvelous idea."

She shook her head, wanting to nip this in the bud. "I am afraid I must withdraw my offer, my lord." She glanced to Sheffington, whose emerald eyes bored into her. "Without meaning to, I twisted your arm in getting you to agree to my proposal. It is much more appropriate for my brother to help you. You were being a gentleman when I tried to force your hand to accept my help. I am merely a woman and should keep my opinions to myself."

"Far from it, Your Grace," he said, his eyes blazing. "You have the experience I need to help set things right at Sheffield Park. Of course, I will continue to consult with Dez on various matters. I value his opinion and intelligence but you are minimizing your own worth." He paused. "Where is the spirited woman I have heard so much about? It seems out of character for you to back down and pretend you know nothing when you are the most capable one among us to help me."

How could she tell him that she was afraid to go with him? That she didn't trust the feelings which he had stirred within her. That if she accompanied him to his country estate she might wind up in his bed.

Her husband had been a gentle lover. He had introduced her to lovemaking slowly and she found the process sweet and satisfying. Lying in Gilford's arms in the aftermath, she thought of how fortunate she was to have a such a considerate man who took such good care of her.

Instinct told her the Earl of Sheffington would not be gentle. He would be passionate and demanding and his lovemaking would be so intense that it might pierce her soul. Even if he were willing and they did make love once or twice, Dalinda believed it would mark her for life. That nothing would ever be the same again and that she would spend the rest of her life craving his touch.

And that was even before they had shared a single kiss.

Before she could reply, the butler announced dinner was ready to be served. Dez took Anna's arm and led her from the drawing room. Lord Sheffington turned to her and offered his arm. Reluctantly, she placed her fingers upon his sleeve and, once more, felt the enigmatic pull to him. Their gazes met and in his, she saw heat—and desire. It thrilled her and frightened her at the same time.

"You *will* come," he told her, his eyes compelling her. "You have a nurturing soul. You sense how desperate I am and will see for yourself how terrible things really are when you arrive at Sheffield Park. You won't leave me in distress. You are a good person, Your Grace. Don't walk away when I need you most."

Dalinda felt herself weakening. She couldn't argue with him and said, "I will only come if Dez and Anna accompany me."

She didn't know if that would keep her from this man's bed but any barrier she could throw up between them must be used.

"Very well. I see my mission is to convince the countess to come."

He smiled at her. "I may not be wed but from my friend's behavior, I have come to realize who holds the real power in his family."

With that, Lord Sheffington led her into dinner.

They arrived at the small dining room, which only seated ten. Dez sat at the head of one end, with Anna to his right. Two place settings were to his left.

"I hope you don't mind us being such a tight-knit group," Anna said. "I didn't wish for us to shout down the table at one another."

"I prefer being seated more closely," Lord Sheffington said. "It does make conversation much easier."

It might aid in the conversation but it did nothing for Dalinda's appetite. The earl seemed far too close to her. Every breath she took, she inhaled his scent, causing butterflies to dance within her belly.

As they finished the soup course, he said, "I have convinced Her Grace that her help at Sheffield Park would be immeasurable. However, she insists that the two of you accompany us so I must plead my case to you, Lady Torrington. Will you and Dez—and Charlie, of course—make the brief sojourn to my new home and help in fixing all that is wrong?"

"First, you must call me Anna. You are as a brother to my husband and I believe we should dispense with such formality." Anna looked to her. "Don't you agree, Dalinda?"

She swallowed. "Whatever you wish, Anna," she said tightly, not wanting the familiarity of being on a first-name basis with the handsome devil seated to her left.

"Excellent," her sister-in-law said. "As to our traveling to Sheffield Park, I think it would be easier to go with Charlie now while he is so small and not mobile. What is it, three hours or so?"

"Closer to two and a half, Anna," Lord Sheffington said, trying out his hostess' name. "And before you both agree—and bring your infant along—I must issue you the same warning that I gave Her Grace."

"What is there to warn us about, Rhys" Dez asked.

"The condition of the estate," the earl said. "I have told Her Grace that I have no housekeeper. No butler. I am down to a single maid and my cook. It will be rough going if you choose to come and far more work than your valet, lady's maid, and nanny might agree to."

"Nonsense," Dalinda heard herself say. "I have told you that I am inviting Mr. and Mrs. Marsh from Laurelwood to come and help."

"Isn't Laurelwood the estate Gilford left you?" Anna asked.

She nodded. "It is. The Marshes run the household for me as its butler and housekeeper. They are efficient and simply the best servants I have ever worked with. I told Lord Sheffington that I can have them meet us. If anyone can put a house to rights, it will be the Marshes. I told Lord Sheffington that they will be able to help him hire an adequate staff and see them properly trained."

Dalinda had no idea why she'd spoken up as she had. It seemed they would be going into an impossible situation, especially with young Charlie in tow. Yet something inside her longed to see Sheffield Park.

As well as spend more time with its handsome owner.

At least she didn't have to worry about Arthur and Harry at this point. Her boys had always been her primary concern from the moment of their birth. With them residing at Dunwood Academy, however, she realized that she had the luxury of indulging herself a bit. She had always put her family first, no matter what, never truly taking time for herself. She had already allotted a few weeks to visit with Dez and Anna and Torville Manor. It wouldn't matter if some of that designated time were spent at Lord Sheffington's estate instead. It would be different if her children were with her but they were being cared for at school. She could help the earl with his difficulties and still return in plenty of time to visit her sons at Dunwood Academy, as well as spend their entire summer term with them.

"Why don't we spend another two days at Torville Manor in order to allow you more time to see how we operate and then we can travel on Friday to Sheffield Park?" Dez suggested. "Is that agreeable, Anna?"

"Yes, I think it a very good plan," his wife replied.

Dalinda kept silent, knowing her protests would be churlish and uncalled for. With Dez and Anna going, it would be much more appropriate and offer a buffer between her and the irresistible earl.

They finished the meal, talking about Torville Manor, discussing everything from what the blacksmith did to the various plantings and harvests throughout the year.

Anna said, "Shall we retire to the music room? Dalinda sang to Charlie today and I would be interested in having her play and sing for us, as well."

She did not want any more attention drawn to her and quickly said, "Oh, I am sure the men would prefer to smoke their cigars and drink their port rather than listen to me. Besides, I am sorely out of practice."

Lord Sheffington said, "Neither Dez nor I favor cigars. I think our time would be better spent in the company of you charming ladies."

For being one who claimed he was a social inferior, the earl seemed born with a silver tongue.

Before a footman could assist her, Sheffington helped her from her seat, his fingers grazing her bare shoulder. Immediately, heat rippled through her and, once more, she thought traveling to Sheffield Park was a terrible idea that she would come to regret.

Dez took her arm and led her away, giving Dalinda a small amount of relief.

"Thank you for helping Rhys," he told her. "He is floundering a bit, which is quite unlike him. He is one of the most self-assured men I have ever come across. Your offer to help him is greatly appreciated."

"I have written to the couple who manage Laurelwood for me, asking them to come and help in this endeavor."

"That's good news," her brother said. "I will send it by messenger to them tomorrow and add my own note, asking them to meet us there on Friday."

They arrived at the music room and Dalinda went straight to the pianoforte. She settled herself upon the bench and opened the keyboard, the ivory keys beckoning to her. Music had always been an escape for her and she didn't realize how much she had missed playing until now.

The others took seats nearby. She allowed her fingers to hover over the keys a moment and then began a composition by Henry Purcell, one of her favorite composers. Though her fingers didn't always move where she wished them to, her mistakes were few and well concealed. She tried an invention from Bach and found the joy in it before singing a few English street ballads. When she finished, she closed the cover to protect the keys and looked up.

Sheffington's gaze was thoughtful and then he smiled, revealing the dimple in his cheek that set her heart aflutter.

"You played marvelously," Anna exclaimed. "Oh, you must play for me every day you are here. And continue to sing to Charlie, as well."

Dez came and put a hand upon her shoulder. "Your performance took me back to a happy time, Dalinda." He pressed a kiss atop her head and turned to his wife. "Anna, dear, you look tired. I believe it is time we retired for the evening."

Anna rose and said, "Please stay. Enjoy a brandy and some conversation while we old, married folks go to bed."

Dalinda said goodnight and remained at the pianoforte. She knew she should leave but couldn't bring herself to do so. Instead, she opened the cover and began to play again. She sensed Sheffington when he came to stand behind her but continued until she reached the end of the Beethoven number.

His hands suddenly rested on her shoulders, the heat from his fingers singeing her skin.

"If that was you without any practice, you must be a formidable musician when you have spent time at the keys."

Gently, his fingers squeezed her shoulders and then his thumbs began moving back and forth in a caress. Her core tightened as need began to throb there, something which had never happened before.

"Your voice is rich and low. What is that called?" he asked softly.

"A contralto," she said unsteadily. "I prefer singing in a lower register than most women."

His fingers went to her nape and stroked it slowly, bringing delicious chills running along her spine.

"You sense what is between us?" he asked.

She closed her eyes. "I do—and it frightens me."

"It should."

Her eyes opened and she looked over her shoulder. His green eyes smoldered.

"Are you afraid?" she asked.

"A little," he admitted.

"Why?"

"Because I want you so badly. I have never wanted a woman as I do you, Dalinda."

It was the first time he had called her by name. It felt . . . *right*. As if he should always have known her.

"I am drawn to you as well, Rhys."

He hissed upon hearing his name come from her. He bent and pressed his lips to her nape, the kiss tender yet scalding. He moved to where her neck and shoulder joined and kissed her there. Her head fell away, giving him better access. Rhys joined her on the bench, his mouth again touching her throat as his hands captured her waist. She had no thoughts of fleeing, though. Dangerous as he seemed, she was compelled to stay.

He lifted his head, his gaze intense. She shuddered.

"May I kiss you, Dalinda? On the mouth?"

"If you don't, I might kiss you first," she replied honestly though it sounded flirtatious to her ears.

His brows arched even as the ghost of a smile drew the corners of his mouth slightly up. One hand left her waist and cradled her cheek.

"You are more than beautiful," Rhys said. "You are intelligent. Caring. I can tell passion lurks just beneath your cool façade."

His thumb stroked her cheek. "We are playing with fire, Dalinda, and that is always dangerous. Someone is bound to get hurt."

"I don't care," she said boldly. "I need to kiss you."

She wanted to taste him. Touch him. Hold him. Have him do the same to her.

"There is no going back," he warned.

"I have learned not to look back," she said. "I live in the present and have hopes for the future."

"We have no future," Rhys said sternly. "You are a duchess. I will never be worthy of you." Desire filled his eyes. "But for a few minutes, I would like to think of us as equals."

His thumb stilled and his mouth covered hers.

CHAPTER NINE

D ALINDA THOUGHT HIS kiss would be demanding. Instead, it was the gentlest she had ever experienced. His lips brushed against hers softly. Sweetly. Achingly slow and tender.

If Rhys meant to light a fire within her, he accomplished it with the delicacy of the kiss. She felt heat generate within her and spiral outward. Her fingers moved to his face and stroked it longingly.

She wanted more. More of his kiss.

More of him.

His tongue slowly outlined the shape of her mouth, sending a shudder through her. Her hands slid from his face down to his chest and she clutched his waistcoat, bunching it in her fingers. His tongue slid along the seam of her mouth, teasing it open. She parted her lips and it swept inside. Suddenly, his scent—coupled with the taste of the wine they'd had at dinner—filled her senses.

Rhys' arms went about her, crushing her to him. His tongue began dueling with hers for control and Dalinda realized it was a war where they both would win. He tilted her head back for better access and deepened the kiss. It went on and on, filling her, causing the blood to rush to her head and pound in her ears. Her breasts began to ache, longing for his touch. The place between her thighs began to pound fiercely, as did her heart.

Still, the kiss went on. She lost all sense of time. There was only this man. In this moment. Bringing delightful shivers and causing her body to tingle with need. Gilford had never kissed her like this.

Rhys broke the kiss, panting. She realized she did the same. His vivid, green eyes swallowed her up.

"You are quite the kisser, Your Grace," he teased.

Her eyelashes fluttered. "I would think after sharing ourselves in such a manner that you would call me Dalinda."

She relaxed her hold and dropped her hands to her lap, suddenly self-conscious with what to do with them. He removed his hands from her waist but his face remained close to hers.

"Are you still the daring girl from your childhood?" he asked huskily. "One who might be willing to come to my bed?"

Her eyes widened. She was not some naïve miss straight from the schoolroom. In the ten years she and the duke had moved through society before he became ill, she had been made aware of how many of the *ton* disregarded their marital vows for their own pleasures. Women who had provided an heir—and sometimes, a spare—were free to find a lover of their choice. Widows, in particular, had a special freedom within Polite Society. As long as they were discreet, their affairs were their own business.

She was now a widow. The mother of two boys. A mature woman who had only been with one man. Her husband. She knew Gilford had given her permission to find a new husband after his death but did she have the audacity to take on a lover? If so, Rhys would be an excellent choice. Instinct told her that this man would know exactly how to treat a woman.

"Do you have any French letters with you?" she asked. "Though I long for another child, I would not make him or her a bastard."

He smiled ruefully. "I did not bring any, thinking I would be closeted with Dez and learning all I could about how to run an estate." A slow smile spread across his face. "I can always pleasure you and then withdraw."

Dalinda knew that a man got his pleasure from spilling his seed.

The fact that he offered to go without said a great deal for him.

"Then I accept your invitation, my lord," she said demurely. "However, I would rather you come to my bed."

Heat filled his eyes. "I see."

"I will go to my bedchamber now and allow my lady's maid to prepare me for bed. I suggest you do the same with your valet. Shall we say half an hour until we meet?"

In reply, he leaned in and kissed her. His hand went to her nape and held her steady as his mouth ravished hers.

He broke the kiss without warning. "I would be delighted to come to your bed, Your Grace."

Rhys rose and offered her his hand, helping her to rise. Dalinda felt unsteady on her feet and hoped her knees wouldn't give out on her as she began to take a few steps.

"We never did have that brandy," he said.

She stopped. "Pour us one now," she commanded.

He went to the decanter and poured some into two snifters and returned to her.

"Take it with you," he said. "Drink it once you are waiting for me. I look forward to tasting it on your tongue." His provocative gaze caused her to shudder.

Rhys accompanied her to the guest chamber Anna had designated for her and he said, "I am across the hall. Listen for my knock."

Her throat grew thick with sudden emotion and she merely nodded, turning away and entering the room. Tandy awaited her, dozing in a chair. Dalinda sipped some of the brandy and then placed it on the table by her bed, which had already been turned back by the maid. She looked at it, thinking that in but a few minutes, she would be in it.

With Rhys.

Taking a second sip of the brandy, she felt it blaze a trail from her tongue to her belly and set the snifter down before gently shaking Tandy's shoulder. The maid apologized for falling asleep and quickly stood, helping Dalinda from her layers of clothing and into her night rail.

"Where is my dressing gown?" she asked. "I am not sleepy. I may read for a while."

Tandy brought it over and helped her slip into it. Dalinda belted the sash.

"You may go. I will ring for you tomorrow morning when I have need of you."

"Yes, Your Grace. Goodnight."

The maid left the room and Dalinda claimed the snifter again, perching on the bed, her focus on the door. Butterflies exploded inside her. She had been impulsive as a child. It was one of the things her father had loathed about her. As a duchess, she had tried to curb that tendency, always being steady in her demeanor and decisions.

Tonight was different. She was going to make love with a man whom she barely knew, beyond what her twin had written about Rhys over the years. Though they were close to being strangers, she was touched he had shared some of his past with her today. He thought himself beneath her, being a former groom, but she had nothing but admiration for the way he had risen in the world. He had made the most of the situation he found himself in. Promotions all the way to colonel spoke of his intelligence and leadership.

Dalinda knew tonight would be the only time they would ever be together. Perhaps she would learn something new about herself—and him. It might give her a better idea of what she wanted as she embarked upon a new chapter in her life.

She took another drink of the brandy, allowing its warmth to fill her.

A soft rap sounded on the door. Nerves danced through her as she shot to her feet. Before she could take a step forward, the door opened and Rhys quickly entered, closing it behind him. He turned to face her.

Though he still wore his trousers, his feet were bare. A dark, silk banyan covered his upper body but she doubted anything was beneath it. She could see his throat and a glimpse of his bare chest. He moved toward her slowly, causing her heart to slam against her ribs.

Taking the snifter from her hand, he brought it to his lips and drank the remainder before setting it aside. His hands gently clasped her shoulders as he gazed down at her. Nervously, she wet her lips.

"Are you certain this is what you wish for, Dalinda?"

Even though she thought her actions foolish, she said, "Yes."

"I am going to explore every inch of you," he promised. "We might be up all night."

A shiver ran through her at the thought of his hands on her. Then she longed to touch him, she asked, "Might I do the same to you?"

A low growl came from him and suddenly she was in his arms. His kiss was demanding. Thrilling. All-consuming. She didn't know when one kiss ended and another began. She tasted the brandy as their tongues collided and mated. He growled again, crushing her to him. She felt small and powerless and wanted him so badly that no words could ever convey that to him. Instead, she let her actions speak for her.

He gentled the kiss, bringing her back to earth, and continued to kiss her as he sought the knot and undid it, slowly tugging on the sash and pulling the dressing gown from her, allowing it to fall to the floor. His eyes roamed over her as his fingers reached behind her head and began pulling the pins from her hair. Moments later, the dark waves spilled about her.

Rhys took her hand and led her to the dressing table, urging her to sit. She did and he placed the pins in his hand on the table. Reaching for her brush, he began pulling it through her locks. Slowly, Sensually. She had never thought the act of brushing her hair could be erotic.

Until now.

Their gazes met in the mirror and she began to tremble, seeing the want in his eyes and feeling the need soar within her. He removed his banyan and she rose, fascinated by the broad, muscular chest and flat belly, a trail of fine, dark hair disappearing into his trousers. She placed her palms against it, hearing his sharp intake of breath. Slowly, she allowed her hands to glide up and down his chest as she explored it. Her fingers went to the flat disks of his nipples and circled them. He swallowed and then caught her wrists.

"I want to see you. All of you," he said, his voice low and raw.

Dalinda nodded. He released her hands, which she dropped to her sides. He caught the hem of her night rail and quickly pulled it upward and over her head, tossing it away. She felt her cheeks blaze with embarrassment and turned her eyes downward.

"What?" he asked softly, lifting her chin in his fingers. "What is wrong?"

She shook her head. "I don't have the girlish figure I once did. After birthing two boys, my breasts are larger. My hips wider. I know I am not—"

His fingertips touched her lips, silencing her. "You are a mature, beautiful woman, Dalinda. The most beautiful woman I have ever beheld. I feel fortunate to gaze upon such beauty."

She bit her lip. "You don't have to ply me with pretty platitudes, Rhys."

His hands cupped her cheeks. "But they aren't, my duchess. Every word from my lips speaks the truth. I will never lie to you. Never."

He brought her against him, enfolded in his arms, his body heat flooding her. Her arms went around him, stroking his bare back. His did the same and she found immense comfort in that gesture.

Suddenly, he swept her into his arms and carried her to the bed, placing her gently upon it. With haste, he rid himself of his trousers and she saw the effect she had on him. His manhood stood proud and erect, so large that a bit of panic flared within her.

Joining her on the bed, he said, "No more words. Just touch. Taste." He leaned close and drew in a long breath. "And smell. My

God, you smell as fresh as a rose garden."

Rhys held to his promise. Dalinda didn't think there was a part of her skin that he did not claim with fingers or tongue. He roamed her body freely and allowed her to do the same to him. She liked the salty taste of his skin and the musk of it, too. He worshipped each of her breasts, fondling and caressing them until they were full and heavy. His lips and teeth teased her nipples and then he sucked on them, causing her nether region to pulse violently.

His mouth trailed down her body, past her belly and beyond. She stiffened but began to relax as his hands soothed and stroked her. Then he parted her folds and, without warning, plunged his tongue inside her. Dalinda nearly levitated from the bed. Her breathing grew harsh, her fingers twisted in his hair as his tongue and teeth worked miracles on her. A tremendous wave broke, shattering her, as she bucked and cried, her head whipping from side to side.

Rhys kissed his way back up her body until he reached her lips. It was quite erotic tasting herself on him. As they kissed, his fingers parted her again and began stroking her. One finger pushed inside and found a sweet nub within her, circling it, causing her breath to come rapidly. Just before she peaked and crashed again, he exchanged his finger with his member, pushing it inside her, filling and stretching her.

Then the dance of love began, the meeting of bodies with each sweet thrust. He buried his face against her throat, nipping and kissing as he pumped into her. She felt her body responding, rising again to those dizzying heights. As she started to cry out, his mouth covered hers and sheer pleasure flooded her.

Rhys withdrew from her and suddenly warmth touched her belly. She realized he had spilled his seed outside her, as he had promised.

He kissed her tenderly and rose from the bed. She heard water splashed in the basin and he returned with a cloth, wiping the white smear from her and dropping the cloth to the floor. He stretched out beside her and pulled her into his arms, her head upon his chest, her ear against his beating heart, their limbs entwined.

"You are magnificent, Dalinda," he murmured.

"And you are a Greek god come to life," she replied. "I have never gone to such heights. I did not know they existed."

He stroked her back, his hand moving slowly up and down.

"Go to sleep," he urged.

Dalinda wanted to stay awake and enjoy his presence but the intensity of their lovemaking was now taking a toll upon her. She yawned wearily and closed her eyes. Rhys continued to run his hand up and down her back and the rhythm pushed her into sleep.

CHAPTER TEN

R HYS SMOOTHED DALINDA'S hair as she slept in his arms. He hadn't closed his eyes, not wanting to miss a single moment with this wonderful woman. He'd even awakened her in the middle of the night and made love to her again before she dropped off to sleep once more.

Tonight would probably be the highlight of his life. When the dawn came, he would go back to being the groom-turned-earl and return to his country estate, which seemed to lack in every way. Dalinda would still be a duchess, albeit a dowager one. She would go on to wed a man of her same social status.

And hopefully, every now and then, she might give a thought to him and this one night they had shared.

He sensed dawn coming. He had never been one to sleep much and that had stayed with him during his army years. Even now, away from the war, Rhys only slept a few hours each night. It probably added to the air of weariness which seemed to constantly blanket him. He felt guilty for having left his men behind on the Peninsula. He worried that he wouldn't be enough of a good earl to help his people.

But for one magical night, he had forgotten all his troubles. In the arms of this remarkable woman.

He smiled, thinking of a few of the stories Dez had shared about his twin. How Dalinda had put a toad in their governess' shoe. How she would climb a tree and dive from its branches into a lake they used to swim in. When she hadn't liked where a gardener had planted a rosebush, she had gone and dug it up in the middle of the night, Dez standing by in support as he held a lantern. Dalinda had moved the rosebush to where she thought it ought to go—and the gardener had only nodded at her in approval instead of chastising her.

A faint streak of light came from the window. Rhys knew his time with the duchess had drawn to a close. His fingers stroked the silky skin of her bare back a final time before he extricated himself from her arms. She slept like the dead, curled up, her cheek snuggled against her pillow. He drew the bedclothes over her, covering the luscious body he had spent hours coming to know. Dalinda sighed and then began softly snoring again, something he found utterly endearing.

Creeping around the room, he retrieved her night rail and dressing gown and placed them neatly across the foot of the bed. She would have to come up with her own explanation to her lady's maid why she had shed her clothes and slept in the nude. Rhys located his trousers and slipped into them and then his banyan. Tiptoeing back to the bed, he kissed Dalinda's brow and stood a moment, admiring her perfection, then he left the bedchamber and returned to his room across the corridor.

Callow had turned back the bed and Rhys shed his clothes and climbed into it, turning several times and punching the pillows to make it appear he had spent the night here and not across the hall with the Duchess of Gilford. Finally, he lay on his back, his hands pillowed beneath his head, and relived every moment of his time with her.

One, short rap sounded and his valet entered the room. Neither of them liked to chat in the morning. Callow poured fresh, hot water into the basin and Rhys rose from his bed. He allowed the valet to shave him, remembering how Dalinda had gotten tickled as his rough stubble dragged across her sensitive belly, the mirth spilling from her. He supposed from now on so many things would remind him of her.

Once he was dressed, he ventured downstairs. He had brought up country hours in the conversation at dinner last night and learned they meant early rising and an early dinner at night, usually at seven. Town hours, especially during the Season, were very different, with many of the *ton* staying out until the wee hours of the morning. He remembered how the viscount he had worked for had come home with his daughter from parties and balls at about the time Rhys rose to go to work. He dreaded thinking of the upcoming Season but knew it would be the best way to find his countess. He didn't expect to land a wife who was especially pretty or intelligent but he did need one who brought a large dowry with her. From his meetings with Mr. Goolsby, Rhys knew his finances were merely adequate at the moment. Within two years, however, things could turn dire unless he found a rich bride, which would enable him to turn things around at Sheffield Park.

"Good morning," Dez said as Rhys entered the sunny breakfast room. "You'll find everything you need on the sideboard. Would you care for coffee or tea?"

"Coffee," he said, moving to pick up a plate as a footman poured the coffee for him and placed it on the table.

Once a mound of food rested upon his plate, he joined Dez and asked, "Where is your lovely wife?"

"I have encouraged her since she became a mother to take mornings slowly and indulge by breakfasting in bed. Of course, the nursemaid brings Charlie in to see her while she eats."

"I gather you make your way up there to be a part of the morning fun?"

Dez laughed. "Of course." He grew serious. "I don't mind Anna getting a little extra rest. Her years in the asylum were difficult ones. Physically, she is still a little too thin, even after carrying Charlie. The doctor has urged her to rest frequently and still get some exercise to strengthen herself. As a matter of fact, he visited Anna yesterday and gave her permission to ride while you and I were out and about on the estate. I am sure she will be eager to join us when we go out again this afternoon after meeting with my steward."

"What of Her Grace? Does she enjoy riding?"

Dez laughed. "Dalinda was born on a horse. She took to it naturally. Since it has been so long since she was here at Torville, you can count on her joining us, as well, wanting to see the changes and familiar sights, as well."

"Did I hear my name?"

Rhys glanced up and his heart flipped over. Dalinda stood in the doorway wearing a pale pink gown that made her cheeks bloom. Her hair again was arranged in a simple chignon, a few stray tendrils framing her face.

"We were talking about riding Torville this afternoon," Dez said.

She moved to the sideboard, asking the footman for tea, and placing a few items on her plate. When she joined them, she sat to Dez's right, opposite of Rhys. She smiled pleasantly at him as she would an acquaintance and focused on her food and her brother. Rhys tamped down the hurt he felt, which was ridiculous. He had known their coupling was just for one night. It shouldn't surprise him that she was coolly polite this morning.

Yet the thought of his hands skimming along her smooth skin and his tongue outlining the curve of her breast had his heart pounding as if he were some randy schoolboy wet behind the ears.

"I showed Rhys most of Torville Manor's lands yesterday. Today, we are to meet with my steward and talk about some of the measures we have in place to increase the upcoming harvest." He grinned. "You know me, though. A few hours with ledgers containing tiny numbers and dry talk about crop rotation and I will be ready to get out of the house and atop a horse."

Dez paused. "You need to join us, Dalinda. Especially since you have offered to help Rhys. You have already been a godsend to me with your advice. It is the rare man that would teach his wife the things Gilford shared with you. We might as well put all that knowledge to good use."

Rhys studied her as she considered her twin's words and then she said, "I am always happy to help one of your friends, Dez."

"Then it's settled." He pushed back his chair. "I am off to see my family for a bit. When you finish eating, Rhys, head straight to Paul Lexington's office and I'll join you. Dalinda, you'll know where it is."

Dez left the breakfast room, leaving them with two footmen. Rhys knew better than to say anything of a personal nature to Dalinda with servants present. They talked about the current weather and the distance between his estate and Dez's and how far Gillingham was from the both of them.

"You mentioned the Marshes coming to Sheffield Park," Rhys said. "How far is your estate from mine? Should I send a carriage for them?"

"That won't be necessary," she said. "Dez sent my message to them this morning. I indicated they were to take my carriage at Laurelwood. They should meet us at noon at Sheffield Park this coming Friday."

"Excellent." He noticed she hadn't eaten much and asked, "Aren't you hungry?"

A slight blush colored her cheeks. "No, my lord."

For a moment, her gaze met his and he thought how hungry he was for her. Rhys pushed the thought aside. They had shared a glorious night. It was in the past, though, and the duchess had told him she didn't dwell on the past.

"If so, are you ready to speak with Mr. Lexington?"

"Certainly, my lord."

As they left the breakfast room and he saw no servants about, he said, "I know you wish to put last night behind you but Anna will notice you being so formal. I thought you agreed to call me Rhys."

She frowned and all he wanted to do was kiss away the worry creasing the bridge of her nose.

"I will do so when it is only the four of us alone. I think formality when servants are present is a different matter."

The crispness in her tone let him know she viewed him as her social inferior. He would have to get it through his thick skull that her spontaneous actions of last night would never be repeated. Of course, the thought of being around her and not touching her would probably kill him. Idly, he wondered who would be next in line to succeed him as Lord Sheffington and decided he should find out from the ever efficient Mr. Goolsby.

"The steward's office is this way," she said and Rhys escorted her to it.

He knocked on the door and they heard a voice jovially call, "Come in!"

Entering, he saw Dez's steward, a rotund man with a bald head and merry, blue eyes. He rose and bowed to them.

"Good morning. I am Paul Lexington, the earl's steward. You must be Your Grace, the earl's sister, for you favor Lord Torrington a great deal. And Lord Sheffington, I presume. The earl told me to expect you."

"It is nice to meet you, Mr. Lexington," Dalinda said. "Dez speaks quite highly of you."

"His lordship is most kind. I must say, Your Grace, you have passed along several suggestions that we have already implemented at Torrington."

"I am fortunate in that my late husband did not think me a featherhead, Mr. Lexington. He took great pride in our homes and he wanted me to do the same. I have spent hours discussing livestock and farming techniques." She turned to Rhys. "Lord Sheffington is eager to hear you speak about those things in regard to Torville Manor and also he would enjoy examining the ledgers."

Rhys didn't think he would enjoy looking at dusty ledgers but he smiled pleasantly. "Quite so. Where shall we begin?"

"Have a seat and we can discuss the estate in general, to start," Lexington said.

The steward spoke at length. Dez slipped into the room and both he and Dalinda interjected at times, adding to what Lexington said and elaborating on things when Rhys asked a question. After an hour, they opened ledgers from different times of the year to illustrate to him what costs could be expected and how much it took to maintain things. By the time several hours had passed, his head was crammed full of knowledge and eagerness filled him.

"You look excited," Dalinda pointed out.

"Actually, I am. I have learned a great deal in your company this morning. I know everything the three of you shared will be worked into how I organize things at Sheffield Park." He paused. "It is a lot to consider, however. I know I will need a talented steward to help me in my endeavors."

Anna appeared in the doorway, dressed in her riding habit. "You have been closeted far too long. It is a beautiful day. Cold but sunny and, surprisingly, there is no wind to speak of."

Dez laughed. "You are itching to get atop a horse, aren't you, my love?" He went to her and slipped an arm about her waist. "Why don't we see if Cook will pack us a picnic? We could stop at the cottage while we are out and dine there."

"An excellent idea, Husband," Anna said. "I'll go arrange that now. Dalinda, you should go and change."

"Very well," the duchess said. "I will meet you at the stables." She looked to Lexington. "Thank you for your time today," she told the steward. "After all we have discussed, I am eager to get back out on the estate and see what has changed since I was last here years ago."

Rhys also thanked the steward, who told him if he had an any additional questions to stop by and ask them.

He ventured to the stables, not needing to change his clothes, and told the head groom of the riding party of four that would depart soon.

"Ah, the countess will be happy to finally take Daisy out. She visited the mare every day once the doctor told her to curtail her riding. I've seen to Daisy myself but the horse will be happy to have Lady Torrington back on her again." The groom chuckled. "And I have just the mount for the duchess. I will see to preparing the horses, my lord."

Rhys wondered why the groom had laughed when he spoke of a horse for Dalinda. He left the stables and paced outside, waiting for the others to appear.

The first to arrive was the duchess, wearing a rust and tan riding habit, her hat perched at a jaunty angle, giving her an air of mischief.

"I see we are the first to arrive," she said.

"The head groom is seeing to our horses," he informed her.

Just then, the four horses were led outside and Dalinda gave a squeal of delight.

"Wilson!"

She ran to the groom and threw her arms about him. Rhys experienced surprise—with a bit of jealousy mixed—as she embraced the groom.

"So, you became head groom. I should have known. You were the one who had the lightest and best touch with our horses. It is so good to see you." She hugged him again.

Wilson, his face beet red, smiled adoringly at her. "I am happy to see you, too, Your Grace. We never got to say a true goodbye. I thought you would return from your come-out Season and wed in the Torrington chapel."

"That would have been my father's plan. He wanted me to wed some ancient fool." She smiled triumphantly. "I found a much better man to wed."

A pang of hurt filled Rhys. The duke had been a lucky man to win Dalinda's heart and give her children. He wondered if she would always love this dead husband and told himself it was of no concern to him.

"I have just the horse for you, Your Grace," Wilson said in a conspiratorial fashion. "She's a temper on her but my, oh my, how she can fly."

Dalinda smiled more radiantly than any sun Rhys had ever seen. "I am looking forward to the challenge, Wilson. What is her name?"

"Stormy." The groom shrugged good-naturedly. "It's her nature." He looked up at the reins he held. "You'll be kind to the duchess now, won't you, girl?"

The horse's nostrils flared and she snorted as if disgusted to be told how to behave.

"May I?" Dalinda took the reins and scratched the horse between her ears. "You're my good girl, aren't you, Stormy love? We're going to get along famously."

She continued stroking the horse and murmuring endearments to it. Rhys wished she touched and cooed to him instead.

Dez and Anna arrived and they set off, Anna taking the lead. Dez rode beside his wife, leaving Rhys and Dalinda to be next to one another. Once they cleared the grounds and reached open land, Anna called out for them to keep up and took off on Daisy.

Before Rhys could react, Dalinda sailed past him, racing to catch up to her friend. He and Dez took off after them, each rider giving their horse its head as they galloped across a meadow. The two women approached and then jumped a fence in tandem. He and Dez followed in close pursuit. As they rode, he couldn't help but admire Dalinda's form and skill in managing the difficult horse. He knew many a man who would have trouble controlling such a temperamental beast.

The pair finally slowed and then reined in their horses, turning and facing the men as they approached. Dalinda's cheeks were flushed with color, making her even more attractive.

"I want her, Dez," she declared to her twin. "I don't care what I have to pay you to have her." She leaned down, stroking the horse's neck and kissed it. "Stormy and I are meant for one another."

Dez laughed. "You can have her. I should pay you for taking her off my hands. No one—not even Wilson—has been able to tame her completely. I might have known you would come in and weave your spell upon her."

"Let's walk our horses through the woods," Anna said. "We're near the lake," she added, looking at Dalinda.

"Near the cottage?" Dalinda asked.

"Yes."

Rhys knew from letters he had received from Dez that the cottage had been a place the three had played at as children. Dez had brought Anna there when he liberated her from Gollingham Asylum and they had remained alone together at the cottage as he slowly brought Anna back to reality.

The four went single file, entering the woods and weaving through the dense forest until they came out at a grove. A cottage stood facing a wide lake.

"The water separates Torrington lands from those at Shelton Park," Dez told him. "Anna grew up there."

"My cousin is the current viscount," Anna added. "He is married and has one child. My sister, Jessa, lives with them."

"Jessa?" Dalinda asked. "Oh, I would love to see her." She looked to Rhys. "Jessa was a good dozen years younger than we were. We would bring her to the lake to swim and picnic. Has she made her come-out yet?"

"She will this upcoming Season," Anna said. "She wants Dez and me to come to town to help chaperone her to events."

"If we don't see her before we leave for Sheffield Park, then we must make sure to visit with her before I return to Gillingham," Dalinda said.

"You'll have to come to town to do so. Jessa left last week with Lord and Lady Shelton. My cousin's wife was going to help see to Jessa's wardrobe."

Dalinda frowned, unease spreading across her face. "I am not sure I am quite ready to return to the social events of the Season," she said quietly. "Though Gilford encouraged me to do so."

Rhys heard the emotion in her voice as she mentioned her husband. Selfishly, he hoped she did stay home though it shouldn't matter to him. As it was, he should be preparing to go to London himself and participate in the whirl of activities in order to find himself a bride.

The men dismounted and helped the two women do the same. As he guided Dalinda to the ground, Rhys inhaled the subtle whiff of roses, which always seemed to cling to her. He dropped his hands from her waist, wishing he could relive last night again with her.

Every night.

Dez handed him a satchel, saying, "Careful. It's got jars of lemonade in it."

They entered the cottage and Dalinda complimented Anna on the furnishings.

"It was all Dez. He prepared it for me." She smiled fondly at her husband. "We still come here sometimes, just to be alone."

The women unloaded the goods from a second satchel while he removed the jars of lemonade, unscrewing the lid from each. While they ate, they talked about the estate and Dalinda asked after various tenants that she had known from her childhood. Rhys was impressed that Dez knew everyone she referred to and made a note that he must get to know all of his tenants—and their families—by name. Knowing something personal about each of them would build rapport. Just another lesson this magnificent woman had already taught him.

Anna sighed and Dez looked at her. "I am concerned, Anna. Have you overdone things?"

Meekly, she said, "Perhaps a bit. If I could lie down and rest for an hour, we could then return to the house." She looked past her husband. "If the two of you wish to ride back—or even ride further along the estate—you can."

"I would like to walk along the lakeshore a while," Dalinda said. "If Rhys is up for a bit of exercise."

"Certainly. When we return, we can all go back to the house together," he suggested.

"Thank you," Anna said. "I am sure I will be better after I lie down. I had forgotten how strenuous riding can be."

Rhys and Dalinda left the cottage and strolled down to the water. They passed a tree and she reached out and placed her palm against its trunk.

"Hello, old friend," she said huskily, causing desire to flare within him.

"Is this the tree you used to climb and dive into the lake from?" he asked.

She looked over her shoulder, her surprise evident. "You know about that?"

His gaze pinned her. "I know a great deal about you, Dalinda. From stories Dez told. From the letters you wrote to him all those years we were at war. From last night."

Her quick intake of breath made him aware of how close they stood together. They remained silent, staring at one another. She turned so that she faced him. He took a step toward her. She took one back, bumping into the tree.

With nowhere to go.

His hands took her by the shoulders. She gazed up at him, her lips slightly parted, her breath rapid.

"May I kiss you again, Dalinda?" he asked.

"Only if you want to, Rhys," she replied, her eyes wide and large.

His mouth hovered over hers a moment—and then he touched her lips.

CHAPTER ELEVEN

D ALINDA REMEMBERED RHYS had told her they played with fire and one of them was bound to get hurt. As his mouth pressed against hers, she realized the danger was to her heart. She had spent one incredible night with this man. He had only left her bed a few hours ago.

Yet already she craved his touch.

It would be a mistake to continue with this kiss. She slid her palms up his chest to nudge him away—and found they glided up and locked around his neck of their own accord, tugging him closer to her. She hadn't known temptation could be so enticing. That her attraction to a man could be so consuming. During her short come-out—before Gilford hastily wed her—she had been popular with the eligible bachelors of the *ton* but had never been physically drawn to any one man. Her husband had introduced her to the art of love and she had found it enjoyable.

But what Rhys did to her body caused it to go up in flames even as she went mindless.

He kissed her as before, starting gently. Almost tentatively. As if he gave her the option to change her mind. When she kissed him back, his hands went to her waist, anchoring her to him, the tree still pressing against her back. Slowly—and very surely—he eased her mouth open.

And then the fire within her burst, flooding her with heat and longing and desire.

Dalinda tightened her hold on him, even as Rhys did the same, and the kiss became wilder. Deeper. Hot and wet and passionate and incredible intense. Her nipples began to ache. The place between her thighs throbbed almost painfully. She could feel his erection, hard and firm against her.

Hungrily, they kissed for an eternity, time standing still. She was aware of the hard trunk against her back. Of a bird chirping its sweet melody. The sound of the water slapping against the shore. And the furnace of Rhys' body singeing her through her clothes.

He broke the kiss and, immediately, she felt bereft. Confused. At sea with no anchor to steady her.

"I promised I would never do that again," he said, his voice low and husky, causing a tingle to race up her spine.

"Why?" she asked, curious.

His crooked grin melted her heart. "Because we are of two different worlds, Dalinda."

She started to cut him off but he placed a fingertip against her lips.

"No. Don't. You know we are. I am rough-mannered though I hold a title. Raised in poverty. All I know is war and destruction and sorrow." He smiled ruefully. "I am now able to meet my financial obligations but my solicitor says that will end within two years. I must wed a woman who will bring me a fortune and be able to overlook my humble beginnings."

His hand stroked her hair. "You, on the other hand, are a duchess. At the top echelon of society. You are still young and beautiful and will have any number of men eating from the palm of your hand next Season. You will make a brilliant match. Have more children."

Rhys kissed her softly, a kiss that Dalinda knew meant goodbye.

"We had our one night, sweetheart. I will never forget it." He paused. "I will never forget you," he added softly.

His finger moved from her lips and fell away. A lump grew in her throat, making speech impossible.

"I think it best that you not come to Sheffield Park. I will have Dez accompany me to the estate. He can give me the advice I need."

She couldn't walk away from this man. He needed so much help.

"No. I have committed to coming and helping get you situated," she said. "Please allow me to do so. I promise I will ask nothing of you in return."

Dalinda wondered if the yearning in his eyes was mirrored in her own. She didn't understand why he thought her so above him. He was a self-made man and one she would be extremely pleased to wed—but she understood Rhys had his pride. It was most likely the only thing he had that was his alone. He had carried it with him from childhood into the army and now beyond as he attempted to settle into the life of the aristocracy.

She would try to be his friend. His adviser. And if she could break through the thick walls Rhys erected about him, perhaps there was a slim chance of finding happiness.

Together.

He stepped back and motioned for her to move away from the tree. Dalinda did so and they continued walking along the shoreline. She told him a few tales of growing up at Torville Manor and the trouble she had gotten them in.

"I was always too curious by far," she admitted. "I believe Arthur gets that from me. Unfortunately, he leads Harry along with him in his mischief. Harry is guileless and always eager to please his older brother."

"You said they are attending a new school?" Rhys asked.

"Yes, one very close to Gillingham, run by a dowager countess. She is formidable and nurturing at the same time. I think my boys will find themselves—who they truly are—at Dunwood Academy."

They spoke of her bringing Arthur and Harry to visit Dez and Anna at Torville Manor this summer and how both boys had experienced an instant rapport with their uncle when they met him for the first time.

"It will be good for them to be around Dez," he agreed.

"I think so, as well. They will also fall in love with Anna. Everyone does. Getting to know Charlie will also be good for them."

"Especially if you do have another baby. It will give them practice."

Dalinda wondered what their child would look like. If it would have Rhys' emerald eyes and height. She shook her head, knowing the thought foolish and yet it wouldn't seem to go away. Becoming a mother again appealed to her a great deal. If a future with this stubborn man proved to be impossible, she would definitely seek a husband in the future. She had a good three decades or more to live and she had no intention of wasting them by being alone.

They returned to the cottage, finding Anna had awakened from her nap and was feeling refreshed. Dalinda tried to ignore the burst of butterflies in her belly when Rhys' hands took her waist, lifting her into the saddle. She kept a firm hand on Stormy until they reached open land and then allowed the spirited horse to gallop all the way to the Torville stables. Though Rhys rode up directly behind her, she made sure a groom helped her to dismount.

Wilson joined them. "What did you think of her?" he asked eagerly.

She grinned. "I have told my brother that I am not leaving Torville without Stormy."

The groom laughed aloud. "She's a feisty one. Just like you, Your Grace."

Her gaze met Rhys' and she thought of how feisty their love play had been. Sensing her cheeks heat, she quickly thanked Wilson and hurried to the house, not bothering to allow Rhys to escort her.

Once inside, she asked Mrs. Abbott to send up hot water for a bath. As she sank into the tub, Dalinda closed her eyes.

And thought of Rhys' kiss.

"HOLD CHARLIE," DEZ commanded, thrusting the baby into a stunned Rhys' arms.

He had never held a baby before. He did remember his arm around his sister, rocking and comforting her when she was young and so very weak. The memory brought an ache to his chest. He had tried to lock away any memories of her or his mother because they all hurt so much. There had never been enough food or medicine. Never enough money for shoes or clothing. He still blamed himself for not doing better. Earning more, even if he had only been a small lad when his father had died.

Charlie gurgled, looking up at him. Rhys smiled at the infant. "Are you ready to travel to Sheffield Park?" he asked.

"I hope you're not expecting an answer," a feminine voice said.

He glanced up and saw Dalinda had joined them. They were journeying to his country estate this morning.

He smiled down at Charlie. "He doesn't have to reply. There'll be time enough for talk between us when he's older."

"I do hope you intend to remain close to Dez," she said. "That what occurred between us will not color your relationship with him in any way."

"No, of course not."

Yet it already had. Rhys felt slightly awkward around his friend, who thankfully seemed oblivious to the change. He knew there was some unwritten code that said a man's sister was hands off to his friends. Surely, a twin sister was even more forbidden. Rhys knew how close Dez and Dalinda were and had been from the beginning, the two of them standing against the world. He would never do anything to come between them. He only hoped, in time, that things would return to normal between him and Dez.

Charlie caught sight of Dalinda and reached out his chubby arms to her.

"May I?" she asked, her features softening.

"He wants you. Not me." Rhys handed the infant over.

She looked so right with a baby in her arms. Over the last couple of days, he had witnessed her holding Charlie and singing to him. Rhys had forced himself to look away. Dalinda glowed with a child nestled against her, like a Madonna. He only wished it could be his babe that rested in her arms.

"I think we're ready," Dez said.

Anna lifted Charlie from Dalinda's arms. "I am going to allow the three of you to ride in Rhys' carriage because all you will do is talk estate business. I will ride in our carriage with Charlie and his nurse. The servants will follow in the other carriage."

Dez leaned down and kissed his son's brow. "Be good, my little man. I will see you once we arrive at Sheffield Park."

Everyone made for the vehicles. Rhys made sure that Dez and Dalinda sat together. Though it would pain him to be sitting across from her, looking upon her the entire time, he didn't think he could have her beside him, that intoxicating scent of roses wafting from her satin skin, tantalizing him for the next few hours.

Anna proved correct and they spoke of Sheffield Park the entire journey. He peppered the pair with questions and they responded with thoughtful advice.

"The key will be hiring a new estate manager that you can trust," Dalinda told him.

He chuckled. "Other than you and Dez, I can't think of anyone I would place in that position." Then a thought occurred to him and he murmured, "Eli. Eli Simpson."

"Who is that?" Dez asked.

"He was Rhys' tutor," Dalinda said.

It touched him that she remembered the man's name. Of course, Rhys remembered everything he'd learned about her, as well.

Dez frowned. "You might have liked this tutor, Rhys, but Sheffield Park is an enormous estate. You need someone with experience to help you run the place."

"That's the thing," he said. "Eli's father was the steward at the country estate of a marquess. He grew up there, learning from his father. The marquess favored both Eli and his father and allowed Eli to be educated alongside his son, sharing the same tutor. He even paid for Eli to attend university."

"Hmm. So Mr. Simpson is both educated and somewhat knowledgeable about an estate's workings," Dez commented.

"Eli had sought a position as an assistant steward and hadn't been able to find one, mainly due to his youth," he continued. "Then he accepted the task of tutoring me in all areas for three years. He was going to begin his search again for work in the country once I left for the army, hoping his age and the recommendation from Lord Sheffington would help."

"I know you mentioned that you chose not to remain in touch," Dalinda said. "Could you contact his father and see if he would share his son's whereabouts with you?"

"I most certainly will. I'm sure by now, though, Eli has found a position and is settled."

He saw the slow smile curve her lips.

"From what you have told me of Mr. Simpson, he was always up for a challenge. Even if he is content in his current position, I don't know a man who wouldn't give his eye teeth to take on a beast of a project such as Sheffield Park and make something wonderful of it. Especially for a close friend," she added.

She was right. He and Eli had been fairly close in age, with Eli having graduated university early at age twenty and Rhys but fifteen when they met. While he had respected Eli's wealth of knowledge, they had become as close as brothers. If Eli called upon him, Rhys would have moved heaven and earth to help him out.

He only hoped Eli might do the same for him.

"I will write to Mr. Simpson the moment we reach Sheffield Park," he declared and then frowned.

"What's wrong?" Dez asked quickly. "Oh, don't worry about getting the message there. I know you have no footmen. We can send the letter along with my driver. Where does Mr. Simpson reside?"

"If he is still employed by the marquess, it is probably thirty to forty miles northwest of my estate. Eli took me there once. We left from London. I am trying to recall the exact distance."

"It doesn't matter," Dalinda assured him. "Write your letter and let Mr. Simpson know how much you think of his son and how Eli is the only one you would trust to help in molding Sheffield Park to your high standards. Prepare one for the younger Mr. Simpson, as well. Once Dez's driver learns of his location, he can take the message to him directly."

For the first time, hope filled Rhys. If he had Eli helping to manage the estate, it would bring huge relief to him.

The carriage slowed and turned to the east. Dalinda looked out the window and then back at the men.

"It looks as if we are almost at Sheffield Park," she declared.

CHAPTER TWELVE

NERVES TRICKLED THROUGH Rhys as the carriage pulled up. He desperately wanted to make a good impression on Dalinda—and even Dez—but knew the outside of his Sheffield Park house to be lacking, especially having come from the pristine Torville Manor and its manicured lawns. At least Dalinda would finally see what he meant. That he wasn't worthy of her, from his lack of fortune to his dilapidated country house.

He climb from the carriage first and held out a hand to assist her. Even with the both of them wearing gloves, Rhys sensed the spark shooting between them at the touch.

Dalinda eyed the house with interest, her lips pursed as she walked to the far end of the front of the house and back.

"I will need to see every room, every nook and cranny, of the inside of your house. It will be most important to have the roof inspected. But so far, the structure itself looks sound, Rhys," she revealed.

"Since I have never lived in a house and most of my years have been spent in a canvas army tent, I will take your word for it—and be grateful."

"No, truly," she insisted. "A few cosmetic changes could make a world of difference. Washing the stone. Some fresh paint. I do see a few defects to be corrected along the decorative, ornamental places."

She could have been speaking Russian to him. He only knew that he trusted her opinion.

"Do you have a blacksmith on the property?"

"No."

"You'll need one. Where is the nearest village?" she inquired.

He told her and she said, "We will seek the local blacksmith's help and also see if any carpenters are available nearby. You should hire men for both positions and have them permanently reside at Sheffield Park. Believe me, on an estate this size, they would have plenty to keep them busy."

By now, Anna's carriage and the second one carrying the servants pulled up. Besides the valets, nursery governess, and ladies' maids, Anna had insisted upon bringing two of her parlor maids and one scullery maid since Rhys had shared how woefully understaffed Sheffield Park was at present.

Before his eyes, both Dalinda and Anna became as drill sergeants, ordering servants about calmly but in a very organized fashion, making sure the coachmen took the horses to the stables to see them watered and fed. The two women entered the house, the men and servants trailing behind them. The two servants Rhys possessed—his cook and a parlor maid—awaited them in the foyer and he introduced them as the Torrington servants were taken in hand by Callow. He told the valet to be sure they were all assigned rooms and should unpack before they reported back downstairs.

Anna said, "I am going to get Charlie settled in. He's due for a feeding and nap."

Dez offered to help and the lone maid offered to show them to their guest chamber. Rhys had sent a message ahead asking for rooms to be prepared for his friends and their servants. With only a single maid to complete the task, he doubted things would be comparable to rooms at Torville Manor or Gillingham.

A loud rap sounded upon the door and Rhys himself answered it, finding a couple in their mid-forties standing before him.

"There you are!" Dalinda exclaimed. "Do come in. Lord Sheffing-ton, this is Mr. and Mrs. Marsh, the couple who runs Laurelwood. This is the Earl of Sheffington."

Mrs. Marsh's gaze roamed the front hall. "I can see you are in sore need of us, your lordship."

He liked that the woman hadn't minced words. "Yes, Mrs. Marsh. Everything has been sadly neglected for some time since the previous Lord Sheffington spent all his time in London. I recently became the new earl and came home from the Peninsular War to assume the title."

"Ah, a military man," Mr. Marsh said, nodding with approval. "Our Johnnie is fighting in Portugal now. We are very proud of him." The butler looked to Dalinda. "Where would you like us to begin, Your Grace?"

"Do you have your pencil and notepad on hand, Mr. Marsh? If so, you and Mrs. Marsh can accompany Lord Sheffington and me as he shows us around the house. Take notes on all that we discuss."

"Yes, Your Grace." The butler removed a pencil and a small sheaf of papers from his inner coat pocket. "Ready when you are."

Dalinda turned to Rhys. "Lead the way, my lord."

He sputtered, "I really don't know much about the house, Your Grace. As I told you, I am living in two rooms until the proper staff can be hired."

She frowned. "Have you not even toured the inside of your new home, my lord?"

Shaking his head sadly, he said, "No. I have tried to spend the little time I have been here to address matters with my tenants."

"Then follow me," she said crisply. "You will need to be made aware of what you own and what work needs to be done." Looking at Marsh, she said, "Your first note—make an inventory of the house's possessions. Furniture. Rugs. China and crystal. Silverware. Paintings."

Marsh immediately jotted something down and Dalinda began

walking the foyer. She bent and inspected the floor. Looked at the railing of the stairs. Touched the walls. All the while, she kept a running dialogue, with Marsh making furious notes as she spoke.

She led them through the entire house from top to bottom. There wasn't a room that they did not enter. No curtain, rug, or bedding went unnoticed. She noted clocks to be wound. Linen to be aired. Rugs to be beaten clean. Silver to be polished. Dalinda recommended rooms which should be painted. Stairs and handrails that needed mending. Mantels that should be taken down and replaced. By the time they reached the foyer again, several hours had passed. Rhys found himself exhausted just thinking about all that needed to be addressed, worried that his finances would take a beating and not last nearly as long as he'd hoped.

Mrs. Marsh said, "Marsh and I will talk through the list and see to the order to address things, Your Grace." She looked to Rhys. "It's a good thing you have our duchess on your side." Glancing to her husband, she said, "Come along, you. Let's see to getting Her Grace and her friends a filling tea. We'll send it to the drawing room, Your Grace."

"Thank you, Mrs. Marsh," Dalinda said and Rhys echoed her words.

Dez and Anna, who had joined them midway through the house tour, both chuckled.

"What?" Dalinda asked. "I wanted to be thorough."

Her brother slung an arm about her shoulders and noisily kissed her cheek. "If I had the king's ear, I would ask him to replace Wellington with you, my dear twin. You would make quick work of the Little General."

Rhys nodded in agreement. "If you are this efficient regarding domestic matters, I am sure you will be downright terrifying when we let you loose upon the estate."

He was teasing but it worried him with all she had found wrong with the house. As Dez took Anna's arm and guided her up the staircase, he offered his to Dalinda.

Taking it, she said, "Your roof is sound. That was my main concern—and something which can eat up loads of money. Much of what I found involves mere cleaning, Rhys. The best furniture polish is good elbow grease. Once we get the proper servants hired, they will attack my list with gusto. The rest? New paint. Some carpentry. It won't be as expensive as you perceive it." She pinned his gaze. "And if you seek a loan, I would be happy to lend you the amount you need. So would Dez."

His pride prickled with her words. "I don't need charity from a woman," he said brusquely.

She gripped his forearm until he almost winced, surprised at the strength in her delicate fingers.

"I wasn't speaking of charity. I believe I said I would be happy to let you borrow the money. I would expect the loan to be paid back with interest. However, I would choose a fair percentage and not take advantage of you."

He would ask her what she knew about such business affairs but realized she knew a great deal more than he did and so he kept silent until they entered the drawing room.

As they waited on tea to arrive, Rhys noted, "The Marshes seem terribly efficient. Mrs. Marsh is both frank and a bit ruthless."

Dalinda laughed. "I think so, too. They are quite loyal, however, and so I put up with them."

"They are at an estate Gilford left you?" Anna asked.

"Yes. It's called Laurelwood and it's in Surrey. It was a favorite of Gilford's and also of mine. He wanted me taken care of when he passed and left it to me since it was unentailed. The Marshes came with it and they are worth their weight in gold."

Her words were another reminder of the husband she'd loved and lost. Rhys had the one dilapidated estate and a decent London townhouse but Gilford, as a duke, would have had a multitude of estates. So many that he could bequeath one to his beloved wife and the new duke wouldn't even miss the property.

Once again, Rhys realized just how far from his reach Dalinda was and vowed to purge her from his system for good.

"I AM NOT sure I am up to this," Rhys admitted to his friends as they gathered in his study.

He was about to address a gathering of his tenants and newly-hired servants and staff on the lawn of Sheffield Park. Naturally, it had been Dalinda's idea to bring everyone together and give him the opportunity to speak to the entire group at the same time.

"What will I say?" he demanded, nerves jangling through him.

Dalinda placed a hand on his forearm to calm him but her touch only made rational thought cease. She must have realized that and removed it.

"Rhys, you have been promoted to commander-in-chief by becoming the Earl of Sheffington," she said, using a military analogy. "You are a former army officer. You have been in charge of troops your entire adult life. Speak to your people as you would your regiment. With confidence and authority."

He had so many doubts. True, addressing his soldiers had been a part of his past existence but he had also known the army inside and out. He still had so much to learn and desperately wanted to do the best he could in order to take care of his people, who depended upon him.

"You are right," he said firmly, wanting to show her that her unwavering belief in him was justified. "I can do this. Better than the previous Sheffington did."

"That's the spirit!" Dez chimed in. "Remember, Rhys—I am still in your shoes, as well. It is coming up on a year since I took the reins at Torville Manor. I discover something new every day."

He remembered how Dalinda echoed the same sentiments. That a person learned throughout his life.

Nodding, he said, "We should go outside. It is almost time."

The four left his study and made their way to the front lawn. He swallowed, seeing the vast number of people gathered there.

His people . . .

Pride swelled within him as he looked out over the crowd, spying familiar faces that he was coming to know. He glanced over his shoulder. Dalinda nodded encouragingly at him.

"Good people of Sheffield Park, I thank you for coming today. If we have not yet met, I would like to introduce myself to you. I am the new Earl of Sheffington."

Rhys paused, deciding to be honest and open, hoping it would bring goodwill and understanding.

"My mother was a distant cousin to the previous earl. She was a gentleman's daughter who married a shipyard laborer. My beginnings were humble but my parents loved me well. My father died in an accident at the shipyard and I became the sole provider for my family, eventually working as a groom."

He heard the murmurings ripple through the crowd but he had committed to and would now stay the course.

"I was fortunate enough to have the previous Lord Sheffington purchase an army commission for me and I fought in His Majesty's Army for a dozen years, ending my career with the rank of colonel. Now, I find myself in charge of a new army."

A titter of amused laughter followed and he continued.

"I am new to this world and these responsibilities but my commitment to you and your well-being is paramount. Will I make mistakes? Undoubtedly. Will I learn from them? I certainly plan to do so, with your patience. I do want you to know that we are in this together, from those who farm the land to the ones who place food on my table. I will be here for you. I will always lend an ear to hear your problems and, at the same time, I promise to take any of your advice under consideration."

Rhys let that information sink in and said, "I have met several of my tenants and have been most impressed by William Shirley. Mr. Shirley, would you step forward?"

This was part of a plan Dalinda had explained to him, one which Dez had implemented at Torville Manor, as well. She had even emphasized to Rhys to always refer to his tenants using the title of *Mister* with their surname, telling him it would show he afforded them respect. He, Dez, and Dalinda had met with William Shirley and a handful of others yesterday in preparation of today's announcements.

The farmer, in his mid-thirties, joined Rhys at the front.

"Mr. Shirley has impressed me with his knowledge of farming and, more importantly, his commitment to the people of Sheffield Park. He will be in charge of three other tenants who will head up teams populated by the farmers who live and work in the surrounding areas closest to those three."

Rhys named the three other men and asked them to join him, explaining how the teams would be divided into various laboring tasks and report their accomplishments to Mr. Shirley, who would act as a liaison between the people and Rhys.

"And also my estate manager, whom I have yet to hire," he added. "This way, communication will be clear for all parties. We have ploughing and planting to do now. Then shearing and an upcoming harvest to manage. If we cooperate and operate as a strong group, we can accomplish tasks much more quickly and efficiently and help Sheffield Park to thrive."

Applause broke out, warming him. He glanced to Dalinda and saw her pleased smile.

He then addressed the household staff and those who would perform tasks about the estate. In the last week, Dalinda, along with help from Mr. and Mrs. Marsh, had hired an entire slate of servants. Rhys now had footmen and parlor maids. Two washerwomen, a carpenter, and a blacksmith. He spoke to these people and told them of his expectations. Dalinda had said he should be firm with his servants but kind, a balance he hoped to achieve soon.

"In conclusion, I want to say how grateful I am to be your new earl. I want what is best for you and your families. I want Sheffield Park to blossom and shine. I know, with your help, that this estate will flourish. To thank you for being a part of my life, I would like to hold a country ball for us to come together and celebrate our new relationship."

Cheers erupted. This, too, had been Dalinda's idea and Rhys saw how well it was received. He doubted the former earl had ever thought to hold such an event. Suddenly, after feeling so adrift ever since he left the military, he thought that he was beginning to make his way and find new purpose in the life he had been given.

"When is the ball, my lord?" called a voice from the crowd.

He thought a moment, having no idea what entailed preparing for something such as this.

"Today is Friday. Shall we say a week from tomorrow?"

More cheers sounded. He glanced across a sea of happy faces and took pride in his people, coming together and uniting for the common purpose of making Sheffield Park and their own lives better.

"That is all," he ended. "Good day to everyone."

He turned, seeking out the person he most wanted to speak with. Dalinda stepped to him, her smile radiant.

"You spoke from your heart, Rhys. You are a natural leader. In time, you will learn of all your responsibilities and become an expert in them, as you were when you were in the army."

He shrugged. "I merely parroted your words. Your ideas."

She grinned, mischief in her eyes. "Well, we need never mention that to anyone."

"Lord Sheffington!" a voice cried.

Turning, he saw none other than Eli Simpson making his way through the crowd.

"Eli? Eli!"

The two men met and Rhys threw his arms about his old friend, pounding him soundly on the back.

"What brings you here?" he asked.

A beaming Eli said, "Are you growing feeble in your old age, my lord? My, you are what–thirty years of age now? You sent for me. I was at my father's house when your note came to him, asking of my whereabouts so he could forward your letter to me. It was a stroke of luck and an opportunity I couldn't pass up."

"What have you been doing since we last saw one another?"

"I did find work as an assistant steward two months after you left with your regiment and then was promoted to steward at the same estate half a dozen years later. The earl recently passed, leaving his son the title. While the son is a good man, his younger brother is a bad apple. The new earl thinks to help his brother improve in character and made him the estate's new steward. I received a generous settlement and recommendation for vacating my position."

"So, you are free to come work for me?" Rhys asked, not bothering to contain his excitement. "You will become my estate manager?"

"If you'll have me, my lord," Eli replied.

He thrust out his hand. "I would be delighted to hire you," and the two men shook.

Rhys realized he hadn't introduced his companions. "Eli, I want you to meet the friends who have been advising me. Her Grace, the Duchess of Gilford. Lord and Lady Torrington. Without them, I would have mucked things up something terrible."

Eli greeted the three and Rhys suggested they return to the house.

"We can talk over luncheon. There is much to be said."

Dez engaged Eli in conversation, bringing Anna along with them. Rhys offered Dalinda his arm and she tucked her hand through the crook.

"It is obvious how pleased you are to have Mr. Simpson in your fold," she said as they strolled behind the others.

"Eli is the smartest man I ever knew. He will be a tremendous asset to Sheffield Park. All I need now are a butler and housekeeper."

Though Dalinda had conducted interviews for those positions, she hadn't been happy with any of the applicants and had told him they might have to reach out to an employment agency in London to find a suitable pair.

"That won't be necessary," she said. "Mr. and Mrs. Marsh will not be returning to Laurelwood. They are staying on at Sheffield Park."

Rhys stopped in his tracks. "What? No, I cannot steal away your butler and housekeeper."

"It has already been arranged," she told him. "While the Marshes have enjoyed managing the household at Laurelwood, Sheffield Park is a vast estate. Their talents are being wasted in a smaller place. I approached them regarding the change and they have agreed it would be best for you—and them—if they remained."

"But what of Laurelwood?"

She chuckled. "I am a duchess, Rhys. Qualified servants will come out of the woodwork once they know I am in need of a butler and housekeeper. I will have my pick of whom to employ." She squeezed his arm. "It is my gift to you."

"It is too much but I will not be churlish. I will accept the Marshes with happiness—and mind my Ps and Qs around Mrs. Marsh, to be sure. I wouldn't put it past her to take me to the woodshed if she felt me lacking in some respect."

She laughed heartily. "Good. See that she keeps you in line."

They started up again and as they reached the house, Dalinda said, "Everything seems to be in order at Sheffield Park, Rhys. Especially with Mr. Simpson's arrival." She gazed steadily at him. "It is time for me to go."

Immediately, sadness washed over him. He would be bereft without her. Though he had maintained control and kept his hands off her, he had grown used to having her here as his friend.

"I haven't a clue how to organize a country ball. Would you at least stay through next Saturday?" he asked, his throat tightening with emotion.

She pursed her lips as she often did when in thought and finally said, "Yes. I will help plan the ball and stay through next week. After that, I must return to Gillingham."

Rhys had Dalinda for another week—and he planned to have her in his bed a final time.

CHAPTER THIRTEEN

DALINDA KISSED CHARLIE and set the sleeping babe into his crib. Cuddling with the infant had been the best part of her trip.

Not her night with Rhys.

Knowing she was lying to herself, she turned and saw Anna stifling a yawn.

"It is time I tucked you in for a nap, as well," she told her friend.

Anna was riding and walking every day but both Dalinda and Dez kept a close eye on her, watching to see if or when she tired. As a mother herself, Dalinda knew how having a baby sapped a woman's energy. Coupling that with Anna's long incarceration at the madhouse, where she was abused and ate very little, it was no wonder the new mother wasn't yet back to full strength.

"I could certainly use one. Are you sure you don't need me for anything?"

She slipped her arm through Anna's and led her from the nursery. "No. Everything is arranged for tomorrow's ball. Our servants know to get the majority of the packing done during the day tomorrow so that we might leave for Torville Manor the following morning."

As they walked down the corridor, Anna said, "I think the idea of a country ball is a lovely way for Rhys to show his appreciation of his workers and servants."

"And also to get to know his neighbors. He needs to establish himself as the leader in the area since he is of the highest rank."

Dalinda had told Rhys that besides his workers that invitations should be extended to the neighborhood and the local village. He had readily agreed, saying he knew nothing of these affairs and she was to plan the event as she saw fit. A few of the tenants and one footman had shared that they played the fiddle but she didn't want any of them to miss out on the fun of dancing. Instead, she had sent a note to London, knowing the Season didn't start for another two weeks, and had engaged her favorite quartet to play at the ball.

They reached Anna's bedchamber and she kissed her friend's cheek. "Get some rest."

"What will you be doing? Or should I even ask?"

Dalinda shrugged. She had worked constantly during the past week, trying to prepare Sheffield Park for when she would depart. The Marshes had been a godsend, helping her prioritize what tasks needed to be accomplished. The pair had thoroughly trained the new household staff which had been hired. Dozens of rooms had been aired and cleaned. Furniture shone and windows sparkled. It was wonderful seeing the beautiful house come to life again.

She parted from Anna and made her way to Rhys' study, which he had told her to use during her stay. Mr. Marsh entered and announced that the London musicians had arrived and were being shown to their rooms.

"They have requested to practice in the ballroom once they are settled, Your Grace."

"Let them. They can entertain the maids and footmen as they decorate for tomorrow evening."

Dipping her pen into the inkwell, Dalinda planned out menus for the coming two weeks. She had found Rhys' cook to be quite talented and now that the woman had a fully stocked larder and scullery maids to assist in meal preparation, her meals had been heavenly. Dalinda was also happy that Eli Simpson had agreed to join them for the evening meal each night. The former tutor had a wonderful sense of humor and keen intelligence. Not only would he be an excellent steward for Rhys but Mr. Simpson would also be a good friend and companion. The two could dine together every night and neither one would be lonely.

Mrs. Marsh appeared and she smiled at the housekeeper. She would miss the woman's no-nonsense approach at Laurelwood. Fortunately, Mrs. Marsh had a sister, Mrs. Franklin, who was also a housekeeper and looking for a new situation. Her employer had recently passed and the new viscount wasn't to the woman's liking. Dalinda had corresponded with Mrs. Franklin and she had agreed to come to Laurelwood in the same capacity. She had written to Dalinda that Mr. Blair, the household butler, would also prefer a new post. Trusting Mrs. Franklin's judgment, Dalinda had accepted the two to head her staff.

"I am glad to see you, Mrs. Marsh. I have the menus for the next two weeks." She passed the sheets of paper to the housekeeper. "You will need to take up this task, consulting with Cook, until there is a Lady Sheffington to manage this."

The thought of Rhys wed to another woman brought a sense of wistfulness to her, quickly followed by jealousy regarding the unknown wife. She still didn't understand the barrier he had erected between them. It wasn't as if she had been born a duchess or even been the daughter of a duke. He placed her on a lofty pillar that she was uncomfortable perching upon. If she had her way, she would climb down from it and box his ears soundly.

And then kiss him as though her life depended upon it.

She had told herself that she would never be able to convince Rhys that they could be together and that she should move on. He had taught her things about herself and her body in their one night together that she would never forget. Things that she hoped she could put into practice with the man who would eventually become her husband. Still, a small part of her hadn't yet given up on the darkly handsome earl.

"I am happy to do so, my lady." Mrs. Marsh said. "I think things have progressed well. Once again, I am grateful to you for releasing Marsh and me so that we might run Sheffield Park. Taking on my sister, too, is such a blessing. You are a good woman, Your Grace. Marsh and I will miss you."

The housekeeper hesitated and then said, "If it's not too forward of me, Your Grace, but I have to ask—is there any chance you might one day come to live here, as well?"

Dalinda sighed. It didn't surprise her that the very astute Mrs. Marsh had picked up on the current that seemed to run between Dalinda and Rhys whenever they were in the same room together.

"I don't think that is a possibility, Mrs. Marsh. While I hope Lord Sheffington and I will always remain good friends, I think his interests lie in another direction."

The servant snorted. "I think you are mistaken, Your Grace. I have seen him look at you when he didn't think anyone noticed. You have most definitely caught his lordship's eye."

"That may be the case but he has indicated to me that he plans to seek a bride on the Marriage Mart during the Season," she said brusquely, tamping down her churning emotions. Dalinda frowned. "I would prefer not to address this topic again, Mrs. Marsh."

"As you wish, Your Grace."

She caught the look of sadness in the older woman's eyes, knowing the same sadness blanketed her.

Mr. Marsh appeared in the doorway. "Your Grace, there is . . . a man here . . . to see Lord Sheffington."

The butler seemed flustered, something she had never encountered before, drawing her curiosity. "Does this gentleman have a name, Mr. Marsh?" she asked.

"He is not a gentleman, Your Grace. He is . . . or rather was . . . a soldier."

"It must be one of his lordship's men come home from the war. I know Lord Sheffington will be eager to visit with him. His lordship— and my brother and Mr. Simpson—are still out and about on the estate. Show him into the drawing room, Mr. Marsh." She paused, thinking the man had come a long way in all likelihood. "Does he look hungry?"

Marsh cleared his throat. "Yes, Your Grace. That . . . among other things."

"Then have a full tea sent up. I will be there shortly."

"Yes, Your Grace."

Mrs. Marsh left but Marsh continued to hover. "Yes?" she asked, impatient to finish what she was doing so she could go and meet Rhys' friend.

The butler cleared his throat. "Prepare yourself, Your Grace. He is . . . that is to say . . ." Marsh's voice trailed off.

"Out with it," she demanded.

"The man was injured in the war. It is difficult to look upon him," Marsh spit out.

"Oh."

The soldier's injuries could be the very reason he had turned to Rhys for help. Dalinda rose. "Where is he?"

"Waiting in the rose parlor, Your Grace." Marsh shook his head. "His name is Robert Morrison."

"I will go to him and bring him to the drawing room myself. See to tea, Mr. Marsh."

She brushed past the butler, steeling herself for what she might see. From Marsh's demeanor, the soldier might be missing an arm. A leg.

Or something much worse.

She drew on the well deep within her. She was a nurturer at heart. If this man needed care, she would certainly provide it to him.

Pausing a moment before the doors to the rose parlor, Dalinda took a deep breath and then stepped inside. The visitor had his back to her as he studied a painting on the wall. She took in his uniform, which had seen better days, and how he leaned slightly to his left, as if favoring that leg or hip.

"Good afternoon. I am the Duchess of Gilford."

The soldier turned and she dug her nails into her palms, thankful she had braced herself. The man looked to be in his mid-forties. The right side of his face was weathered but handsome. The left, however, was another story. He wore an eyepatch over his left eye, which led her to believe it was missing or severely damaged. The flesh of his cheek and lower chin were mottled red and blotchy. Though his hat was pulled low, she could tell there was just a nub where his ear once sat.

She smiled brightly at him.

"Your Grace," he said, bowing to her. "I am Robert Morrison, late of His Majesty's Army. I was Colonel Armistead's batman."

Dalinda knew what a batman was from Dez's letters to her. "I know the colonel—now Lord Sheffington—will be delighted to see you, Mr. Morrison. He, his steward, Mr. Simpson, and my brother are out on the estate now. Would you care to come to the parlor for tea? We can wait for them to return."

Tears welled in the man's lone eye. "I think it best I wait here, Your Grace. You do not have to play nursemaid to me." His eye fell to the ground. "I know I'm a fright."

She crossed to him and slipped her arm through his. "Nonsense, Mr. Morrison. You'll come with me and we will share a spot of tea together. I insist."

Pulling on the reluctant soldier, she slowed her gait when she saw his was a bit unsteady. She led him upstairs to the drawing room and saw he was seated as a maid rolled in the teacart. She didn't know how Cook had put something together so quickly but she was grateful to have something to do with her hands. Willing them not to shake, she poured out and handed Morrison a cup and saucer. He eyed the abundance of food and then looked away.

"Lord Sheffington's cook is a fine one," she told him. "She is a bit sensitive, however. If we don't do justice to what she's sent to us, she will be quite upset."

"Oh. Well then, I should have a little something."

Dalinda chuckled. "Have more than a little something, Mr. Morrison. We don't want Cook in a temper when she's preparing the evening meal. I do hope you will stay and join us for it."

He looked baffled by her words. "I am not a guest, Your Grace. I have come in the hopes that the colonel—I mean, his lordship—might help me obtain a job."

"Hmm. Lord Sheffington already has a valet. Callow. That would be the job you would be most suited for. What did you do before the war, if I might ask?"

"I worked in a stable, Your Grace. I have been around horses all my life. It's something the colonel and I had in common."

"Oh!" she exclaimed. "You are the one who whispers to horses, aren't you? The one who could calm them with but a gentle touch and soft word in their ear."

His brow creased. "Yes, how did you know that?"

"My brother was Major Bretton, now the Earl of Torrington."

Morrison's face lit up. "I know the major well. He and Colonel Armistead were quite close." He nodded. "I should have known. You favor Major Bretton quite a bit."

"We are twins. I came to visit my brother and his wife at the same time Lord Sheffington paid them a visit. The four of us, along with my nephew, came back to Sheffield Park to help the earl become more established."

Morrison took a large bite of his sandwich, nodding, and then said, "It's a large place."

"I agree. Both Lord Sheffington and my brother never expected to become peers. They are leaning upon one another for advice on how to run their estates."

"If anyone can do it right, it's those two. They each had a good head on their shoulders and the respect of their men. I can tell you they were sorely missed after they both departed the Continent."

Wanting to know more about Rhys's time in the military, she thought Robert Morrison would be the perfect person to ask.

"Naturally, I know my brother well. We are twins and grew up being very close. I don't know much about Lord Sheffington's military career, though. What was he like in the war?"

The veteran chewed a bite of his sandwich thoughtfully a moment and then replied, "Smart. Smarter than any of the other officers. No disrespect to Major Bretton."

"None taken," she said. "Why do you say your colonel was smart?"

"It's as if he had a sixth sense about things. Oh, he was strict about the rules we had to follow. He made sure his men were trained and trained well. We marched better and shot better than any regiment on the Continent. What's important, though, is that he got to know us. We weren't just another soldier in the rank and file. He knew our names. The places we came from. A bit of what we liked to do and something about our families. If we left behind a mother or a sweetheart. He always fought to get us extra rations or clean socks, too. His men were quite devoted to him, Your Grace.

"But it was going into battle where we placed all our trust in him. He had experience all right—but it was more than that. Like intuition, I'd say. Some premonition about how the enemy would act or react. As if his gut and brains aligned when all the bullets began to fly. He carried out orders from above and we obeyed him without question. There were times, though, he'd pull us back or send us around another way and let me tell you—those were the times he saved a good number of hides." Morrison nodded. "Yes. The colonel was beloved."

"More tea?" she asked, glad to see him opening up.

Dalinda asked him about his life before the war and how he became a soldier. Eventually, he began talking about his injuries, sharing how he received the burns on his face and lost his ear.

"It's hard, knowing how I scare others now, from little children to old men. I'm a right friendly sort, Your Grace, but it's like I'm being swallowed whole by a black hole, one so deep I might never climb out of it." Tears welled in his eye. "I tried to get a job. The army had no need of me anymore. No one else has wanted to take me on. I'm still strong. I can work. I limp a little but my one eye and ear do their jobs just fine."

He put down the saucer. "I didn't know where else to turn. The colonel was such a good man. I thought if anyone might could help me, it would be him."

"I guarantee that he will find a position for you, Mr. Morrison. He has been hiring staff for the household and—"

"No, nothing inside, Your Grace. I don't want to frighten his guests or other servants. Maybe the stables since I know horses so well. Or I am good with my hands and can make all sorts of things from wood. I'd even give farming a try. All I am asking for is a chance."

Dalinda's heart went out to this man who had lost so much defending Great Britain.

And then an idea began forming. One she would share with Rhys the minute he returned.

CHAPTER FOURTEEN

R HYS MOUNTED HIS horse and Dez and Eli did the same and they rode to the Sheffield Park stables after a full day out on the land. Everywhere they had gone, people were buzzing about tomorrow night's country ball. So many had thanked him for holding it to celebrate his arrival. None could remember a time when an event such as this had occurred.

He handed off his horse to a groom, one of two, and thought he would like to add at least one more. Perhaps one who might serve as his driver, as well. He wanted to invest in more horses and he could certainly use a new carriage though both of those would have to wait until after the house repairs had been completed. Most likely, it would be wise to delay such purchases until after he wed.

Dez had asked him if he would partake in the Season, which started in two weeks. He had no inclination to do so, preferring to stay at his new country estate and make sure things were up and running for the coming harvest. Of course, now that he'd hired Eli and saw how experienced his new steward was, he could probably go to London for some of the time. The city was only four or five hours away by carriage. He could possibly go for a week at a time throughout the Season and then return here to help oversee things when necessary.

He assumed Dalinda would also be in London and at events he attended despite her mentioning she didn't feel ready to participate in social events. Her duke had encouraged her not to mourn him and instead find another husband once he was gone. Knowing how she longed for more children, he doubted she would waste any time. Unfortunately, it would be impossible to avoid her.

The three men headed toward the house, Dez commenting how ready he was for tea.

"I won't be able to join you," Eli said. "I have more work to complete."

"You are far too dedicated, Eli," he told his friend.

The steward grinned. "For what you are paying me, my lord, I should put in double the number of hours."

He hated the formality between them now. At least Eli would join them as usual for dinner this evening. It was already an established pattern and one Rhys hoped would continue once his friends departed.

"Very well," he told his steward. "I will see you at seven."

They parted ways inside the house and Marsh approached them.

"Are the ladies in the drawing room?" asked Rhys.

"They are, my lord," the butler answered.

"Good. I am famished," Dez declared.

"You have a visitor, my lord," Marsh continued. "A Robert Morrison is with Her Grace and Lady Torrington."

"Morrison? He's here?" Rhys asked. "That certainly surprises me." Glancing to Dez, he said, "You remember my batman."

"Of course," Dez said. "I wonder why he has come."

"We shall certainly find out."

As they started toward the staircase, Marsh called out, "My lord, you need to—"

"Not now, Marsh. I'll deal with whatever it is after tea," Rhys told the servant, eager to see Morrison again and find out why he had come to call when he should be at war.

They arrived at the drawing room and entered. He heard laughter and saw both Dalinda and Anna engaged at something his visitor had shared.

"I hear Morrison has come to pay a call," Rhys said, striding across the room.

The soldier rose and turned to face him, causing Rhys to stop dead in his tracks.

Morrison had been a few years past forty when they had parted and still a handsome man for his age, full of vim and vigor and always one with a ready story. While one side of his face remained intact, the other had been set afire. Whether from a rifle backfiring or being caught in cannon fire, he couldn't say. All he knew was that Morrison's face had been ruined and he'd lost both an eye and an ear. It would be hard for anyone to look upon him without disgust.

Yet Dalinda and Anna had been sitting with Morrison, laughter coming from them, as if everything were perfectly all right.

The former batman came to stand before him. "I know how hideous I look, Colonel. I'm sorry, my lord."

"Do your injuries pain you, Morrison?"

"Some." He smiled wryly. "Not as much as when they first happened, though."

"Come and sit," Dalinda called to them.

Rhys looked to her and saw a placid expression on her face. No one would ever know the guest she entertained would strike horror in most people.

"Mr. Morrison, you need to finish your sandwich," she said. "Anna, would you ring for fresh tea now that Dez and Lord Sheffington have joined us?"

His gaze returned to the former soldier and he thrust out his hand. "It is very good to see you again, Morrison. I hope you have received a warm welcome to Sheffield Park."

"Her Grace has been most kind to me."

Dez also shook Morrison's hand and the three men returned to where the ladies sat.

Dalinda said, "Mr. Morrison is eager to find a position, Lord Sheffington. We have been discussing horses and he simply knows everything about them. I believe he would make for a fine head groom at Sheffield Park."

"Your Grace?" Morrison questioned uncertainly, looking from her to Rhys.

He steadied himself and met Morrison's gaze. "Horses were always something you and I had in common. I would like to purchase a few more for my stables and for use in London. Your advice on which horseflesh to buy would be helpful, as would you staying on and seeing to them."

The hope that filled Morrison's eye almost did Rhys in. He could only imagine what this man had been through and how many places he had been rejected before he had turned to his former commanding officer.

"Are you certain, my lord?" Morrison asked hesitantly.

"I can think of no man better suited to the position."

"Then it's settled," Dalinda said, smiling her approval.

New tea arrived and they spent a pleasant hour in conversation. Morrison shared what he knew of the war since Rhys' and Dez's departures and the three men spoke of soldiers and officers they all knew.

Dez set aside his empty cup and said, "It is time for Anna and me to make our way to the nursery and spend some time with Charlie. It has been good to see you again, Morrison. You will make valuable contributions to Sheffield Park."

"Thank you, Major." Morrison flushed. "I mean, Lord Torrington. I apologize, my lord."

Dez laughed. "It has taken some getting used to on both my and Sheffington's part, answering to a title."

Dez and Anna left the drawing room and Dalinda said, "Lord Sheffington is holding a country ball tomorrow evening, Mr. Morrison. It will be a good way for you to get to know the staff which has been hired and meet his tenants, as well as some of the locals."

A look of horror crossed Morrison's face. "I cannot go!" he sputtered. "It would ruin the occasion for everyone who comes. I won't do that, Your Grace."

She frowned. "I know you are concerned about your physical appearance, Mr. Morrison. Does your war injury make you know any less about horses?"

"No," he said uncertainly and Rhys wondered where she was going with her questions.

"The two grooms may find it hard to look upon you at first but once they see how knowledgeable you are about horses and how well you take things in hand, they will see beyond your marred flesh. The same will be true for others. You are a kind, thoughtful, and very charming man, Mr. Morrison. You have proven that to me during the past few hours we have been together. Why, I have completely forgotten about your war injuries during our conversation."

Morrison fidgeted in his seat. "You are most kind, Your Grace, but most people won't be. I know. I went to enough places. Applied for too many positions. Wasn't even given a chance to show what I could do. No one could see past my mutilated face. The fact that Lord Sheffington is willing to hire me on is enough. I will avoid others when I can. I don't want to cause a stir. And I certainly won't ruin his lordship's ball tomorrow night by upsetting his guests."

Steely determination filled Dalinda's eyes and Rhys prepared himself for what might come.

"Mr. Morrison, I insist you come to the ball because I plan to dance the first set with you."

"What?" the man proclaimed, clearly confused by her declaration.

"You heard me. I am a duchess. If I accept you, others will, as well." She gazed at him intently. "If you choose not to attend the ball, then I will forgo going myself."

"Dalinda," Rhys said, a warning in his voice. "You have planned this ball. Everyone is expecting you to be there. You have promised to help me in hosting it."

Her mouth set firmly. "I will go only if Mr. Morrison does. If he refuses to do so, you are on your own, Sheffington."

He turned to his batman. "Help me out here, man. You must come."

Morrison's gaze flicked from Rhys to Dalinda and back again several times. Finally, he said, "You're a stubborn one, aren't you, You Grace?"

She bit back a smile. "You have no idea, Mr. Morrison."

After hesitating a moment, he said, "All right. I will come. I can't guarantee I'll stay long but I will dance with you." Then he grinned. "Me, Robert Morrison, dancing with a duchess. My, that'll make a grand story."

Dalinda beamed at him. "And you will tell it so well. I am sure each time it will get even better."

She rose and both men shot to their feet. "I will leave you to discuss the position. I am sure Lord Sheffington wishes to escort you to the stables and show you his horses. Be sure to pay special attention to my Stormy. She's a handful but so sweet."

After Dalinda vacated the room, Morrison looked at Rhys in wonder. "She is quite a woman, my lord."

"I couldn't agree more," Rhys said, wishing she were his woman—and no other's. "Shall we go down to the stables? I can show you your room and introduce you to the other two lads."

As he led Morrison from the house, Rhys determined that he would have Dalinda in his bed a final time and then force himself to let her go.

RHYS AND HIS friends dined together for the final time. As he looked around, he was grateful that Dez and Anna lived so close to him. Who knew that his only friend and he would wind up as earls, much less own country estates in the same county?

He did see how good Anna was for Dez and how Dez doted on both his wife and son. They had been childhood sweethearts separated for many years but would fortunately spend the rest of their lives together. Part of him envied the love match they had, seeing how right things were between the pair. His expectations would be much lower when it came to marriage. From the little he knew about Polite Society, marriages were a business arrangement and a matter of convenience. He would provide his wife the title of Countess of Sheffington, while she would bring much-needed funds to their marriage. He would do his duty in the bedroom and make sure they had an heir and hoped that the two of them would get along. She would be responsible for household affairs and he would take care of the estate and his business holdings. Hopefully, they would be respectful of one another and provide love and support to whatever children they were blessed with.

Rhys avoided looking at Dalinda tonight. Instead of drinking her in, knowing she would soon be gone, he tried his best to remain distant and polite. The sooner he could cut the invisible ties that seemed to want to bring them together, the better it would be for him. He had spent enough time mooning after her like some silly schoolboy. He needed to get used to the idea that she would soon wed a high-ranking peer and be satisfied by another man in her bed.

The meal ended after much talk of tomorrow night's ball. As Dalinda and Anna discussed things related to it, he realized how much work had gone into organizing such an affair.

"I think you will make quite a good impression on not only your tenants and workers but your neighbors, as well," Dalinda said. "Two barons and their wives, along with a viscount and his wife and daughter, will be attending."

"Along with all the villagers," Anna added. "Everyone is curious to meet the new Earl of Sheffington. The last one hadn't been seen at Sheffield Park in well over a decade and from what I gather, he wasn't very highly thought of."

"I only met Lord Sheffington the one time," Rhys said. "He seemed like any other peer of the land to me. Not that I knew many. A few used to call on Viscount Mowbray and I would attend to their horses. Then the viscount's daughter made her come-out and a few other eligible bachelors came sniffing around."

"That reminds me of the upcoming Season," Anna said. "Dez and I will be going for part of it to support Jessa." She looked to her husband with a fond smile. "I only hope my sister is fortunate enough to find her true love this year."

Dez took his wife's hand and kissed her fingers. "I only hope Jessa doesn't find me too protective of her. I know what scoundrels dwell among the *ton*. I want only the best for her." He looked to his twin. "Will you reconsider and attend the Season, Dalinda? I know Gilford's death is recent but he did encourage you to get out and about in public."

Rhys couldn't help but watch her steadily as she said, "I don't think so."

"Why not?" he demanded. "You have mentioned wanting to re-marry." He thought he knew the answer, though. Dalinda was still in love with her dead duke.

"I am not ready to become involved in the social swirl," she admitted. "Arthur and Harry will be coming home from Dunwood Academy. I want to spend time with them, especially now that their father is gone. I neglected them for far too long and it is time I made it up to them and show them just how much their mother loves them." She paused. "I am planning to move to Laurelwood and want them to become familiar with the property. Also, I want to return to Torville Manor when Dez and Anna leave London and allow the boys to visit them and meet their cousin."

"Why would you leave Gillingham?" Anna asked, perplexed. "It is your home and close to where the boys are going to school."

Dalinda said firmly, "I have given this much thought. With Reid now being the Duke of Gilford, he will want to wed and start a family. His duchess shouldn't have to look over her shoulder and see me hovering. Besides, Gilford provided Laurelwood for me. I adore the estate and feel quite comfortable there. Perhaps next year I will be ready to attend parties once again."

Rhys thought she looked sad and wanted to comfort her. Any comfort, though, would turn to kisses—and beyond. She had acted impulsively coming to his bed once. Most likely, she regretted having done so. While he had hoped they could spend a final night together, he now saw that Dalinda needed to finish grieving for Gilford. It would be selfish of him to lure her to his bed, knowing nothing come ever come of anything between them.

Still, he longed to hear her sing a final time and asked, "Would you consider singing and playing for us tonight, Dalinda?"

Their eyes met and she said, "I would be happy to do so."

Dez and Anna begged off, saying they were both tired and wanted to go to bed. Something told Rhys that the couple had more than sleeping on their minds by the looks in their eyes.

He and Dalinda retreated to the drawing room and he closed his eyes as she sang a few country ballads, knowing any time he heard them her image would come to mind.

The last note sounded and he opened his eyes, seeing her rise from the bench and come to sit with him.

"I have a suggestion to make," she said. "Mr. Morrison's arrival today spurred an idea within me."

Intrigued, he asked, "What do you wish me to consider? You have already given me food for thought on so many different subjects."

"I know you have felt as if your life has gone topsy-turvy ever since you left the military."

He chuckled. "You are correct in saying so. Thank goodness Eli Simpson showed up and is helping to right things about the estate. I also express my gratitude to you—and Anna—for seeing the household put back in order and hiring the proper servants. I know Mr. and Mrs. Marsh will never allow me to be blown off course in the future."

"That is all true. Mr. Simpson is a huge asset and he will relieve you of many burdens regarding the day-to-day management of Sheffield Park."

"What does this have to do with Morrison?" Rhys asked.

"Look at how shabbily he was treated once he left the army. They didn't want him anymore after he was injured and neither did anyone else. He is still able-bodied and of sound mind, ready to fully contribute in any manner of ways that he can. You hiring him to be in charge of your stables will change his life."

Dalinda leaned forward. "What if you could do this for other former soldiers? Surely, there are many who find themselves in Mr. Morrison's position, not having any family to go home to and no job to be had."

"You're saying I should hire disabled soldiers?"

"I am. Moreover, I think you could help those that are injured even more severely than Mr. Morrison. Your house is quite large. The entire east wing is not even in use now. What if you turned it into a kind of hospital? Offering medical care for those men who have been harmed in battle. Perhaps you could even help them learn other, different skills from those they possess, allowing them to be able to seek work once they left Sheffield Park."

Her idea excited him. He'd been seeking direction in his life. A way to fulfill his responsibilities and still feel useful. Taking in discharged soldiers and nursing them back to health—and even helping to train them for different occupations—would be a worthwhile pursuit.

"I could write my former commanding officer, General Shepherd," he said. "Broach the subject with him. He receives the lists of casualties and those injured in battle."

"Perhaps he could funnel certain cases your way," Dalinda said. "Of course, you would need a medical doctor on staff. Perhaps two, along with a few women to help nurse the men back to health."

Enthusiasm filled him. "This would be a worthwhile endeavor. I could help soldiers that would otherwise be forgotten. Put this large house to good use." He smiled. "As always, you are full of excellent ideas, Dalinda."

She rose and he did the same. They stood facing one another, not speaking. He could feel the air charged between them and wanted nothing better than to pull her into his arms and kiss her senseless.

Instead, he played the gentleman. "I think I will go and write to General Shepherd at once so that the letter can be posted first thing tomorrow morning."

Rhys thought he saw disappointment flicker in her eyes as she said, "That is a wise use of your time. I think I shall retire for the night. I will be up early tomorrow since there will be much to be done to finish preparations for tomorrow's ball." She paused and then said, "Goodnight, Rhys."

Dalinda turned away and he watched her as she crossed the drawing room and exited. Hurt in letting her go mingled with the excitement of the prospect of helping others. Besides caring for the people of Sheffield Park, he finally felt as if some good might come from him being named a peer. He would concentrate on this part of his future—and not the brown-haired beauty who had stolen his heart.

CHAPTER FIFTEEN

DALINDA, ALONG WITH Dez and Anna, joined Rhys in a receiving line. Normally, these weren't a part of such an informal occasion but Rhys had insisted upon one, wanting to personally greet every attendee and speak to them by name. He had asked the three of them to join him since they acted in part as hosts for the country ball along with him.

She thought he looked splendid, his superfine coat a deep hunter green, causing his emerald eyes to stand out even more than usual. He had asked her what he should wear, noting he didn't have any formal evening clothes yet, only a few items the local tailor had made up for him. She had told him black evening wear wouldn't be expected at this type of event. Dez had provided Rhys with the name of his London tailor, saying if he were to take part in the Season that he would certainly need proper clothes for the various balls, routs, and concerts.

For her part, Dalinda had decided to skip the Season altogether, as she had shared with the others the previous evening. She did yearn for a husband and knew the best place to meet a new one would be in London among the *ton*. Her heart told her, though, that she wouldn't want any part of it. She had found the only man she would ever consider marrying—and he didn't seem to want her. Actually, Rhys did want her. She could see desire in his eyes anytime he spoke with her. There was no hiding the passion whenever he gazed upon her, which was rare these days. It was as if he pulled away, wanting to be rid of her as soon as possible. She still didn't agree with him that he was unworthy of her. Oh, why did Gilford have to be a duke? If she had wed a viscount or an earl, she doubted Rhys would be resisting the pull between them.

Of course, it was because Gilford *was* a duke that her future had been secured. He had—through sheer willpower—pushed her father into a corner and demanded that Dalinda be given to him as his bride. She didn't think a man less powerful would have been able to bend Torrington to his will. It had worked out, giving her a life of security and peace for many good years, with their boys an added blessing to their marriage. Her husband had taught her all manner of things and offered her friendship and respect. She viewed herself as fortunate that she had become the duchess of such a kind, thoughtful man.

Would she ever be able to change Rhys' mind? If he left Sheffield Park and went to London for the Season to seek a bride with a hefty dowry, she would have no chance with him. Perhaps she should reconsider and go to London at least for part of the time. It would give her more opportunities to interact with him. Perhaps she could boldly tempt him back into her bed.

Dalinda also hoped that her idea in turning a part of Sheffield Park into a place to house and train injured veterans might keep Rhys so busy that he wouldn't have time to find his countess. At least not immediately. With her planning to move to and spend a great deal of the year at Laurelwood, she would only be an hour or so away from him. Coming to see the former soldiers under his care might be an excuse for them to be thrown together more frequently.

She would have to act as her own advocate because she could only see a future with Rhys in it. It wasn't just the one, magnificent night they had spent together that clouded her judgment—though the physical attraction between them wasn't something she could lightly dismiss. Rhys himself was the draw. He was hardworking. Honorable. Loyal. Intelligent. Flexible. Decent. It was as if she were a gambler and her entire life centered around the next throw of the dice or the card the dealer passed to her.

Turning to him, she saw his brow furrow slightly and she whispered the name of the tenant about to reach them. He greeted the man and his wife with enthusiasm, using their names.

As the couple left to enter the ballroom, he told her, "You have done an outstanding job of planning this ball, Dalinda. I also believe you know the names of more of the guests than I do," he said wistfully.

"You will learn them all soon. Going out on the estate and meeting regularly with tenants was something Gilford and I did twice a week. Sometimes, I even went on my own, bringing baskets of food and medicines to those in need and helping to deliver babies."

"You acted as a midwife?" he asked, his brows arching.

"I did. It is hard work bringing a child into the world. I was able to offer comfort and support to those who gave birth."

Rhys shook his head. "You continue to surprise me at every turn."

"Lord Sheffington!" a voice cried and they turned, seeing the local doctor and his wife stepping to them.

A quarter-hour later, the line ended, the last of the guests now entering the ballroom.

"I am glad that is over and done with," Dez declared. He slipped his arm about Anna's waist. "Let's go inside, my love. I am ready to dance with my beautiful wife."

The couple left, leaving Dalinda and Rhys alone. She hoped he would ask her to dance at some point this evening. The thought of being in Rhys' arms seemed heavenly. Not during the opening of the ball, though. She had promised to dance with Mr. Morrison and would keep to that promise. Then she saw the uncomfortable look on Rhys' face and realized that wouldn't be the case.

"You don't know how to dance, do you?" she asked softly.

Sadly, he shook his head. "No. I never had an opportunity to learn how. As a lad, I was working too hard trying to put food on the table. Then when Lord Sheffington plucked me from obscurity and assigned Eli as my tutor, the notion of dancing never came up. I learned Latin and Greek. Advanced mathematics. Read classic literature. We walked the streets of London daily and Eli showed me various styles of architecture and took me to museums to view famous paintings. A few times we went to a play or concert. We had no social life, though.

"From there, I went straight into the military with the commission the earl purchased for me." He grinned. "The only dancing I did then was as the bullets flew by and I tried to avoid them."

She laughed at his joke and then grew serious. "I am sorry I did not think to give you dancing lessons, Rhys. Here you are hosting a ball and will not be participating."

"It doesn't matter. As long as my guests enjoy themselves, it will make me happy."

Dalinda touched his arm, feeling the jolt that seemed to be ever-present between them. "Promise me you will find a dance master to teach you the waltz and basic reels. You can't go through the Season without dancing."

He gazed at her steadily. "I have decided not to go to London anytime soon. I am learning too much about my estate to run off and participate in frivolous activities. Besides, I have given quite a bit of thought to your idea of helping wounded and injured veterans. I quite like it. It would give me additional purpose and make all this worthwhile." He chuckled. "It also sounds far more interesting than pursing a wife."

His words confirmed her decision not to go to London. She would rather spend time with Arthur and Harry anyway.

And hopefully, Rhys.

"Since you are so willing to learn and I will be close by at Laurelwood, I would like to offer to teach you how to dance before next Season comes around."

She removed her arm from his sleeve but he caught her wrist. His thumb slowly rubbed back and forth on the underside, causing her breath to hitch.

"I would like that, Dalinda. Very much."

His smoldering eyes made her skin heat. She was surprised that she didn't erupt in flames.

Slipping her arm into the crook of his, he guided her toward the ballroom. The crowded room buzzed with conversations. Rhys caught the eyes of the musicians, who were tuning their instruments, and they ceased.

Dalinda leaned closer and told him, "Say something to commence the opening of the ball and welcome your guests."

"Very well."

She pulled away and took a few steps back, wanting the Earl of Sheffington to be the center of attention. He made his way to the quartet of musicians and she noticed those gathered fell silent.

Rhys faced the room and said, "Tonight is a celebration of the beginning of our relationship together. Enjoy the food and music. Dance until your poor feet ache. For a few hours, leave work behind and become swept up in the gaiety. Welcome to Sheffield Park!"

He turned and nodded. The quartet picked up their instruments and began to play. As Rhys left the dance floor, partners hurried to form their lines. Dalinda took the opportunity to move toward Mr. Morrison. She had seen him hanging back from the others, trying to melt into the wall. She knew he must be terribly worried about his facial disfigurement and she wanted to help launch him into life at Sheffield Park.

"I am here to claim my dance with you, Mr. Morrison," she told him brightly. "You are remiss not to have sought me out before now."

"Your Grace, I must—"

"No protests. Come!" she said gleefully, snagging his arm and leading him to the center of the room. "I asked for a Scotch reel to be played first. I hope you know the steps."

They lined up with the others and the dancing began in earnest. She was impressed with how light on his feet the new head groom was, as were others. When the set finally came to an end, applause broke out and Dalinda saw several people go up and begin talking to Morrison. She winked at him and he smiled gratefully at her before turning his attention to those gathered around him.

"That one dance may have changed his life," Rhys said in her ear, causing a shiver to run along her spine. "Thanks to you, people will see him for the man he is and what he can offer—not the damaged soul who slunk home from the war."

"I like Mr. Morrison a great deal. Others will, too," she proclaimed.

"Your Grace? Would you care to dance?" asked William Shirley, the lead tenant.

She faced the farmer. "I would enjoy partnering with you, Mr. Shirley."

Two hours later, Dalinda's feet began to protest. Thankfully, it was the supper dance, which she had spent with a young man who was about fourteen. His mother called him back over, leaving her free. She entered the room where Cook had set up the lavish buffet. Both she and Anna had spent hours with Cook, talking about a blend of hearty country dishes and some which were more refined. The buffet looked elegant and the room had been decorated to perfection. She gazed out and saw many happy faces and knew the ball had been a success.

"Would you care to dine with me?" Rhys asked. "Dez and Anna have a table over to the left and asked if we wished to join them."

"I can think of no others I'd rather spend the meal with."

Rhys and Dez left her with Anna as they went to make plates for them.

Anna turned to her. "The ball is certainly a success and you are a large part of that, Dalinda. You dancing with Mr. Morrison also made a huge difference. He hasn't been shunned but rather embraced by those present."

"I am happy that Rhys is meeting his neighbors and showing his tenants how much he cares for them."

"And what about how much he cares for you?" her friend asked.

A hot blush spilled across her cheeks. "You are mistaken, Anna. There is nothing between us."

Anna snorted. "Not from the heated glances I have seen him toss your way. Have you rejected his attentions? Are you not over Gilford's death yet? I know you cared for your husband a great deal."

"Gilford has nothing—and everything—to do with it," Dalinda complained. "Rhys thinks that, as a duchess, I am too far above him. He cites his humble origins and everything Gilford was and had that Rhys claims he is not. Yet it is his beginnings and what he has done with his life that impress me so. He has made the most of every opportunity given to him. He will make for an excellent earl." She sighed. "But he thinks himself beneath me and claims that I want a lord with a lofty title and numerous properties." Tears welled in her eyes.

"When all I want is to find love."

Anna took her hand. "Perhaps the old saying may prove true—absence makes the heart grow fonder." Anna squeezed her hand. "You have been a constant presence in Rhys' life, helping him put Sheffield Park back together. Once you are gone, he is bound to miss you."

"He may but he is a very stubborn man, as I am sure you can tell. He would rather wed a stranger and wealthy bride than me, keeping his new wife at a polite distance in a marriage of convenience." Dalinda shook her head. "Gilford left me quite well off. Besides the Laurelwood property and providing for Arthur and Harry, I have access to an obscene amount of funds. I could easily help shore up Sheffield Park and barely make a nick in what Gilford provided for me."

"Give it time, Dalinda," Anna advised. "Here they come."

"No word of this to Dez," she pleaded.

Anna grinned. "Do you think my husband would box his closest friend's ears for having taken his sister to bed?"

Dalinda gasped.

Her friend nodded. "I *knew* I was right. Don't worry. I haven't said a word to Dez. He hasn't a clue."

Rhys and Dez joined them, heaping plates in their hands.

"Do you really think I can even eat half of that?" Anna asked her husband playfully.

Dez grinned. "No. It just leaves more for me, I suppose."

Rhys sat next to Dalinda and set her plate before her. She scanned it.

"You seemed to have chosen all my favorites."

"Cook was helpful. She was at the buffet supervising. She said you had worked with her on creating every dish tonight and had an idea what might please you."

His gaze was warm, causing her to swallow and glance away, her face flaming. She wondered if it was obvious to others how much she cared for Rhys. Of course, Anna knew her well, almost as much as Dez did. Still, her twin had not mentioned anything to her regarding Rhys. She wondered if he had spoken to Rhys about her.

The four enjoyed a pleasant supper, discussing the guests who were in attendance and the music that had been played so far by the London musicians. When they finished eating and saw others were heading back to the ballroom, Anna told them she and Dez would be retiring for the night.

"I know country balls end early but I am exhausted after the dancing I've done. I know we are leaving early tomorrow and I must get some rest."

They all rose and Rhys kissed Anna's cheek. "Thank you for everything you have done to make tonight special. If Dez hadn't already married you, I would have to do so myself," he teased.

Dez and Anna said goodnight and Rhys escorted Dalinda back toward the ballroom. Before they entered, he stopped.

"I must tell you the same as I did Anna. Tonight is a success in no small part thanks to your contributions. The whole of Sheffield Park has seen your hand upon it. I am grateful to you, Dalinda. More than I could ever say." He paused. "My only regret is that I cannot ask you to dance with me tonight. I would have enjoyed that," he said wistfully.

She spoke from her heart. "There is another kind of dancing we can do, Rhys. If you are willing to come again to—"

"Your Grace." Marsh appeared before them. "You are needed at once."

Of all times for the butler to interrupt.

"What is it?" Dalinda asked sharply.

Marsh looked sheepish as he said, "Mrs. Abernathy has just gone into labor, Your Grace."

"Oh!"

Dalinda had learned earlier in the evening in the receiving line that the local midwife would not be in attendance because one of the estate's tenants had gone into labor with her first child, which meant she would be tied up most likely until tomorrow morning. Mrs. Abernathy, on the other hand, had not been due for two more weeks with her second child.

Turning to Rhys, she said, "First babies take their time in coming. Those that follow can arrive swiftly. There is no time to see Mrs. Abernathy back to her cottage."

"Do what you must," he said and she caught the regret in his eyes at their unfinished conversation.

"Mr. Marsh, see that hot water is put on to boil and that Mrs. Marsh gathers clean linens. I will take Mrs. Abernathy to a guest bedchamber."

"Yes, Your Grace."

The butler left swiftly and Dalinda entered the ballroom. She located Mr. and Mrs. Abernathy in a corner. Mr. Abernathy looked perplexed, while his wife sat in a chair and grimaced.

"Hello, Mrs. Abernathy," she said calmly. "I hear that your labor has started."

"It has, Your Grace," the woman replied. "My water broke." She indicated the floor underneath her. "I was dancing and probably shouldn't have been and suddenly felt lightheaded. My husband led me to a seat . . . and this happened," she said in dismay.

Rhys appeared. "We are going to take you to a room upstairs, Mrs. Abernathy."

"Oh, my lord, I couldn't impose upon you." Then a labor pain struck her and she sucked in her breath, wincing.

"It is no imposition at all. Her Grace will attend to you."

The woman's eyes grew round as she looked at Dalinda. "You will?"

She smiled. "I have done this often, Mrs. Abernathy. Here, let your husband and Lord Sheffington assist you upstairs."

The two men got on either side of her and helped her to stand. The dancing still went on and they were able to slip from the ballroom unnoticed. Once upstairs in a guest room, Mrs. Marsh appeared and told Dalinda preparations were being seen to as she settled the mother-to-be in the bed.

She said, "Mr. Abernathy, I know your child is with you tonight. The ball will be ending within the hour. You are welcome to remain here and wait for your wife to deliver the baby or you can take your boy home and put him to bed and await word from me."

The farmer nodded. "I think it best for us to go home. I can get someone to come and watch my boy and then return and wait. If that's not too much trouble," he said worriedly.

"Not at all. I will take good care of Mrs. Abernathy."

"Thank you, Your Grace." He took her hands and squeezed them.

"Thank you."

"Lord Sheffington, you might want to go with Mr. Abernathy. His wife needs her privacy."

"Of course, Your Grace," Rhys said. "Let me know if you have need of anything."

The two men left and Dalinda smiled at Mrs. Abernathy. "You will certainly have a story to tell. Giving birth at a country ball!"

The woman chuckled and then gripped the bedclothes as another pain struck her. As Dalinda examined her to see what progress had been made, she prayed that all would go well as she delivered this babe—and tried to put aside all thoughts of making love with Rhys.

CHAPTER SIXTEEN

R HYS ACCOMPANIED HIS departing guests to their waiting carriage. Anna held Charlie up and he kissed the baby's head, a sudden rush of unnamed feelings pouring through him.

"Take care, Rhys," Anna said. "And do come visit us. If not at Torville Manor, then come to town for a few days."

He kissed her cheek. "I will consider it, Anna, but I have much to do at Sheffield Park."

Dez offered his hand. "Work is important but so is play, Rhys. You never had a day off in the army and haven't taken one since you've become Lord Sheffington. Do think about a visit to town."

He had noticed that neither of them referred to London by its name. They always seemed to call it *town*. Yet another quirk of the *ton* that he'd best remember.

He shook his friend's hand. "Thank you for coming to see my estate and all the knowledge you've shared with me."

"We are not far from one another. I expect there will be many visits back and forth between Torville Manor and Sheffield Park over the years to come."

Dez assisted Anna into the carriage, leaving Rhys standing with Dalinda. His heart pounded fiercely and he swallowed, his mouth dry.

"Thank you for inviting me to see Sheffield Park," Dalinda said. "It is on a lovely piece of land and your house is quite beautiful."

"Thanks to you, things are falling into place," he said lightly, keeping a tight lock on his feelings for this woman. "I must thank you for all the advice you've dispensed. Perhaps you should start a service for peers coming into an unexpected title. Dez and I could certainly recommend your services."

"Hmm. It's a thought. Ashlyn started her own school when she became a widow and she's proven to be quite successful." Her eyes lit with mischief. "It might even lead to me finding another husband. A lord who is floundering and needs the steady hand of a capable woman in his life."

Rhys imagined her hand gliding up his chest and swallowed. "I might need to claim a percentage of your business since I gave you the idea for it," he teased, trying his best to keep things cheerful between them.

"Why don't we call ourselves even?" she asked, her eyes bright. "I have helped you. You have helped me." She paused. "In ways I never thought possible," she added softly.

They stood speechless for a moment and then she said, "Goodbye, Rhys," regret in her eyes. Regret he wished he hadn't put there and had no way of removing. It was best to let her go now, before either of them suffered heartbreak. She would be free to find herself another wealthy duke, while he would make the most of reviewing the Marriage Mart for a bride.

Just not yet. He wanted to savor his memories of Dalinda and do what he could to get Sheffield Park to be more profitable. Only then would he consider offering for a bride.

She leaned up on tiptoe and pressed a kiss to his cheek and then turned away. The waiting footman assisted her into the carriage. Rhys gave a wave as the vehicle started up and then watched it until it was out of sight.

He turned to Marsh and said, "Ready my carriage for town. I've business to see to."

"Yes, my lord," the butler said. "I will notify Callow to pack for you. Will you be gone long?"

"Only a few days, I believe."

Though he fully intended to spend the majority of his time at Sheffield Park, he couldn't rid himself of Dalinda's suggestion to help returning, injured veterans. What good was it to have a large country estate and this title if he couldn't put it to good use?

Of course, starting a hospital at Sheffield Park would prove to be expensive. He would need to hire a doctor and some nurses. The men would have to be fed and housed. Already, he'd hired additional servants, as well as a butler and housekeeper in the Marshes. While Goolsby had assured Rhys that he was solvent for a couple of years, that hadn't included the idea of a hospital, though. Rhys now had a burning desire to see this plan come to fruition. He couldn't fund it now without help. If he mentioned the idea to Dez, his friend would insist upon loaning Rhys the money and he didn't want that. Knowing Dez, he would call it a loan and then refuse to accept Rhys paying back the monies owed. He would never accept funds from Dalinda, whom he knew would be generous to a fault if he asked.

As far as the army was concerned, they never even gave discharged soldiers a by-your-leave. Once a man wasn't equipped to be an able-bodied soldier, His Majesty's Army washed its hands of him. Rhys would never see a farthing from them for his hospital. As for General Shepherd, he knew the man came from a wealthy family but as a second son, the commanding officer possessed no true wealth of his own. If Rhys was going to find a way to finance this type of operation, he would be on his own. If he had a wife, he assumed she would be involved in charitable affairs and she might be able to raise monies for this cause. Since no countess existed at the current time, it was up to him to figure out how to get the capital to begin.

One thought had occurred to him, which was why he was willing to leave Sheffield Park for a short while in order to go to London. While his country estate was dilapidated, his London townhouse shone like a crown jewel. Surely, he could find some items within it that he could sell. The walls were lined with paintings. The carpets and furniture appeared to be of excellent quality. Silver and china had to be plentiful. Parting with some of those things wouldn't bother him in the least and the proceeds could easily be used to begin the hospital. Doing so would allow him to concentrate on a worthy effort.

And put off perusing the Marriage Mart for now.

Rhys arrived in Mayfair close to noon. Before he could knock on his own door, Wiggins opened it.

"It is good to see you, Lord Sheffington," the butler said, unflappable as usual.

"I am sorry I did not send word of my arrival, Wiggins. I will only be here a day or two at most. Would you join me in the study?" he asked.

"Of course, my lord."

The two men closeted themselves, Rhys taking a seat behind the desk and Wiggins sitting in the chair in front of it.

"I want to share with you an idea that I want to see put into place," he began and then fully outlined what he wished to accomplish at Sheffield Park.

"That is a worthwhile endeavor, my lord," Wiggins agreed. "I am proud to serve a peer who thinks of the welfare of others, especially the less fortunate."

"Thinking and doing are two different things, Wiggins. I need a way to have the funds to pull this off."

Quickly, he explained his idea of selling a few of the possessions in the London townhouse since nothing of real value remained at Sheffield Park.

The butler said, "You do have a few paintings that are quite valuable, my lord."

"Show them to me."

Wiggins took Rhys to the drawing room and pointed out a landscape. "This is a Thomas Gainsborough. A painter who became known more for his portraits but early in his career he produced landscapes such as this one."

"Do you know how much it might bring?" he asked eagerly.

"No, I am afraid not. For that, you would need an art appraiser. Once validated as an original by the artist, then it would have to go to auction."

Impatiently, he asked, "What else?"

The butler led him upstairs to the earl's rooms and indicated a painting on the wall. "This is a Vermeer, my lord. An artist of Dutch origin and quite well-known. He didn't live very long and only produced a finite amount of work. Because of that, this painting would be of great value, I would think."

"Perfect," Rhys proclaimed. "I will go and see Mr. Goolsby now. He should be able to put me in touch with an art appraiser and begin the process. Thank you, Wiggins."

The butler nodded deferentially. "I am happy to be of service, my lord."

As he turned to go, Rhys added, "You made the better decision, staying in town. Things were quite atrocious at Sheffield Park when I arrived. Fortunately, I have a new butler in hand and his wife serves as my housekeeper. The Marshes have proven themselves to be quite capable."

"That is good to know, my lord."

He summoned Callow and had his valet help him change from the clothes he had traveled in before he called upon his solicitor. By the time he arrived at Goolsby's offices, it was mid-afternoon.

"I don't have an appointment," he told the clerk. "But I would like to see Mr. Goolsby as soon as possible."

"Mr. Goolsby is with a client now, my lord, but he is free after that and could see you then."

"Thank you."

Rhys only had to wait a quarter-hour before he was ushered into Goolsby's office.

"It is very good to see you, Lord Sheffington," the solicitor said. "What brings you to the city?"

Once more, he explained the notion of beginning a hospital for wounded veterans and how he needed the capital to do so.

Goolsby sighed. "It is a noble venture, my lord. You could start on a very small basis so that it wouldn't be so costly." He frowned. "We have spoken of your financial situation so you understand it would be unwise to follow through with your idea at this particular time. However, if you chose to attend the Season and married well, this wouldn't be a problem and you could begin the venture once the marriage contracts were signed and your bride's dowry became yours."

"I want to focus my efforts on Sheffield Park for now," he revealed. "That and this hospital. Not on finding my countess. I do, though, have a way to raise some money for the near future."

Rhys shared the names of the artists of the two paintings that he wanted to sell and asked Goolsby about how to go about it.

The solicitor steepled his fingers. "I do know of someone who could appraise the works. If you'll allow me to—"

Suddenly, the door flung open and a man in his mid-forties barged in. Ignoring Rhys, he said, "Goolsby, you must help me. The house I leased has burned. At least a part of it has. The kitchens. The drawing room. The ballroom. Thank God the bedchambers remained untouched. But Maria is making her come-out this Season. I simply must have a house. I've been about all day with a leasing agent and there is nothing decent to be had. Lady Furleigh is most upset. And when my wife is unhappy, I cannot be happy."

Rhys sat up. It had never occurred to him to lease his London townhouse. As it was, it would sit empty without its owner for months, if not a couple of years. He was paying an army of servants to maintain it when that wasn't necessary at all. Even when he did decide to come to town and peruse the Marriage Mart, he wouldn't need such a large space. As a bachelor, he wouldn't be expected to host events, merely attend them. He wouldn't even need a drawing room since he was the one who would make the calls upon eligible ladies. He could get by with living in a couple of rooms instead of a grand townhouse.

"Lord Furleigh," Mr. Goolsby began. "While I understand your predicament, I am with a client at the moment."

The nobleman glanced over his shoulder and surprise lit his face. "Oh, dear. My lord, please forgive me for interrupting. It's just that things are dire, especially with the Season on the verge of starting."

Rhys gave what he hoped was a charming smile. "Not a problem, Lord Furleigh. I am Lord Sheffington. My business with Goolsby had just come to an end." He paused, ready to reel in the man. "But I might have a solution to your problem."

Furleigh collapsed into the chair next to Rhys. "Please. I could use your help, my lord. My daughter must make her come-out as planned. And she has five sisters after her who will be doing the same in the next few years. We prefer the country to town and never come, which is why I have no place of my own. If you know of someone who might let me his townhouse, I would be forever in your debt."

"I have recently come into my own title," he explained. "I was a colonel in the army. I find my country estate needs much of my attention since it had been sadly neglected by the previous earl. That means I must forgo the upcoming Season. It would be foolish to let my townhouse sit empty when you have such need of one."

He glanced to Goolsby, who chimed in, "Indeed, Lord Furleigh. Lord Sheffington's place is in the heart of Mayfair, whereas the townhouse you were renting merely sat on its edge. Of course, that would entail paying a higher fee to rent such a prime property."

Lord Furleigh waved a hand dismissively. "That is of no consequence, Goolsby. Having an adequate place is what is important. One which Lady Furleigh approves of, naturally."

"Why don't you and your wife come to dinner this evening?" Rhys suggested smoothly. "Bring all your girls along. You may view the townhouse before we dine. If it is appropriate, we can strike a bargain regarding its rental." He turned to the solicitor. "In fact, Goolsby, why don't you join us? Draw up the papers ahead of time in case Lady Furleigh deems the property suitable. If she does, we can sign the documents tonight."

"With no leasing agent?" Furleigh asked.

"Why use a middleman when we can allow Mr. Goolsby to handle the situation for us?"

"Very well." Furleigh's head bobbed up and down. "You may have saved my daughter's Season, Sheffington."

Rhys added, "If you and your wife find my home suitable, we might even consider adding an option to purchase the property in the paperwork."

He gave Lord Furleigh the address and said, "Dinner will be served at eight. Come an hour early so that you and your family may tour the house."

He returned home and told Wiggins they would have guests for dinner—and why.

"It was fortuitous that Lord Furleigh was in need of a place for his family to live."

"And clever of you to suggest leasing your own home to him, my lord. It would provide an enormous income for you."

The Furleighs arrived with a bevy of daughters in tow. Rhys allowed Wiggins to lead the tour. When they reached the ballroom, the oldest girl sighed aloud.

"Oh, Mama, this is perfect," she exclaimed. "I can see myself dancing here with my future husband. It's much better than the place we were before."

Rhys watched Lady Furleigh as she took in the room. "Yes, it is quite nice," she said. Looking to her husband, she nodded subtly.

Lord Furleigh looked to Rhys. "We will take up your kind offer, my lord, and lease your house for the Season."

Lady Furleigh frowned at her husband and he added, "And we might exercise the option to purchase it at Season's end." He glanced to his daughters. "After all, we will be in town for several years. There are many come-outs to be made."

They dined on roasted pheasant and, afterward, Lord Furleigh put his females into their carriage, instructing the driver to return for him in an hour. The three men adjourned to Rhys' office, where they commenced signing the documents prepared by Goolsby.

When the last had been executed, Furleigh smiled and said, "I am sorry you will not be partaking in the Season this year, Sheffington."

"Too many matters to attend to in the country," he replied, relieved that Lady Furleigh had agreed the house to be suitable and that all the papers had been signed.

"I will arrange for the funds for the first and last month's rents to be placed into your account first thing tomorrow morning, Lord Sheffington," the solicitor said.

Goolsby had shared with Rhys how much Furleigh had been paying for the original townhouse he rented and the price they had agreed upon was double that. Even renting out the townhouse for the upcoming five months would ensure Rhys would have enough to not only begin the hospital but keep it running for several years.

As they went downstairs and the solicitor took his leave, Lord Furleigh hung back, which indicated to Rhys that the man wanted a private word with him.

Once Goolsby had left, Furleigh said, "Though you may not be a part of this Season, my lord, I do hope you will attend in the future." He beamed. "After all, I have a plethora of girls that need husbands—and they all come with a hefty dowry."

Rhys supposed he could do worse than wed one of the pretty if shy Furleigh girls.

He smiled. "We will see what next Season holds, my lord."

CHAPTER SEVENTEEN

Four months later . . .

R HYS ALLOWED CALLOW to help him dress for the day. His valet already looked weary and yet the day had only begun.

Guilt filled him. He had pressed Callow into heading affairs up for the injured soldiers who had been sent to Sheffield Park. General Shepherd had thought it at excellent idea for Rhys to house soldiers discharged from His Majesty's Army who needed further time to mend and so men had begun to dribble in over the last month. His commander had replied to Rhys' original letter, saying while officers usually had a family and resources to be had if they returned home to heal from their wounds, the rank and file rarely did. Though the general said he easily could send a hundred men to Sheffield Park, Rhys had requested that his former commander be more circumspect and only send a handful to begin with. Once he had an idea and worked out a system on how to care for a small group of veterans, more could certainly be added to the fold. With the goal to eventually give these former soldiers training in skills that would see them capable of earning a living, there would be men rotating in and out over a long period of time, depending on how much longer the war with Bonaparte dragged on.

After additional correspondence to firm up the details, Rhys had taken in soldiers three different times in the last month, all men formerly under his command except for Garfield, who had been transferred to the unit after Rhys departed. He had thought requesting those who knew him might help in their rehabilitation and adjustment to civilian life. Thank goodness he had pressed for taking things slowly. Even with Callow assuming additional responsibilities and heading up the arrivals and their care, it was already too much. Rhys hadn't been able to locate a physician willing to come live fulltime at Sheffield Park. The local doctor promised to stop by two or three times a week but he, like Callow, seemed overwhelmed with even a handful of patients numbering less than ten. He had thought money would be his problem and once he solved that issue that things would fall into place. Instead, funding had turned out to be easy when compared to all the rest.

"We have two new arrivals coming sometime today, my lord," his valet informed him. "And still no nurses."

Rhys had pressed two parlor maids into helping with the wounded. Neither seemed good at caring for the men or their injuries. Already, his washerwoman was working day and night with the additional linens and clothing to be washed and hung to dry. Cook was on the verge of quitting because she had so many more mouths to feed.

"I know we are struggling, Callow, but so are these men. I am working on something that will help us simplify the process so that we can facilitate all stages of the men's recovery with ease."

"Have you written to Her Grace?" the valet asked eagerly. "She would most likely have suggestions for you."

His heart sank at the thought of Dalinda. "I will let you know. Right now, I am scheduled to meet with Mr. Simpson during breakfast."

"Yes, my lord," the servant said dejectedly. "I will go and attend to the men now and will notify you when the additions arrive."

Rhys made his way to the breakfast room. He tried to dine each morning with Eli so they could have a friendly chat regarding the estate and any pressing matters Rhys might need to attend to. He entered and found Eli already present and eating.

"Good morning," his friend called as Rhys took a seat.

Immediately, a footman placed a large mug of coffee before him and Rhys doctored it with a single cube of sugar and a generous pour of milk. Moments later, another footman set a plate in front of him and removed the cover. He thought of all the times he had struggled to buy food to put on the table when he was supporting his family and swore never to take small favors such as a timely meal for granted.

"What do we need to discuss today?" he asked before biting into the ham he had sliced.

"Everything on the estate is going exceedingly well," Eli replied, detailing what his agenda was for the day.

"If you have time and can meet with me and William Shirley after breakfast, my lord, we'll be talking about the upcoming harvest."

"Yes, I'd like to do so," Rhys replied, wanting to put off going to see the group of soldiers. It was ridiculous to avoid them when he was responsible for bringing the veterans to Sheffield Park but he was at his wit's end on how he was supposed to help them with little medical help and no ideas on how to provide them training for a new occupation which took their injuries into consideration.

They went to Eli's office and found Shirley waiting. The farmer outlined a few ideas he had for harvesting the crops more efficiently and Rhys gave his approval to go forward with his tenant's suggestions.

"If you don't mind me asking, my lord," Shirley said, "I would like to bring up another matter."

"Go ahead," Rhys said, worried what new problem the farmer might throw out.

Shirley looked sheepish as he said, "Well, it's a request from my missus. And all the other wives, it seems." He hesitated and then said, "They're wanting a harvest festival to be held."

"What would that entail?" he asked, knowing how hard Dalinda and Anna had worked to plan the country ball several months ago.

"It wouldn't need to be held inside Sheffield Park, my lord," Shirley assured him. "It could take place outside on the lawn in front of the house. The women, they've been talking about it, and would love to have food. Tea cakes and buns. Ale and cider. Dancing. Games for the children. Perhaps a bonfire. It could take place at harvest moon. A way to bring the community together again after all their hard work reaping and threshing."

It made his head ache to think of what would go into this.

"I am not sure if—"

"Mrs. Shirley is perfectly happy to organize it, my lord. She would have lots of help. She just needs your approval to proceed in planning it." The farmer looked hopefully at Rhys.

"Why not?" he exclaimed. "My cook can contribute to the food but the tenants' wives will have to do the rest, Mr. Shirley. My staff is stretched rather thin these days."

The farmer beamed. "Oh, that's very good news, Lord Sheffington. Very good, indeed." He rose. "If we are finished here, I want to go and tell my missus. She'll be ever so pleased."

"Tell away," he said, hoping the news would lift the tenants' spirits.

Once Shirley left, Eli said, "Actions such as that will not only make you a popular landlord but will, in fact, get your workers to toil harder on your behalf."

"Their lives are hard ones," he noted. "I see no harm in a little fun after they have worked for so long. Especially the number of hours they will put in in the weeks leading up to and during the harvest."

He had already put off visiting the patients long enough so he ventured to the east wing. Going first to Private Finnerty's room, he spent a few minutes talking with the foot soldier, who had lost his left hand and was now deaf in one ear. Next, he stopped to see Pimmel, who was missing his left eye and whose leg might need amputation. The local doctor kept putting off making a decision and Rhys hoped it wouldn't cost Pimmel his life.

Hayward was his next stop. Both he and Garfield suffered from some kind of battlefield fever which the local doctor hadn't been able to diagnose. Rhys had heard of men been hipped—unable to focus and feeling useless—or being blue-deviled—haunted by what they had seen in the war. He himself had hated everything about the war but he had no idea how to help these two soldiers, who showed no physical signs of injury but carried emotional scars deep within them.

Rhys decided to go for a ride. It was the only place he could truly be alone and sort out his thoughts. Morrison saddled his horse for him and he took off, galloping for over two miles before bringing his mount to a halt. He dismounted and, taking the reins in hand, began to walk and think.

Reluctantly, his thoughts turned to Dalinda. He hadn't had any contact with her since she, Dez, and Anna had departed from Sheffield Park. He had wanted a clean break between them and yet he spent parts of every day thinking about her. She would know what to do with the situation he faced. How to fix the soldiers under his care. He knew from a letter Dez had sent that Dalinda had moved to Laurel-wood two months ago after her stepson, the Duke of Gilford, had wed and now she lived there with her two children.

Should he go and see her? Place his burdens at her feet—and hope he could keep his heart intact?

Uncertainty filled him. Perhaps when Dez and Anna left London for Torville Manor and Dalinda and her sons went to visit them as planned might be a better time to see her. That wouldn't be for another couple of weeks, though, based upon what Dez had written. Frankly, Rhys didn't know if he could hold out that long. Desperation filled him. He so wanted to help the men General Shepherd had entrusted to him but still floundered with how to do so.

With no ready answers, Rhys flung himself into the saddle and rode back toward the stables. When he reached the front of the house, he saw a wagon had pulled up. Callow assisted two men from it. He realized these must be the latest injured General Shepherd had sent.

He dismounted and greeted the newcomers, whom he did not recognize. He didn't know if they were like Garfield and had transferred into his unit or if he had simply never met the pair.

"Good morning. I am the Earl of Sheffington, formerly Colonel Armistead. Welcome to Sheffield Park."

"Wharton," the first man barked as he leaned upon his crutches for support. "Bullet in my thigh. They say it's healing but it hurts like the dickens." He nodded to his companion. "This is Hensley. His right arm got blown off just below the elbow. He's complained of a fever."

Rhys looked at Hensley, who stared out morosely, not making eye contact. His skin and eyes spoke of jaundice.

"Go with Callow. He'll see that you are assigned a room. The local doctor should be here the day after tomorrow to look over you both."

Wharton sighed noisily and shrugged. He placed his crutches and good leg in front of him and swung his body up to meet them. Hensley followed wordlessly.

Callow looked at him. "Something must be done, my lord. I never thought I would be a man to give an ultimatum to my employer but I am issuing one to you now. Either get me help—or I shall resign my post—both as your valet and . . . whatever I am the rest of the time."

Callow hurried after the latest arrivals before Rhys could reply. He couldn't lose the valet. The servant's words gave him the needed push and he determined to ride to Laurelwood tomorrow and beg Dalinda for her help. Mounting his horse again, he rode to the stables and handed the horse off to Morrison, who met him.

"I will need my carriage tomorrow morning after breakfast," he informed the groom, hoping Dalinda would choose to return with him for a few days. "I would like you to drive me to see the Duchess of

Gilford. Rather, the dowager duchess, that is," he said, knowing enough about Polite Society to realize Dalinda had been replaced by the new Duke of Gilford's bride.

"About time you came to your senses," Morrison grumbled. "You've been a first class idiot, my lord, if I say so myself."

Surprise filled Rhys. No one had spoken to him this way in some time and annoyance flickered through him. Perhaps he was becoming more of a peer than he thought.

"What do you mean?" he challenged.

"Her Grace can solve all your problems. Have this mess organized and running like a fine timepiece in no time. As for you?" Morrison eyed him.

"What?"

"You know," his groom said mysteriously.

"No, I do not. Know what?" he demanded.

"She's for you, my lord. No ifs, ands, or buts."

Anger filled him at the servant's brash declaration. "You have overstepped your place, Morrison," he ground out.

Morrison gazed at Rhys in defiance. "And what if I did? Will you fire me, my lord?" He snorted. "No, you wouldn't have the heart, knowing what I would suffer if I was forced to leave Sheffield Park. I see *you* suffering, Colonel. You need Her Grace in your life. No one else will do for you."

Rhys' rage dissolved instantly. He sighed. "No one could feel more inferior than I do, Morrison."

The groom grunted. "What with how I look now? Yet Her Grace told me that I am the same man I was before that shell exploded and ruined my face. She made me believe that I am still capable. Intelligent. And that I can tell a mean story. Yes, it takes a while for others to get used to my horrendous face but then they see me—the inside, real me—not the ugly shell I am now."

Morrison's gaze bored into him. "You are the same, Colonel. You still see the little boy who lost his father and had to fight to keep his family alive and a place in the world without being swallowed whole. Well, you're not that lad now. You are a titled peer with a lovely estate and I've heard a fine townhouse in London, as well. You've high standards. You're caring. Just see how you're trying to help these wounded veterans arriving here each week."

The groom placed a hand on Rhys' shoulder. "If Her Grace wasn't interested in you, then she wouldn't be interested. There's no artifice to her, Colonel. For a duchess, she is as grounded and practical as anyone I've ever met." He grinned. "Fine to look at, as well. If I were you, I'd stake my claim before it's too late."

Had he been a fool? Was Dalinda still clinging to her past with her husband? Missing her duke and the lofty position they had held in Polite Society?

No, he didn't think so. She had moved on. Vacated her longtime home in order to give the new duke room to have his own family. Made her sons her priority. Rhys had pushed her away at every turn, thinking himself unworthy and undeserving of one of her beauty and intelligence and position in the *ton*. She might never love him—but how many in society did love their spouses? Rhys knew she liked him a great deal. They always had things to talk about and never seemed to grow bored in one another's company.

Moreover, they were well-matched in the bedroom. He had done things which had surprised her. Things her much older husband hadn't done to please her. Things that Dalinda had thoroughly enjoyed.

Was that enough to build a marriage upon? It would be foolish on his part to wed a stranger he cared little for, simply using her for her money, when he could be with the one woman he wanted above all others.

The one he loved.

For the first time, Rhys admitted it to himself. He loved Dalinda. And even if she couldn't return his love, he believed they could make a go of it and have a successful marriage. He could give her the children she so desperately wanted and she could provide him with an heir. It would be a lot taking on two boys he had never seen—but he was up to the task. Hadn't the army taught him to believe in himself?

Rhys turned to his former batman. "You are absolutely right, Morrison. I have been a dunderhead. Ignored what was before my eyes all along. I've been too stubborn to admit it."

He grinned. "Ready the carriage now. I want you to drive me to Laurelwood immediately."

CHAPTER EIGHTEEN

Laurelwood

D ALINDA BREAKFASTED WITH her boys and Mr. Selleck. The four had been at Laurelwood almost two months now. Though Reid had told her she didn't need to vacate Gillingham, she knew with his marriage to Ashlyn, Lady Dunwood, that the couple needed some privacy and a bit of peace. Thornhill, the property which housed Dunwood Academy, had burned to the ground, thanks to Eden Martin, the local viscount's daughter. Eden's mother had been touched with madness and her daughter must have inherited it, though no one had suspected the depth of the young woman's madness. She had become fixated on Reid, wishing to marry him. Eden had almost shot and killed Ashlyn shortly before the wedding, with Reid coming to the rescue. Unfortunately, Eden had died tragically, deliberately rushing back into Ashlyn's cottage and perishing in a fire.

Her stepson's wedding to the schoolmistress had gone off without a hitch and Reid had generously offered for Dunwood Academy to be located within Gillingham. His gesture had added prestige to the small school, being housed inside a ducal mansion, and kept the taint of gossip away. School had been dismissed for the summer break and, with that, Dalinda had brought Arthur and Harry to Laurelwood.

Though she planned to spend a great deal of time with her sons, Dalinda had thought to hire a governess to keep them occupied and out of mischief when she was engaged with her estate responsibilities. Both Arthur and Harry had clamored for Mr. Selleck to be allowed to take the position instead. The tutor was a favorite of her boys and she had contacted him, asking if he would be willing to spend his time off this summer at Laurelwood. Not only would Mr. Selleck continue her children's lessons in languages, but they would also read together and Harry would work on his handwriting, which was atrocious.

The tutor believed in fresh air and exercise and had the boys outside every day. They went for nature walks, observing various species of birds and having botany lessons. Mr. Selleck took Arthur and Harry fishing and swimming. Dalinda joined them on their daily rides. She had found Mr. Selleck to be a godsend for her active, rambunctious sons. The tutor made sure they kept to a schedule and yet provided many breaks for the boys to explore nature and pursue their own interests. Both Arthur and Harry were fascinated with geography and the three had spent time poring over the atlas in Laurelwood's library, with Harry claiming he was going to be a ship's captain someday and Arthur vowing to be a trader who traveled the world, buying exotic goods and bringing them back to England.

Though she stayed busy throughout the long days, her nights proved lonely. She missed Rhys terribly. Their bantering. Their conversations. She thought several times of writing to him but thought it too forward on her part. She did know from Anna's weekly letters that Rhys hadn't come to any events during the London Season. She wondered how his project with injured soldiers fared and if his estate was beginning to thrive. She didn't know she could miss someone so much that it produced a physical ache. Even her soul, that unseen entity, hurt deep within her.

Perhaps she could write to him in a neighborly gesture and ask if he would like to come to Laurelwood for the day. Or she could offer to come to Sheffield Park to see the injured veterans he had taken in. She could bring Arthur and Harry to act as a buffer.

"Your Grace, a letter has arrived from Lord Torrington," her butler said.

"Thank you, Mr. Blair." She claimed it from the silver tray and eagerly opened it, reading the contents quickly.

"Boys, your uncle and aunt are returning to Torville Manor in two weeks. They'll be there by the first of August and they've asked us to come and visit them."

"We finally get to meet Cousin Charlie," Harry said, beaming.

Her younger boy had a tender heart and would do well playing with the baby.

Arthur, on the other hand, frowned. "I am eager to see Uncle Dez and Aunt Anna but what do you do with a baby?" His nose crinkled in disgust.

"Your impatience is showing, Lord Arthur," Mr. Selleck admonished. "There are all kinds of things to do with a baby. Observing them as a scientist is but one of them."

"How?" Arthur asked, his natural curiosity betraying him.

"We have studied probability and outcome, for instance, and that can be applied to a baby. Which hand will they use to take an object? Which direction will they crawl? What are the signs of hunger they display? How often do they nap?"

Mr. Selleck's gaze met hers and she saw he bit back a smile.

Arthur looked thoughtful. "Hmm. I suppose I do want to meet Cousin Charlie and study him."

"No dissecting him!" Harry said, laughter bubbling up. "He's not one of our frogs."

"That will be the beginning of August, Mr. Selleck," Dalinda said. "Please feel free to return to Gillingham. I am sure you need a respite from my two before the next school term begins."

"Mama, Mr. Selleck must come," Harry implored. "We want him to see Torville Manor."

She looked to the tutor, who said, "I wouldn't mind accompanying you and the boys, Your Grace. I enjoy visiting new places."

"Like Madagascar and India!" Harry said with glee. "Arthur and I are going to both places someday."

"And China," Arthur added. "Paris, too, if the war ever ends. Even the colonies interest me."

"Remember, they are their own country now," Mr. Selleck reminded. "The United States of America."

Arthur wrinkled his nose. "That's far too grand a title for a backwater place. Still, we do trade with them a great deal. I suppose I will have to become familiar with them if I plan to do business and sail my ships there," he said thoughtfully.

"I have some correspondence to deal with and then we can go riding afterward," she told them. "I will meet you at the stables at eleven."

Dalinda went to her sitting room, where she kept a desk, and wrote several letters. One would be sent to Dez and Anna, confirming that she and the boys would come for a visit that first week in August and letting them know Mr. Selleck would accompany them. She also wrote to Rhys but after she read over the letter, she tore it to shreds. It sounded too stiff and formal and would never do. She would have to think on its wording and make another attempt at it later.

After she changed into her riding habit, she ventured to the stables. Just as the groom brought out their horses, a carriage rumbled up and stopped.

"Who's coming to visit, Mama?" Harry asked excitedly.

She knew exactly who, thanks to the crest on the door. Blood pounded in her ears and raced through her limbs. She grew lightheaded and willed herself not to faint.

Rhys bounded from the carriage, looking more handsome than ever in a dark blue coat and buff breeches that showed off his muscular legs, leaving nothing to her imagination.

"I hope you don't mind me dropping by, Your Grace," he said, a twinkle in his emerald eyes that made her tingle.

"Not at all, my lord." She looked to her sons. "Lord Sheffington, I would like to present to you Arthur, my older boy, and Harry, my baby."

"Mama!" protested Harry. "I am not a baby!"

"No, you are fine young man," Rhys said. "Your mama is merely proud of you, Lord Harry." He offered Harry his hand and after they shook did the same with Arthur.

"Lord Sheffington and your Uncle Dez are close friends," Dalinda said. "They fought on the Continent together."

"You were an officer with Uncle?" Arthur asked, looking much more impressed now with their visitor. "What is war like?"

Rhys said solemnly, "War is sometimes necessary but a very ugly reality, Lord Arthur. I hope you will never have to be placed in harm's way as your uncle and I were, much less all those who still fight on the front for England."

"We were about to go for a ride, Lord Sheffington," Harry said. "With Mama and Mr. Selleck, our tutor. Would you like to join us?"

"Why not?" He turned to the groom who had lingered. "Do you have a mount I might borrow?"

"Right away, my lord."

"Mount up, boys," Dalinda said and Mr. Selleck saw to putting them into their saddles.

Rhys stepped to her. "How have you been?" he asked softly.

Her heart skipped several beats, like a rock skimming a pond's surface. "Well. And yourself? What of—"

"We will talk later," he said and then clasped her waist.

Dalinda forgot to breathe the moment his hands touched her. She found herself lost in his mesmerizing eyes. She wet her lips nervously and thought he might have groaned but, suddenly, he lifted her to the saddle. She took up the reins, trying to rein in her own wild emotions.

Rhys was here. At Laurelwood.

After the boys and Mr. Selleck were situated, the groom returned with a horse for Rhys.

"Is this one as spirited as Stormy?" he asked.

"You know Stormy?" Arthur looked intrigued and glanced from Rhys to her and back again.

"Yes. Your mother is an excellent rider. Probably the most skilled I have seen and one of the few women who could control Stormy so effortlessly."

"Is Lord Sheffington the earl you and Aunt Anna helped?" Harry asked guilelessly.

Dalinda did her best to reply, keeping her voice even. "Yes, dear. We went along with your uncle to Sheffield Park and helped Lord Sheffington become established. Come along. Let's ride and show his lordship Laurelwood."

Arthur spurred on his horse and took off, Harry following in his wake. The three adults took up their reins and followed.

Dalinda pointed out several things to Rhys as they rode about the estate, which was half the size of Sheffield Park and yet still quite large. When they returned to the stables, Mr. Selleck said it was time for a language lesson and the boys followed him away from the house.

Confused, Rhys asked, "Aren't lessons usually taught in the school-room?"

She laughed. "You don't know Mr. Selleck. He is a tutor at Dunwood Academy, which is owned and run by the new Duchess of Gilford. Mr. Selleck believes that young, active boys need plenty of fresh air. He holds many of their lessons outdoors." She chuckled. "Arthur told me that, yesterday, they went fishing and conjugated Latin verbs aloud as they waited to hook something on their lines."

He laughed, too, and she loved the rich sound of it.

"Would you care to go to the drawing room? I can ring for tea."

"Yes, I have things that need to be said to you. In private."

His words made her wonder what they would be speaking of.

Most likely, Rhys would talk about the soldiers who had come to stay at Sheffield Park. Still, her insides fluttered and she had to force herself to take air into her lungs and expel it calmly.

As they waited for their tea to arrive, Dalinda told him about how Dunwood Academy would be permanently located within the walls of Gillingham and how Reid and Ashlyn had recently wed.

"I wanted to give them their privacy and also allow the boys to get to know Laurelwood. It's not as if I am taking Arthur and Harry away from Gillingham for they will spend a majority of their year there at the school."

"Why is Mr. Selleck here?"

"I was going to hire a governess for the boys but they clamored for Mr. Selleck. He teaches languages and literature at their school, as well as riding, and they are mad for him. Mr. Selleck can be a little unconventional at times but he is very good with them. He is even going with us in two weeks when we visit Dez and Anna at Torville Manor."

A maid rolled in the teacart and Dalinda poured out for them. She was conscious of Rhys watching her carefully and she concentrated to keep from spilling it. She handed him a cup and saucer but he immediately put it down.

Instead, he took her hands in his and raised them to his lips, kissing them tenderly. A rush of emotion swept through her at his unexpected gesture.

"Rhys?" she asked cautiously.

"I should have contacted you before," he began and then hesitated, a pained expression on his face.

"Why didn't you?"

"I have been a clot, Dalinda." Tears swam in his eyes and he blinked rapidly. "I have never cried. Not even when I lost my beloved sister and mother."

She squeezed his hands encouragingly. "What is it?"

"I've missed you."

She smiled gently, her heart melting at his honesty. "I have missed you, too."

"I love you," he blurted out. "I think I always have. Your mind. Your body. Your spirit. Morrison helped me to understand."

"He did?" She reeled from his declaration, her heart pounding against her ribs.

"Morrison helped me to realize that the obstacles I had placed between us were ridiculous. The *ton* will only see that I have a title and am an earl. They won't know of my humble origins and background. Only that I succeeded the former Sheffington."

He gazed at her longingly. "I have a right to be here. I am an earl. I may not always be the best man I can be but when I am with you, I want to be a better one."

Tears cascaded down her cheeks now. Rhys' palms cupped her face, his thumbs wiping them away.

"I know it is only a few months since your cherished husband's death. I know how much you loved him and that—"

"I didn't love Gilford," she said simply, beginning to see part of why Rhys had kept her at arm's length.

Shock filled his face. "You didn't? But . . . the way you speak of him. I . . . ." His voice trailed off as he tried to understand what she had just told him.

She placed her hands over his. "Gilford was my savior. He swept in and by offering for me, kept me from being forced to wed a horrible man. My father sought to punish me for my role in trying to help Dez and Anna elope to Gretna Green. From the beginning, Gilford told me that he would always love his first wife but that we could create a good life together—and we did. We were the closest of friends. We respected one another. We loved our sons."

She gazed at Rhys intently. "But we never loved one another. Never. And I have never loved anyone. Except you." Her voice broke and a fresh flood of tears erupted.

"Dalinda," he said huskily. "I didn't know."

His arms came about her and their lips met for a tender kiss. She didn't want tender, though. She wanted to possess him and be possessed by him. Her fingers thrust into his hair, fisting and bringing him close. She opened to him and they kissed hungrily. Greedily. Trying to make up for the months they had spent apart. Their tongues waged war, both of them becoming winners, as desire sizzled through her, heating her flesh and melting her bones.

Rhys broke the kiss and stared at her in wonder. "I thought home was a place with four walls and a roof. I never understood it was a person. *You* are home to me, Dalinda. I realize now that a man who doesn't love can never truly be whole. You said Gilford was your savior—but you are mine. Now and always."

CHAPTER NINETEEN

RHYS KISSED DALINDA for a good hour. Just kissed her. Drank her in. The heady scent of roses surrounded them. He would plant rosebushes throughout Sheffield Park so wherever he looked, he would always be reminded of this magnificent woman and his love for her. He realized in telling her he loved her that it only strengthened him. He wanted to slay dragons for but a single smile from her.

He finally broke the kiss, his forehead resting against hers.

"I love you," he said again, the feel of these words right on his tongue.

Her fingers stroked his face. "And I love you. Oh, Rhys, I never knew I could be so happy."

He pulled away but laced his fingers through hers. "I will speak to Arthur and Harry about us marrying."

She looked alarmed. "You are going to ask their permission? I am afraid Arthur might prove resistant. Ever since Gilford passed, he is quite protective of me."

"Not their permission," he reassured her. "But they are a part of you. Which means they will be a part of me. Of us. We will be a family. Along with any other children you might bear."

A dreamy look crossed her face. "Oh, Rhys, I do want more children. I was made to be a mother."

"I hope I can give you a dozen more," he teased. "Or perhaps half a dozen."

Dalinda laughed. "As long as one or two are girls. I love my boys but I would love to see a girl with your dark hair and piercing, green eyes."

He kissed her. "We will need to start working on it immediately. How soon will you marry me, Your Grace?"

Radiance filled her face. "As soon as possible." Dalinda chuckled. "I don't know if I can wait the three weeks for the banns to be read."

"Then it will be a bishop's or special license for us. Can you wait at least until we get to Torville Manor so that Dez and Anna might be present at the ceremony?"

"I suppose so." Mischief lit her eyes. "Of course, that's only two weeks. Do you think I could come to your bed during that time? While I can wait a while for our vows, I am not certain I can wait on that."

Rhys kissed her soundly. "I knew I was marrying the right woman."

"I am definitely marrying the right man," she replied. "You are dedicated to your people. You are loyal. Intelligent. Handsome as sin."

"You think so?" He waggled his brows at her and she laughed in delight.

"I know so." She kissed him again, marveling that this man was going to be all hers.

"Well, you are beautiful and nurturing and the wisest person I know." He grew serious. "I must speak of my finances, though, Dalinda. You are not wedding a wealthy duke as you did before. I do not have endless estates at my disposal. My income is limited to a few investments and my share of the crops grown by my tenants. You'll never go hungry—but I cannot shower you with jewels or other magnificent gifts."

"You think that is important to me?" she asked. "I would wed you if you were poorer than a church mouse, Rhys. I want to marry you because I love you. Not for what you can give me."

He stroked her cheek. "I can give you love in abundance. Of that I am certain."

He kissed her slowly, reveling in the fact she wanted him, despite the fact he was no highborn duke with limitless wealth.

Dalinda broke the kiss. "Once we wed, money will never be a problem. Everything I have will be yours."

Rhys frowned. "Exactly what do you have? I know you own Laurelwood outright."

"Yes, Laurelwood is mine. It brings in a very steady income. Gilford also left money for the boys' education and to help them establish themselves in society. They will come into their inheritance when they each turn twenty-five. The will stipulated that I would keep all the jewels given to me during our marriage. I own several racehorses. A trading ship. I also have ample money."

She named a figure and his eyes widened. "You have that much?" He was astounded that her wealth exceeded his tenfold.

"*We* have that," she emphasized, her fingers running through his hair. "When we wed, everything I have legally will become yours."

"It will be ours," he said firmly. "You will always have a say in our financial affairs. You have experience far beyond mine where that is concerned." Rhys paused. "I have need of your counsel, Dalinda. Things are in a quandary regarding the soldiers General Shepherd has sent to me." He sighed. "I need you to help make it work because it certainly isn't being run well now."

"Tell me," she urged, snuggling close to him, his bergamot and musk scent surrounding her.

He explained the current arrangement and the unfortunate lack of a doctor and nurses. How Callow was ready to abandon him entirely and Cook and his washerwoman might not be far behind. Frustration poured from him but her hand in his assured him they would find the answers together.

"First, I think new men arriving should be placed upon cots in the ballroom," she said. "It will be easier to nurse them if they are closer together. It might help them having nearby companions, as well, instead of being so isolated. Once they are well, they can be relocated to their own room for privacy if they choose."

"I like that idea," he said. "Then the parlor maids I've asked to be nurses wouldn't be run so ragged."

"You need a fulltime doctor. We may have one here near Laurelwood. Dr. Robinson recently arrived from the Continent because his wife was dying. I have heard he doesn't wish to return to the front and would rather stay with his daughter, who helped nurse her mother during her illness. Our village already has a physician. Dr. Robinson might be willing to come to Sheffield Park. With his battlefield experience, he will know better how to help these wounded veterans, much more than a country doctor who has never seen such devastating injuries."

"Would he up and leave his grieving daughter?" Rhys asked.

"Miss Robinson is a nurturing soul. I think she is almost twenty years of age. If she came with him, she would prove valuable as a nurse. We should call upon them now and offer them the positions."

Rhys smiled. "Why not? I like how you aren't reluctant to act swiftly."

They returned to his carriage and she greeted Morrison.

"It's good to see you, Your Grace."

Dalinda glanced at Rhys. "I have an idea," she said quietly and turned back to Morrison. "How busy are you at the stables, Mr. Morrison?"

"Not much at all," he replied frankly. "His lordship hasn't bought any new horses yet. I help exercise those he does own and I am driving him about some in his carriage."

"I think you should take over from Callow," Dalinda declared.

He looked puzzled. "As his lordship's valet?"

"No, Mr. Morrison. Callow should remain Lord Sheffington's

valet. *You* would be in charge of the soldiers arriving at Sheffield Park. Because of your army career and injuries, they can relate more to you." She smiled. "You are also quite the raconteur. I am sure your stories and your way with people would be appreciated and help in the healing process for them. These men need friendship and camaraderie as much as they need for their bodies to heal."

Morrison's face lit up. "I would be honored to serve in this capacity, Your Grace." He glanced to Rhys. "What do you think, my lord?"

"I think my future countess is brilliant." He slipped his arm about Dalinda's waist and kissed her temple.

Morrison beamed from ear-to-ear. "I knew coming to see Her Grace would be the right move to make." He looked to Dalinda. "All his lordship needed was a nudge. I can see he did all the rest on his own."

"We are going to the local village, Mr. Morrison," Dalinda said, giving him directions to Dr. Robinson's cottage. "Let's hope we find a doctor there for the men."

Rhys helped her into the carriage and they began making plans. She told him that she had a scullery maid who showed great talent and could come to Sheffield Park as an assistant cook, preparing all the meals for the soldiers and enabling Cook to focus on her usual tasks. They would need to seek an additional washerwoman to lessen the burden on the current one.

He brought their joined hands upward and kissed her fingers. "Already, relief floods me. You are going to make for a wonderful countess, my love."

The vehicle stopped and Rhys assisted her from the carriage. He knocked on the door and a servant with kind eyes opened it.

"Oh! Your Grace!" she exclaimed. "I didn't know you were coming. Dr. Robinson didn't tell me."

"He didn't know, Mrs. Nathan."

It didn't surprise him that Dalinda would know this servant's name.

"Please, come in," the woman said, leading them to the parlor. "I'll fetch Dr. Robinson at once."

"If Miss Robinson is available, we would like to speak with her, as well," Dalinda said.

"Of course, Your Grace." The servant hurried from the room.

Moments later, both the doctor and his daughter appeared. Dalinda introduced Rhys to them and Miss Robinson invited them to sit.

"Would you care for tea, Your Grace? Lord Sheffington?" she asked.

"No, thank you," Dalinda said. "We are here to discuss a worthwhile project his lordship has become involved with." She glanced to him.

Rhys took over, explaining how he had recently come into the earldom and had left his army career behind but still wanted to use his new position to help some of his former men, many of them amputees.

"General Shepherd is sending injured soldiers from my previous command though a few who were stationed with my troops are new to me. One is Private Garfield, who was transferred to my regiment after I returned to England. Two other soldiers arrived this morning, ones I will need to get to know."

"I admire you for wanting to give back to those greatly in need, my lord," Dr. Robinson said. "But what does this have to do with me?"

"Her Grace told me you had recently returned from the battlefront and plan to remain in England with your daughter. I have great need of a doctor to remain on staff at Sheffield Park to see to the men on a daily basis. Her Grace also informed me that Miss Robinson helped nurse her mother." He looked to the young woman. "I could certainly use a nurse or two, as well."

The pair glanced at one another and Miss Robinson nodded to her father.

"My daughter and I would be happy to come to Sheffield Park, my lord. We have nothing to tie us to this area now that my wife has passed."

"What of Mrs. Nathan?" Miss Robinson asked. "She has been with our family since before I was born. She would be an excellent nurse herself, my lord."

"If Mrs. Nathan is willing to come, we would be happy to have her. I can provide rooms for you in the east wing or see to a cottage on the estate in order to offer you more privacy."

"For now, I would rather stay closer to my patients so providing rooms for us would be best. When do you want us?" Dr. Robinson asked.

"As soon as possible," Dalinda said. "My two sons and I will be going to live at Sheffield Park. Lord Sheffington has asked for my hand in marriage and I have agreed to wed him."

They received congratulations from the Robinsons and a commitment from the physician that they would arrive by week's end.

"Then I will see that everything will be ready for your arrival," Rhys promised.

He and Dalinda returned to Laurelwood and she said, "It is teatime. Arthur and Harry join me every day. Would you like to speak to them now?"

"I think after tea," he suggested. "Our conversation will call for privacy."

She laughed. "Oh, man talk," she teased.

They arrived at the drawing room and found the boys already present as a maid came in with the teacart. Rhys saw it filled with sandwiches and sweets. The boys filled their plates as Dalinda prepared the tea. He noticed Arthur subtly eyeing him and knew the older boy had an inkling of why Rhys had come to Laurelwood.

He got Arthur and Harry to talk about their time at Dunwood Academy and they freely shared about their lessons and the friends they had made. He told a few stories about him and Dez in the army, all ones that were lighthearted and fit for young ears.

When tea ended, Dalinda said, "I must excuse myself. I have some correspondence to attend to. Will you boys entertain Lord Sheffington for half an hour while I am busy?"

"Yes, Mama," Harry said, always eager to please.

Arthur merely nodded.

Once Dalinda left, Rhys looked at the two.

"I am glad your mama had work to do because I wanted to address the both of you in private." He paused and saw he had their full attention. "I have grown quite fond of Her Grace and have asked to marry her but I wanted to talk it over with the two of you."

Arthur scowled but Harry grew thoughtful.

"Would we come live with you and Mama?" Harry asked.

"Definitely. If Sheffield Park is your mother's home, it certainly will be yours, as well." He paused, wanting to phrase his thoughts delicately. "I know I am not your father and can never replace a man you loved so dearly but I would be proud to be your stepfather, Harry. Yours, too, Arthur. Your mother has told me many things about both of you. I look forward to getting to know you myself. What do you think?"

Arthur sullenly said, "It doesn't matter what we think. You've already gone and asked for Mama's hand."

Rhys could understand the young boy's hesitation. "I did. However, I would hope you would each give your approval to the match."

Harry nodded enthusiastically but Arthur said, "We don't even know you, Lord Sheffington. How can we consent to Mama marrying a stranger to us?"

He moved to kneel beside the reluctant boy and met Arthur's gaze. "I know you want to protect your mother, Arthur. You have been the man of the house ever since your father passed. I will say this on my behalf—that I am an honorable man and I love your mother very much. I am your Uncle Dez's closest, oldest friend. I know you hold him in high esteem. He will vouch for me if you have any doubts."

Then he added, "Most of all, you should trust your mother. She is a remarkable woman. She has raised two excellent sons. She cared for your father during his long illness. She is very wise. I would ask that you trust her judgment. She would never rush into something as important as marriage without giving it—and me—her full consideration. She has confidence that we are suited for one another." He looked at the boy beseechingly. "Have faith in her, Arthur."

Rhys could see the boy mull over the argument and saw when he came to a conclusion.

"All right, my lord. You have mine and Harry's blessings. Mama and Uncle Dez are not ones to take anything lightly, especially friendship and marriage. As long as you don't try to replace Papa, I think we will be fine."

Arthur stood as Rhys rose and offered the boy his hand. Rhys shook it and did the same with Harry.

"One thing we should all be clear about," he said. "I may be your stepfather and I will certainly hold you to rules and a high standard but know this—you are now my family. I will always love you. I will always fight for you. Just as I will your mother. Is that clear?"

Arthur nodded his approval while Harry asked, "What should we call you, my lord? Lord Sheffington sounds very stilted. And Stepfather is a mouthful."

"We are to be family, Harry. Why don't you both address me as Rhys?"

Harry brightened. "Rhys. I like that name. I like you, too. When will you and Mama get married?"

As Rhys told them about marrying Dalinda at Torville Manor so that Dez and Anna could be present, Arthur said, "I think we should invite Reid and Ashlyn. They are our family, too."

"That is an excellent idea, Arthur. The wedding will take place before your new school term. Hopefully, they will be able to join us."

"What is Sheffield Park like?" Harry asked, his curiosity obvious, reminding Rhys of Dalinda and what she must have been like as a child.

"It's large. Very large. It is located in Surrey, less than three hours from your uncle, Dez."

"So we can see him often?" Arthur piped in.

"Yes, of course. I don't have a brother but your uncle is like one to me. We entered the army at the same time. Fought alongside one another. He will become my brother-in-law once I wed your mama."

"What else?" Harry demanded.

Rhys told the boys about the land the estate was situated upon. How it had a pond where they could fish and swim. How they would be able to ride as often as they liked.

"I know Mr. Selleck has been with you this summer and you've ridden frequently with him and had lessons. He is welcome to join us anytime."

"For our holidays next summer?" Arthur asked eagerly.

"Yes, if Mr. Selleck chooses to do so."

"We like Mr. Selleck," Harry said. "He is an adult but he is interesting. He teaches us all kinds of things and half the time, Arthur and I don't even realize we are learning. It's a bit sneaky on his part."

Rhys laughed. "I am already liking Mr. Selleck more and more." He grew serious and then said, "There is something else I wish to discuss with you both before you arrive."

"What?" Arthur frowned deeply, his face wary, and Rhys knew it would take longer to gain this boy's trust than his brother's. Harry had a sunny nature but Arthur seemed far less likely to trust someone unless given cause to do so.

"I have embarked on something important. Something very dear to my heart. I was an officer in Her Majesty's Army and in charge of large numbers of men. Sometimes, soldiers are injured in battle and can no longer fight for the crown. They return to England and need weeks—sometimes, even months—to heal. I have started a hospital at Sheffield Park, devoting the east wing to the care of some of my former men who need special care."

"What's wrong with them?" Harry asked, his eyes round.

"Some of them are missing limbs, Harry. An arm or a leg. Some have even lost an eye or ear."

Harry's face fell, sadness overtaking it. Dalinda was right, seeing much of herself in this boy. Rhys glanced to Arthur and saw him sitting very still, his face void of emotion. Arthur would always be one who kept his feelings to himself.

"Some are disfigured in other ways. They may have damage to their faces and bodies. Scars from the burns of exploding shells."

"They sound like they're sad," Harry said.

"They are. Very sad. And lonely. I am taking in veterans who have no families to go home to. I am giving them the luxury of time to heal in the fresh country air. I hope to help them train for jobs so they can become self-supporting."

"What do they have to do with us?" Arthur asked.

Rhys noted the boy didn't sound superior, as someone of his class might be. He merely wondered what role he and his brother would play once they arrived at Sheffield Park.

"I am hoping you will visit with the men. I know just by you speaking to them that it will lift their spirits. They are lonely and could use a friend."

"We could be friends with them?" Harry asked. "But we're just boys."

"You can be friends with whomever you like, Harry. Friendship isn't limited to a certain age. I hope you will get to know these men. They won't want your pity. They merely want to be treated as humans, with a dash of kindness. They are brave men, soldiers who have given their all for their country."

"We will be happy to meet them," Arthur said firmly. "Mama would want us to be nice to them." He hesitated. "Is it . . . is it hard to look at them?"

"Some of them," Rhys admitted. "But once you get to know them, you will see they are the same as you or me. You will be able to look past the fact they are maimed and damaged." He sighed. "They are a big part of life at Sheffield Park. I hope you can accept this."

"Mama knows about them?" Harry asked anxiously.

He smiled. "It was your mama's idea for me to help them."

Arthur looked pleased. "Mama is very smart. And she cares about people. I'm glad your hospital was her idea."

"She does care very much for others, Arthur. It is one of the reasons I love her."

Dalinda entered the drawing room again and both boys ran to her, telling her about asking their older brother and his wife to the wedding. She readily agreed that Reid and Ashlyn should be in attendance and the four of them sat and talked over plans for the small affair and wedding breakfast. Harry begged for his favorite cake to be served.

Arthur told his younger brother, "The day is for Mama and Rhys to celebrate their vows. They should have the kind of cake they want."

Harry, round-eyed, looked at his mother. "What do you think, Mama?"

Dalinda ruffled his hair. "You and I both like the same kind of cake so it looks as if both of us will be pleased."

"What about you, Rhys?" Arthur asked. "What is your favorite kind of cake?"

He warmed at hearing the boy address him naturally after being so reluctant only a short time ago. These two might not be his flesh and blood but Rhys believed they would, in time, become true family.

"I like anything sweet, Arthur," he replied. "Absolutely anything. I went for years at the front without having any sweets at all so I am happy with whatever cake is baked for us."

Mr. Selleck appeared at the door. "It is time for our reading, my lords."

"Mama is getting married!" Harry shared excitedly. "To Rhys. I mean, Lord Sheffington."

The tutor inclined his head. "Congratulations, Your Grace."

"Thank you, Mr. Selleck. We are leaving for Sheffield Park in the morning and will stay there until it is time to go to my brother's estate. Would you see that the boys' things are packed?"

"Yes, Your Grace. Come along," he urged his charges.

The door closed and Dalinda let out a long sigh. "I paced in the corridor the entire time you were alone with them. It seems as if they took it well." She hesitated. "I was a bit worried about Arthur. While Harry is more open to change, Arthur is always reluctant."

Rhys decided not to mention Arthur's earlier surliness and merely said, "I think both boys are pleased for us. All they want is your happiness, Dalinda. The same as I do."

Her lips twitched in amusement. "I know one way you could make me very happy, my lord."

"Tell me, Your Grace," he said, wrapping her in an embrace.

"You can make love to me tonight."

Rhys touched his lips to hers for a brief kiss and then said, "I plan to make love to you every night, my love."

CHAPTER TWENTY

DALINDA GAVE LAST-MINUTE instructions to Mr. Blair and Mrs. Franklin and then allowed Rhys to assist her into his carriage. Arthur and Harry already waited inside, sitting opposite each other. Arthur indicated for her to sit next to him and Rhys took the seat beside Harry. She thought it interesting that it seemed as if her older boy wanted her apart from Rhys as they journeyed to Sheffield Park this morning. It probably was a good idea to have a little distance from Rhys, especially after the night they had spent together in her bed. Her cheeks heated thinking of his touch in very intimate places. His teeth. His tongue. His hands. They all seemed to conjure magic in them, turning her from a sedate widow to a writhing wanton.

She glanced to her newly-betrothed and saw he appeared totally captivated by Harry's constant chatter and questions. Harry always took to people quickly and was open to new relationships and experiences, much like Dalinda herself. Arthur, on the other hand, proved to be more like his father, circumspect and slow to warm to others. It still amazed her after all this time that Gilford, usually so methodical and shy, had offered to marry her after only a brief conversation.

As they rode, she sensed Arthur wanted to talk and so quietly, she asked, "Are you happy to be visiting Sheffield Park?"

He glanced to the pair across from them and seeing they were engaged, told her, "I suppose so."

"I know this is a lot for you and your brother to take in," she began. "It is right for me, though. There will be times in your life, Arthur, when you will take your time, weighing a decision from all sides. Sometimes, though, you must go with what your gut and heart tell you to do."

"Do you love Lord Sheffington?" her son asked.

"I do. I feel very fortunate at this stage in my life to have found a good man, one I have much in common with, and one who is willing to build a life and family with me. Rhys loves me and I do love him. Very much."

She saw a shadow cross Arthur's face and she added, "Just because I love him doesn't mean I love you any less."

His expression let her know she had discovered what troubled her son.

"Think of it this way. When you were born, your father and I were over the moon in love with you. We thought you perfect in every way. Yet your father already had a son—Reid—and he loved him first. Just because Reid already existed didn't mean your father loved you less and Reid more. He loved both of you."

She pushed a lock of hair from his brow. "When Harry came along, it was the same. We both loved him tremendously. Harry was very different from you or Reid yet your father couldn't have been prouder of Harry or loved him more. He loved all three of his boys with all his heart and said many times he was grateful for having a second chance at marriage because it enabled him to be a father to more children."

Arthur grew thoughtful as he mulled over her words. Dalinda gave him a few minutes and then continued.

"Just like Gilford did in his second marriage to me, I hope to do the same and have children with Rhys. Legally, they will be your half-brothers or half-sisters. I hope what you will learn is that that word—half—doesn't really mean much. You will be related by blood to any children I have with Rhys. I hope you will accept and grow to love those new babies I bear."

He frowned. "I don't know anything about babies."

She chuckled. "Well, you will begin to learn a little about them when you meet your cousin. Charlie is a happy baby. I hope as he grows that you and Harry will teach him many things and offer Charlie friendship."

"Rhys will love his children more than us," Arthur said glumly.

"That is a possibility. I know I love you and Harry more than I do Reid, who is my stepson as you and Harry will be stepsons to Rhys. That may be because Reid is an adult and close to my age and I never served as a mother to him. However, if your father had had a young child when we wed, my heart tells me I would have loved him as my own. Adding you and Harry to our family only multiplied the love."

Dalinda paused. "All I ask is that you give Rhys a chance. He has told you he doesn't wish to replace your father and he will hold to that promise. I have learned Rhys is truly a man of his word. However, he can serve as a father figure to you and teach you much as you grow to manhood. Will you try? For me?"

Arthur slipped his hand into hers. "I love you, Mama. I will do the best I can. I want you to be happy. So does Harry. He already likes Rhys. I told him not to forget Papa, though."

She squeezed his hand. "Accepting Rhys as a part of our family doesn't mean we will ever forget your father. He will always be with you, in your heart and in your memory. Never forget that, Arthur."

He released her hand and settled back against the cushion. She hoped she had helped alleviate any fears her older son had. It would take time to blend Rhys into their family of three. She believed if she and Rhys did have a child that her sons would accept the baby. They were good boys at heart.

An hour later, the carriage pulled up the lane leading to Sheffield Park. Rhys pointed out various structures and talked about the farmland as they drove to the manor house.

When Harry spied a field with a few horses, he asked, "Will we get to bring our ponies here and ride when you and Mama are wed?"

"Of course. If you are as horse-mad as your mama, which I suspect you both are, I expect you to bring them. I enjoyed our ride together yesterday and hope we can make that a daily occurrence. I want to show you boys the entire estate and have you begin meeting our tenants."

"Why?" questioned Arthur, not belligerently but with curiosity.

"It is important for the family to get to know those who live on the land and work for us. We are entrusted with seeing to their needs and protecting them while they are our workers."

"Will we be your family, Rhys?" Harry asked.

Rhys smiled at the boy. "You already are, Harry. When I asked your mama to marry me, I knew I wasn't just marrying her—I was bringing you and Arthur into the fold. I have no family. My parents and sister are long dead. I have been on my own for many, many years." He paused. "Truth be told, you are part of the reason I wanted to wed Her Grace. It means not only do I get a countess but I also have two fine sons from the very start."

Dalinda's eyes brimmed with tears at his words. She hadn't really known how Rhys would feel taking on another man's children. She should have realized how lonely he was and that because her boys were an important of her life, they would be equally important in his.

She glanced to Arthur and saw a smile on his face. Just as he had accepted being at a new school and thriving there, she thought her marriage to Rhys would have positive benefits for both her and her boys. Another thing that she felt would be important was for Arthur and Harry to meet the wounded men that Rhys had been entrusted to care for. She wanted her sons to understand how fortunate they were and teach them the importance of goodwill and charity toward others. In her mind, it was essential to give to the community. Helping these injured veterans back into the fold of society would have lasting effects.

The carriage door opened and Rhys climbed out after a footman placed the steps down. She allowed Harry and Arthur to follow and then Rhys assisted her from the vehicle. She saw Mr. and Mrs. Marsh standing there and greeted both of them. They also said hello to the boys.

"I am happy to inform you that Her Grace has consented to be my wife," Rhys shared, a broad smile on his face, which was then matched by the couple.

"We are delighted with that news, Lord Sheffington," Mr. Marsh said. "It will be as it should."

"I agree," Rhys said, giving Dalinda a wink.

As the butler instructed footman to bring up the trunks from the carriage that followed with Mr. Selleck, Tandy, and the scullery maid, Dalinda saw Harry staring in fear at Morrison, who had served as their driver from Laurelwood to Sheffield Park. He had climbed down from the coachman's seat to confer with Rhys.

When they finished their brief conversation, she said, "Mr. Morrison, I would like you to meet my sons."

Morrison smiled tentatively as Harry inched closer to her. Arthur stood without speaking.

"Boys, please introduce yourselves," she said firmly.

Arthur recovered first, obviously trying to mask his repulsion. "I am Lord Arthur Baker. This is my brother, Lord Harry Baker."

Morrison bowed to the boys. "I am Morrison and have served as head groom at Sheffield Park until now. Her Grace has asked me to help work with the soldiers who have been brought to the estate."

Harry said, "A head groom?" ignoring what Morrison had mentioned after that. "Arthur and I adore horses. We get that after Mama."

Morrison smiled. "Your mother is probably the finest rider I have seen. And Stormy? Not many men or women could handle such a spirted mount."

"You know Stormy?" Arthur asked.

"I do."

Morrison began talking about Stormy and then some of the horses at Sheffield Park. Dalinda stepped back and Rhys slipped an arm about her waist as they listened to the boys pepper the groom with questions.

"Their enthusiasm is unbridled when it comes to horses," he noted.

"I had hoped Morrison would talk horses with them. I wanted them to see him as a knowledgeable man, not a damaged one."

"I think it's working. I saw at first they were a little unsettled by him but looking at them now, they are seeing past his physical appearance."

Harry turned and said, "Mr. Morrison has two mounts we can use while we are here, Mama. Before we bring our ponies to Sheffield Park."

"Morrison knows all about breeding horses," Arthur added. "It's something I'm interested in."

Rhys nodded. "I have been thinking of adding to my stables here. I, too, was once a groom and worked with horses for many years. Perhaps starting a small breeding farm might be a good idea. We can discuss this after dinner tonight, Arthur."

"You want . . . my opinion?" Arthur asked, bewildered.

"You are interested in horses. You said so yourself. What better way to contribute to the estate than by getting involved in an important aspect of it?" Rhys asked. "Of course, we will need to discuss the advantages and disadvantages of the idea. You'll also be going back to school in a few weeks so this may be something we talk about during the year at length before we act upon it. It will take much to get organized and take on such an enterprise."

His words prompted Dalinda to say, "A new venture such as this might give some of the former soldiers a new outlet. Working with animals can be quite soothing."

"Hmm. I hadn't thought of it. It's certainly worth considering. It will definitely take more manpower to run that type of operation." Rhys paused. "Let's go inside and let Arthur and Harry choose their own bedchambers."

"We don't have to share?" Arthur asked. "Mama always makes us share."

He place a hand on Arthur's shoulder. "I think you are of an age now where you value your privacy. Sheffield Park is large enough for you to take advantage of that. What do you think, Dalinda?"

She liked how Rhys had phrased things and said, "I think that is a decision you and the boys can arrive at."

Harry whooped loudly and ran into the house. Arthur paused long enough to thank Rhys and then quickly followed his brother inside.

Rhys dropped a light kiss upon her lips. "Mrs. Marsh can direct you to the rooms designated for the countess. Mind you," he said softly, "you will only sleep in there for propriety's sake until after the wedding. Then I expect you to use the rooms only for dressing and bathing. I claim you nights, Your Grace."

Butterflies fluttered in her belly as she thought of what last night had entailed. The fact that Rhys wanted her in his bed every night thrilled her. She and Gilford had their own separate chambers and he had visited her in hers. They had never spent an entire night together. Going to sleep and awakening in her new husband's arms made her smile.

"I will look them over," she said. "You may deal with Arthur and Harry fighting over which bedchamber will be theirs."

She found Mrs. Marsh waiting for her in the foyer and accompanied the housekeeper upstairs while Rhys went to sort out whatever problems arose between her sons. She had a small regret that he was being thrown into the fire as far as fatherhood was concerned but she knew if any man could handle two rambunctious boys, it was her husband-to-be.

As Dalinda supervised Tandy's unpacking, Mrs. Marsh talked over the next few days of menus with her. She informed the housekeeper they would be at Sheffield Park for two weeks before departing for Torville Manor, where she and Lord Sheffington would be wed.

Mrs. Marsh's face softened at the mention of the wedding. "We are so happy for you, Your Grace. Lord Sheffington is a very fine man."

"I think so, too. I will be proud to be his countess."

The housekeeper left as her sons hurried into the room.

"Come, Mama," Harry urged. "You need to see my room."

"Mine, too," Arthur begged. "Harry and I are next door to each other."

"That way we can knock on the wall and hear one another," Harry noted. "And if I am scared—I won't be, but if—I can go and slip into Arthur's bed."

Dalinda knew Harry had a tendency to hear noises at night and was the more fearful of the two. It was one of the reasons she'd had them share a room, knowing Arthur would look out for his little brother.

"Show me the way."

They took her hands and led her a few doors down from her rooms. Harry's bedchamber came first and he pointed out all the reasons he had selected this particular room.

"I think you did a fine job in choosing, Harry," she told her son, who beamed at her praise.

"Come to mine, Mama," Arthur urged, tugging on her hand.

He, too, showed her around the large, airy bedchamber and noted where he planned to read and the area he could set up the small army figures he favored playing with.

Rhys appeared in the doorway. "Do you like their choices?" he asked.

"I do. It doesn't seem as if they argued about the decision at all."

"Not a bit," he assured her. "I do need the three of you to come downstairs with me now."

"Are we having an early tea?" Arthur asked. "I am famished."

"I can arrange that," Rhys said. "Come along."

As they reached the final landing before arriving at the ground floor, Dalinda saw the foyer lined with people and realized it must be all of the household's servants and many of the others who worked outside on the estate.

The four of them came to stand on the last stair and Rhys said, "I asked you to gather because I have some excellent news to share with you. Her Grace has consented to become the next Countess of Sheffington."

Applause rang out and she felt the hot blush stain her cheeks as attention was focused upon her.

Rhys placed his hands on her sons' shoulders and added, "This is Lord Arthur and Lord Harry. They are the sons of the Duke of Gilford—and I am proud to claim them as my new family members, along with the duchess."

Dalinda glowed with happiness, seeing how Rhys had truly accepted her boys as his own. More importantly, it seemed as if Arthur and Harry were also happy at being part of a new, hopefully, growing family.

CHAPTER TWENTY-ONE

"Y OUR GRACE," MRS. Marsh said, "a carriage is approaching."

Dalinda looked up and said, "It must be the Robinsons and Mrs. Nathan. Are their rooms ready?" she asked the housekeeper.

"Yes, Your Grace. And Cook has asked me to pass along her thanks at the new cook you brought with you from Laurelwood. It has made a significant difference in getting meals to the soldiers and relieved Cook greatly."

"A house can only be as happy as its cook is," she said as she rose to go and meet the new arrivals.

The two women went downstairs and outside where Mr. Marsh and two footmen awaited. The carriage, which Rhys had sent, pulled into the drive and came to a stop.

First out was Dr. Robinson, who assisted his daughter and then their servant from the vehicle. Dalinda went to greet them.

"Welcome to Sheffield Park, Doctor. We are happy to have you, Miss Robinson, and Mrs. Nathan here with us. We have rooms ready for you in the east wing. Would you like to go to them now and freshen up?"

"No," he said. "Our journey was short. I think we are all eager to meet our patients."

His daughter and Mrs. Nathan nodded in agreement.

"Very well. If you'll follow me. We are using the ballroom as a clinic and a barracks in which to house the veterans."

As they entered the house, she explained how they had moved the majority of the men from individual bedchambers to the ballroom in order to streamline their care and allow them the camaraderie they were used to experiencing in the military.

"Since you will now be living here and tending to the men fulltime, our local doctor has left their care and all medical decisions in your hands," Dalinda revealed. "There is one case, a Mr. Pimmel, whose leg will probably need to be amputated."

Dr. Robinson frowned. "And the local physician decided to allow me the privilege of making that decision and informing the patient of it?"

"Yes," she admitted. "Mr. Pimmel is reluctant to lose the limb. The doctor was wishy-washy in making a determination. He said with your war experience that you would be better suited to arrive at a diagnosis for Pimmel."

"I see I have my work cut out for me," he said grimly.

"Mr. Marsh is our butler," she said, indicating the servant who hovered nearby. "He will see that your things are placed in your rooms. We dine at seven each evening and hope you and Miss Robinson will join us."

"We would be happy to, Your Grace," Miss Robinson said.

Dalinda led them to the ballroom. Over the last few days, she had spent time with each of the men who had been brought to Sheffield Park. All were soldiers formerly under Rhys' command with the exception of Mr. Garfield. He had transferred to the unit after Rhys had sold his commission and returned to England. General Shepherd had written to Rhys and said that Garfield was a special case and that he hoped being around men he was familiar with might help him to recover his equilibrium.

She doubted it. Both Garfield and Mr. Hayward suffered from battlefield fatigue. Rhys said that it went by various names with soldiers. Used up. Worn out. Dogged. He called Mr. Hayward hipped, which meant he was unable to focus and that the soldier often felt useless, tearing up and moping. Mr. Garfield was what Rhys termed blue-deviled. He, too, lacked the ability to concentrate that Mr. Hayward demonstrated, but Garfield's case went further. He had a haunted look in his eyes, which could turn wild at times. Being around the former private had made Dalinda very uncomfortable.

Though she had the boys come with her when Rhys first introduced her to each individual, she had asked Morrison, who was now in charge and in the ballroom a majority of the day, to keep an eye out for Arthur and Harry whenever they came around. She had also told her sons that she preferred Mr. Morrison being there when they came to visit and that they should always have Mr. Selleck with them, as well. Neither had questioned her request, for which Dalinda was grateful. Mr. Selleck brought the boys by each morning after breakfast to tell the men hello and they stayed for half an hour or so before they left for their lessons.

They arrived and she motioned Morrison over, introducing him to the trio. In return, he pointed out each former soldier by name and told Dr. Robinson why they had come to be at Sheffield Park.

"Two new arrivals also showed up today, Your Grace."

He indicated a man sitting in the corner, talking to another man she was unfamiliar with.

"The one with the missing arm is Davis," Morrison revealed. "He was left-handed to begin with so he's having to learn everything over with his right hand. Next to him is Brown."

Dalinda didn't observe anything physically wrong with Brown and asked, "What is his story?"

"He's blind now, Your Grace. Had a head injury and forgot who he was for a few weeks. Brown asked that the cloth around his eyes be removed. He said he felt too boxed in with it about his head."

"Amnesia," Dr. Robinson said. "It can happen. He is fortunate to have regained his memory. Many soldiers never do."

Morrison assessed the physician with a new eye. "You were on the front, Dr. Robinson?"

"I was."

The two men spoke of places they had been stationed before returning to Brown's case.

"He has stitches and some deep bruising," Morrison said. "Other than that, it's the blindness that has him feeling so helpless."

"My mother was blind," Miss Robinson said. "From birth. I especially would like to work with Mr. Brown," she said softly.

Rhys joined them and explained how he planned to hire skilled workers who would train the recovered men in various occupations, helping them to leave Laurelwood and make their own way in the world.

Morrison led them in rounds after that so that Dr. Robinson could examine each individual. Dalinda liked the doctor's easy yet professional manner with the men. He didn't brag about his war experience but when it came out in conversation, she saw each former soldier felt a greater connection with him than they had the local doctor, who only came around infrequently and hadn't seemed sympathetic to their plights.

The bullet wound to Wharton's leg was healing nicely. Hensley, who still ran a slight fever, was suffering from jaundice. He still experienced pains in his missing right arm, which Dr. Robinson explained to him was called phantom pain.

"They seem as real as anything," the physician said. "You feel the limb burn. Tingle. You may have these shooting pains for weeks or even months—or they might disappear tomorrow. The point is when a pain strikes, you should look anywhere except where your arm once was. I have discovered in working with other soldiers who were haunted by phantom pain that physical activity can take your mind off the ache. Also, anything that can serve as a distraction helps. Try any activity. Eating. Talking to someone. Something that will keep you from fretting about the hurt."

Hensley nodded. "I understand, Doctor. That is good advice."

They reached Pimmel, who was missing his left eye and was the one Dalinda had mentioned who had the leg that wasn't healing properly. Dr. Robinson evaluated the eye socket first and found the cauterization had prevented any infection. He recommended Pimmel continue to wear the eye patch and discussed some exercises with him that would help him with his balance as he viewed the world from a single eye.

Then the physician moved to examine the injured leg. Pimmel winced the entire time, gritting his teeth, tender to any touch.

"I am afraid that the leg will have to come off, young man," the physician said. "Immediately."

"Why?" the young private asked, agony on his face and present in his voice as his lone eye brimmed with tears. "It's bad enough I'm missing an eye. I won't be a man without my leg."

Dr. Robinson said bluntly, "You won't be a man at all, Mr. Pimmel. You will be a corpse lying in a grave if I don't take your limb within the hour. It's your choice. Life—or death."

The room had grown silent and the doctor's stern words echoed through the room. Dalinda held her breath as she watched Pimmel's indecision.

"You've told me you enjoy carpentry, Pimmel," Rhys said. "I could use another carpenter on the estate. I am thinking about starting a horse breeding operation and, in time, will need to expand my stables. I can promise you if you learn the trade, there will be plenty of work for you."

She saw Rhys' words had an effect and that they would influence Pimmel enough so that Dr. Robinson might save the veteran's life.

"You'd hire me, my lord? Even with one eye and one leg?"

Rhys chuckled. "I hired Morrison, didn't I? You are a far sight prettier than he is."

Pimmel stared a moment—and then burst out laughing. Soon, laughter filled the entire ballroom. Dalinda saw that Rhys had gotten through to the young man.

"All right," Pimmel said. "I agree. Let's do it. Now."

Dr. Robinson glanced around and then back to her. "Your Grace, I would like to use one of the bedchambers as my surgery," he said quietly. "While I have morphine to give my patient, I think it best if there's no audience during this amputation."

"I can assist you," Morrison volunteered.

"I will help, too, Father," Miss Robinson said. "Mrs. Nathan can start with the men here."

The physician turned to Morrison, telling him what would be needed in order for the room to be prepared. He excused himself, taking his daughter and medical bag to the bedchamber they would use.

Rhys shook hands with Pimmel. "I expect a swift recovery."

Pimmel grinned. "I am motivated by knowing I will have a job when this is over, my lord. I hate losing my leg but I'd rather live to be an old man without one than die at nineteen."

Once Pimmel had been carried from the ballroom, Dalinda told Rhys she wanted to stay a while.

"They aren't saying it, but I know they are worried about their friend's surgery," she said. "I think it best to try and take their minds off what is happening now."

They stayed another hour, until news came from Dr. Robinson himself. He joined them.

"The surgery was a success. Mr. Pimmel is now resting comforta-bly. Mr. Morrison and my daughter are watching over him."

"Would you share that with the men?" she asked.

"Of course, Your Grace."

The physician address the room, letting the veterans know Pimmel had come through surgery with no complications. Cheers erupted.

"They are a close group, Doctor," she told him. "You have gained their trust by taking good care of their friend."

"I am glad to be here, Your Grace. Thank you for this opportunity, Lord Sheffington."

"We are glad to have you here," Rhys replied.

"I hope you and Miss Robinson will join us for dinner tonight at seven," she said.

"Thank you for the invitation. We will see you then."

As Dalinda and Rhys exited the ballroom, an odd feeling rippled through her. Dalinda looked over her shoulder and saw Garfield staring at her. The unnatural look in his eyes caused a shiver to run along her spine. Quickly, Dalinda turned away, her heart pounding. She said nothing, however, knowing that Garfield was at Sheffield Park to be helped. She would do her best to avoid contact with him in the future.

Rhys led her to his study and closed the door, taking her into his arms.

"You are good with the men. You are a true nurturer." He kissed her softly. "I cannot wait for us to have children. To see your belly swell with our child."

"I long for that, too."

"I just returned from speaking to the local clergyman about our wish to wed at Torville Manor within two weeks. He explained that we aren't eligible for a bishop's license. Though it would allow us to wed within seven days of purchasing it, we don't meet one of its requirements."

"What is that?" she asked.

"One party has to have resided in the parish where the wedding takes place for four weeks. You haven't lived at Torville Manor in many years. We could wed here but I think it would be nice if we could have our vows take place in the Torville chapel."

Dalinda frowned. "Does that mean you must purchase a special license? It's what Gilford did when we married years ago."

Rhys nodded. "I will leave now for London and go immediately to Doctors' Commons. I want to have the special license in hand before we journey to see Dez and Anna."

"By the time you reach London, it may be too late in the day to purchase it," she pointed out.

"If that is the case, I will stay overnight at my London townhouse. I may even see my solicitor, Mr. Goolsby, while I am in town. If I do wind up having to spend the night, I will return by midday tomorrow."

He kissed her at length, until her toes curled and her bones liquified. "I will miss having you in my bed tonight," he said huskily, nuzzling her ear.

She chuckled. "We both might actually get a little sleep tonight by being apart."

"Sleep is highly overrated," he answered and kissed her again.

Rhys finally broke the kiss. "I could stay here all day kissing you, you know." He smoothed her hair.

"Or you could go see to our marriage license," she said lightly, knowing how hard it would be to be apart from this man for even one night.

"As a soldier, I understand when I've been tasked with a mission." He kissed her hard and swift. "I will bring back the special license tomorrow."

She placed her palm against his cheek. "I love you, Rhys Armistead. I cannot wait to be your wife."

CHAPTER TWENTY-TWO

Torville Manor

ANTICIPATION GREW WITHIN Dalinda as they turned up the lane leading to Torville Manor. By this time tomorrow, she and Rhys would be husband and wife. They had written to Dez and Anna and arranged for the wedding to take place in the morning at the small chapel on the estate. Dez had promised he would arrange to have a clergyman present.

"It's a very pretty place, Mama," Arthur said. "Did you have fun growing up here with Uncle Dez?"

"I did. Aunt Anna lived on the adjacent estate and the three of us spent quite a bit of time together."

"What about your mama and papa?" Harry asked.

"I never knew my mama, Harry. She died giving birth to Dez and me."

Harry leaned close to her, resting his head against her shoulder. "I am glad Arthur and I know you."

She kissed the top of his head. "Thank you, dearest."

"What about your papa?" Arthur asked. "Our grandfather. You told me once he died a long time ago."

She didn't want to sound judgmental, much less let her harsh feelings for her long-dead father infringe upon her current happiness, and so she said, "My father preferred living in town. My older brother, Ham, was often with him since he would become the earl one day."

"But Uncle Dez is the earl," Harry protested.

"He is now. That is why he came home from the war. Until then, Hamilton had been Lord Torrington. Ham accidentally drown, making Dez the new earl."

"Charlie will be the next earl, isn't that right?" Harry asked.

"It's always the oldest son," Arthur said, rolling his eyes. "That is why when Papa died Reid became the Duke of Gilford."

Harry leaned out the window. "I see Reid's carriage!" he exclaimed. "It's just now turning behind us."

Dalinda was thankful that Reid and Ashlyn had accepted the invitation to the wedding. She knew how the boys loved both of them. Though she was just beginning to know the couple, they were family. She wanted to impart the importance of family to her sons. Knowing how Rhys had been without a family for so many years, she hoped he would take to being a father to her sons, as well as any children she might bear him. The thought of having Rhys' babies brought a sweet surge of love within her.

Arthur and Harry began waving wildly and she knew they had spotted Dez and Anna. She glanced to Rhys, who sat opposite her. He had been quiet for most of the journey. She wondered if he contemplated their marriage and hoped he hadn't changed his mind about marrying her tomorrow.

As if he could hear her thoughts, he leaned over and took her hand, squeezing it gently, giving her a smile.

"This time tomorrow, we'll be at our wedding breakfast," he said. "And then after that?"

She felt a hot rush of desire run through her as his eyes heated, assuring her he was just as eager for this union as she was.

They descended from the carriage and she fell into Dez's arms. No one knew her quite like her twin and she relished the thought of him being at her wedding. He had missed her first one to Gilford, having already been sent away to the army by their father. It meant a great deal to her for him to be present at this one and share in her joy.

Dalinda hugged Anna and asked, "Where is Charlie?"

"He just went down for his nap. It will be at least an hour before he can meet his cousins."

By now, the Gilford ducal carriage pulled up, followed by another one carrying servants and luggage. Reid helped Ashlyn from the vehicle and Arthur and Harry ran to greet them. Where once they had been sullen and standoffish with Reid, the boys now flung themselves at him and then embraced Ashlyn, too. Harry took her hand and led her back to where Dalinda stood with Dez and Anna.

"This is Her Grace," Harry said formerly to his aunt and uncle. "The Duchess of Gilford. That used to be Mama's title but it is Ashlyn's now."

"We only call her Ashlyn around family," Arthur explained solemnly. "When we are with our schoolmates or others, she is Her Grace."

"This is Uncle Dez and Aunt Anna," Harry said with pride.

"The Earl and Countess of Torrington," Arthur added. As Reid approached, he said, "This is the Duke of Gilford, our brother."

Handshakes were exchanged and Anna urged everyone to come inside to the drawing room.

Rhys said, "We've been cooped up in a carriage for a few hours now. Perhaps the boys would like to see a bit of Torrington lands since they are visiting for the first time."

As Arthur and Harry cheered, Dez said, "That's a fine idea. Shall we men go riding? Your Grace, do you care to join us?"

Reid agreed and the men started away from the house. Dalinda caught Rhys' arm.

"Thank you for looking out for them," she said.

He leaned down and dropped a light kiss on her lips. "We will see you later."

She turned and accompanied Anna and Ashlyn inside.

"Since it is just the three of us," Anna said, "we can go to my sitting room. It's light and airy and I enjoy spending time there."

The three went to the room. Anna rang for tea and they settled in for a chat.

"How is Gillingham without all of its boisterous students?" Dalinda asked.

Ashlyn laughed. "Quite peaceful, actually." She briefly explained to Anna how her school was located in a wing of Gillingham. "All the boys are away enjoying their summer holiday now. Because of that, it has given Reid and me time to visit a few of his other properties."

"I remember doing the same thing when I wed Gilford years ago."

They spent a few minutes talking about which estates Ashlyn had visited and Dalinda asked after some of the staff at the various properties.

"Torville Manor is lovely," Ashlyn told Anna. "How long have you and the earl been wed?"

"Since last year," Anna replied. "Dez had been on the Continent with his regiment and came home after he came into the title."

"Reid was in the same situation. We met when Dalinda's boys enrolled in my school, Dunwood Academy." She chuckled. "I was a widow, bound and determined never to wed again. My duke is a very persuasive man, however."

Dalinda smiled. "So was his father. He convinced me to wed him after our first meeting. Harry has Gilford's charm, while Arthur has his father's sense of duty."

"It seems we have all married—or at least by tomorrow will have wed—military men," Anna noted. "Dez and I have a son, Charlie. I look at him and cannot imagine sending him to war someday."

"I feel the same about Arthur and Harry," Dalinda confided. "No matter how old they become, they will always be my babies."

The tea arrived and Anna poured out for them as they continued chatting. Naturally, talk turned to the upcoming wedding.

"I have done as you asked, Dalinda," Anna said. "The chapel is being decorated with simple greenery this afternoon. The only guests I have invited are our neighbors, Viscount Shelton and his wife, and my sister, Jessa, who lives with them."

"I am eager to see Jessa again after all these years," she said. "I am sorry it did not work out for me to visit with her on my previous stay at Torville Manor."

"Well, we did spend a good portion of that time at Sheffield Park," her friend said.

"What is your new home like?" Ashlyn asked.

Dalinda told her a little about the property and invited her and Reid to come stay with them.

"We would like that. Of course, a majority of our year will be tied up with the school. Reid is very supportive of my endeavors on behalf of my pupils. How has it worked out having Mr. Selleck with you this summer?"

She told of some of the lessons the tutor had given to the boys and how the three had roamed every inch of Laurelwood.

A maid appeared and said, "My lady, the nurse wished to know if you'd like for Lord Charles to be brought to you now?"

Anna's face softened at the mention of her son. "Yes, please." When the servant left, she said, "I hope you don't mind Charlie coming down."

"Not at all," Ashlyn said. She paused, an odd look on her face and then her words came out in a torrent. "I must tell someone. My courses are very regular. They did not come last week. I believe I am with child."

Dalinda leaned over and embraced the duchess. "That is wonderful news, Ashlyn."

"Yes, congratulations," Anna said with enthusiasm. "I cannot imagine our lives without Charlie. Having a baby will be so much fun."

"I haven't told Reid yet because it's so early. I haven't been sick at all but I know that will come."

She took Ashlyn's hand. "He will be so pleased. Reid is already so good with Harry and Arthur. With all of the boys at the academy, actually."

Tears welled in Ashlyn's eyes. "I never thought I would be wed again. Be a mother again." She paused. "I had a child with my first husband. My son's name was Gregory. He died in an accident when he was four."

Anna took Ashlyn's other hand. "I am so sorry you lost your boy, Your Grace. That must have been horrible."

"It was the worst thing that ever happened to me." Ashlyn closed her eyes and Dalinda squeezed her hand encouragingly. Ashlyn opened them again and said, "This second chance with Reid means the world to me, especially since I now know love."

"I feel the same way," Dalinda shared. "Meeting Rhys has changed my life. While I was very fond of Gilford and he was a wonderful husband and father, I finally know what it is to love a man. To think Rhys will be my husband—and that one day we may have children together—is a blessing I never imagined."

The door opened and the nursery governess entered carrying Charlie in her arms. She brought the baby to Anna, who nestled him in her arms, cooing to her son softly. Dalinda saw the expression on Ashlyn's face and hoped that her and Reid's baby would be born healthy and without any complications.

Anna kissed Charlie's head and with an impish grin said, "Who wants to hold him first?"

"HOLD STILL, MY lord," Callow admonished gently.

"I am trying to," Rhys said impatiently, knowing he was wiggling and not being able to stop the restlessness running through him.

Not until he slipped the gold band upon Dalinda's finger and made her his forever would he find peace.

"Grip the arms of the chair, my lord," his valet suggested.

Rhys did as he was told and concentrated on keeping his feet still and his knees from bouncing up and down. He wondered if every groom became a bundle of nerves on his wedding day. He had no regrets in asking Dalinda to be his countess. He looked forward to a lifetime with her.

If they could just get the damned ceremony over and done.

"There," Callow said, satisfaction in his voice. He stepped back and held up a mirror to Rhys. "You look ready to be wed now, Lord Sheffington."

He studied his image in the mirror a moment. Callow had tied the cravat's knot perfectly. The valet had also trimmed Rhys' hair and, for once, the unruly waves seemed to behave. He was clean-shaven and as ready as he would ever be.

"Thank you, Callow." He stood and panicked. "Where are—"

"Here, my lord," the servant said, locating the ring box and other small box with the lapel pins for Arthur and Harry.

He'd stopped at a shop in London when he went for the special license, buying rings for both him and Dalinda to exchange. When he had mentioned to the jeweler that he was wedding a widow with two sons, the man had made an interesting suggestion. He had told Rhys about a family medallion ceremony, something which could be incorporated into the actual wedding ceremony and involve Arthur and Harry. Rhys purchased two lapel pins from the jeweler for the boys and while out riding the estate yesterday, he had called upon Reverend Harris, explaining to the clergyman his idea. Harris had been enthusiastic and promised to make presenting the pins to Arthur and Harry a part of the vows.

Rhys slipped both boxes into his pocket and hurried downstairs. Dez awaited him, along with the Duke and Duchess of Gilford.

"My carriage will take us to the chapel," his friend said. "His Grace's ducal carriage will convey Dalinda, Anna, and the boys in a few minutes. Beyond that, the only other invited guests are Viscount and Viscountess Shelton, our neighbors, and Jessa, Anna's sister who lives with them. They will meet us there."

The four climbed into the carriage for the short ride to the chapel. The day was sunny, without a cloud in the sky. A perfect day for a wedding.

"You look quite handsome, Lord Sheffington," Her Grace said.

Gilford took his wife's hand. "As long as you find me more attractive, my love, I am good with the compliment paid to the earl," he said with a smile, bringing his duchess' hand to his lips and kissing it tenderly.

Rhys liked the duke. Dalinda said Gilford favored his father quite a bit physically and that she thought he would make for an excellent duke. Rhys was also impressed with the duchess, hearing more details about her school at dinner last night. He could see why this remarkable woman had caught Gilford's eye and was grateful that she was in charge of Arthur's and Harry's education.

They arrived at the chapel and he went immediately to speak with Reverend Harris, giving him the box holding the lapel pins. They briefly discussed what Rhys wanted to say and then he found Dez and gave him the wedding rings for safekeeping.

Dez accepted them and said, "Who would have thought my closest friend would wed my twin? I cannot think of a better man for Dalinda than you, Rhys. I know you will love and care for my sister better than any other man could."

"I do love her, Dez. I have a feeling I will love her more with each passing day." He paused. "I want you to know how much I care for your sister. How I will love and honor her all the days of our lives. How I will be a good husband to her and take care of her and the boys."

His friend grinned. "If you are lucky, that is exactly what will happen. Your love grows stronger every day you are wed. And if you are blessed with children, that love will explode."

"I know how you dote on Baby Charlie."

"Don't worry," Dez assured him. "Charlie is staying back at the house with his nanny. Ever since he has discovered he has a voice, he constantly uses it at full volume. Anna and I didn't want him to interrupt your ceremony."

A few minutes later, Reverend Harris summoned them. "Your bride has arrived, my lord."

Rhys and Dez went to stand at the front of the small chapel. The Duke and Duchess of Gilford were seated on the bride's side, while Viscount and Viscountess Shelton and Miss Browning sat on the opposite side. Anna appeared and came up the aisle to stand up for Dalinda. Then the doors opened again and his bride appeared, the sun shining down upon her as a radiant beam from heaven. Arthur and Harry stood on either side of their mother and the boys escorted her up the aisle.

Dalinda glowed with happiness. Her gaze never left his as the boys brought her down the aisle and handed her off to him. They went and joined the Gilfords, taking seats beside them. Rhys took Dalinda's hand and kissed it before slipping it through the crook of his arm. His heart beat rapidly as the importance of what would now take place blanketed him.

Reverend Harris had performed many marriage ceremonies and smoothly took charge, addressing the handful of guests and helping the couple to repeat their vows to one another. Rhys and Dalinda exchanged rings and then the clergyman cleared his throat.

"I have been asked by Lord Sheffington to extend today's ceremony." He withdrew the velvet box and opened it, showing it to Dalinda and allowing Rhys to take the lapel pins in hand.

She turned to Rhys, her gaze questioning.

He took a deep breath and said, "We have made our vows to one another today, Dalinda, but my commitment extends not only to you but the children you bring into our marriage."

Turning, he found the boys and said, "Arthur, Harry, would you please join us at the altar?"

They stood and made their way toward the front.

"I have taken your mother as my wife and we have exchanged rings that are a symbol of our love for one another. I have a small token for you, as well. A family medallion."

Rhys slipped the first lapel pin onto Arthur's coat and then did the same with Harry's.

"These pins represent that you are also a part of this marriage and our new family. It has three interlocking circles. They represent the commitment between your mother, the two of you, and me. These tokens are a visual affirmation that you are loved and an integral part of this marriage. I promise to love you and support you—as well as any other children that may result from my union with your mother. I hope you will wear these lapel pins with pride and always remember my pledge to you this day."

Tears streamed down Dalinda's cheeks as his new sons threw their arms about him. Rhys felt love pour through him for these two young boys and he looked forward in leading them to manhood.

"Thank you, Rhys," they both echoed, blinking back tears of their own.

"You may sit, my lords," Reverend Harris said gently.

Once Arthur and Harry had returned to their seats, the clergyman said a few more words about love and commitment and then told Rhys he could kiss his bride.

He turned to Dalinda, whose radiant smile warmed him to his soul. Cradling her face in his hands, he kissed her tenderly, sealing their vows.

Breaking the kiss, he whispered, "I love you will all my heart, Countess."

CHAPTER TWENTY-THREE

D ALINDA ALLOWED RHYS to escort her outside to the waiting carriage. He handed her up and then climbed in after her. The moment the door closed, he pulled her onto his lap for a long, leisurely kiss.

Once he broke it, she said, "You touched my heart with the vows you spoke today, Rhys, but you touched my soul in the promises you made to my sons."

He cupped her cheek. "They are a part of us. They are my family now as much as yours." He grinned. "I am sure there are times I will take their side against you."

She swatted him playfully. "You better not," and then kissed him soundly.

She had no idea how she had come to deserve the love of this wonderful man but she wouldn't question it. She would simply savor it each and every day.

They arrived at the house and Meadows and Mrs. Abbott greeted them.

"The wedding breakfast is laid out, Lady Sheffington," the house-keeper said. "Cook outdid herself with the menu."

"I know it will be exceptional, Mrs. Abbott," Dalinda said.

Soon, their guests arrived and she was happy to see a very grown up Jessa Browning, as well as meeting the new Viscount Shelton and his lovely wife. They gathered around the table and dined upon so many delectable dishes that she lost count. Champagne toasts were made in their honor and Dalinda knew she was blessed to have such a loving, close family.

Her boys eagerly showed off their lapel pins to her. Harry declared he would wear his every day while Arthur said the token was exceptional and he would only wear it upon special occasions.

"I am still grateful for it, Mama," Arthur told her. "Rhys really does seem to love us."

"He does," she assured her son. "He will be a good father to you and Harry. Rhys is new at it, though, and he may make a few mistakes but he will always have your best interests at heart."

Arthur smiled shyly. "I am glad you married him, Mama."

She hugged him. "I am, too, Arthur."

When it was time for them to depart, Dalinda thought she and Rhys would leave for Sheffield Park. She and Anna had spoken about the boys staying on for the next two weeks as planned. It would give her and Rhys some private time together, especially since they had discussed not taking any type of honeymoon for now. With the upcoming harvest, he wanted to be present at Sheffield Park and experience that process for the first time. They would also most likely go to Laurelwood for a day or so and help in supervising the harvest there, as well.

She had decided to remain in her wedding gown instead of changing for the journey home. When Rhys led her outside, though, his carriage was nowhere in sight. Only a cart attached to a single horse stood in the drive. Dez's valet, Coral, sat with the reins in hand, his bald head shining in the sunlight and his blue eyes merry.

"Where is the carriage?" she asked. "Aren't we going home?"

"Not tonight," Rhys said mysteriously. "Let me help you up."

There was only enough room on the bench for her to sit next to Coral. Her new husband climbed into the back of the cart.

Anna called out, "Don't worry. I've seen some of your things taken there."

Dez handed up a hamper to Rhys. "Treats from Cook. It will be enough to see you through until tomorrow morning." He winked at Dalinda. "Enjoy!"

Coral flicked his wrists and the horse took off. She waved goodbye to everyone, still curious as to where they might be headed. It soon came to her, though, as they drew closer to the lake. She remembered the cottage they had played in as children. Dez had refurnished it when he had come into the title and he had brought Anna to it when he had liberated her from the madhouse. The couple went to the cottage occasionally, using it as a getaway in order to be alone with one another with no intrusions from the outside world.

It would be perfect for her wedding night with Rhys.

Coral pulled into the small glen. "I hope you have a lovely time, my lady," he said, a twinkle in his eyes as he tipped his cap to her.

Rhys jumped from the bed of the cart and set the hamper onto the ground and then captured her waist, swinging her down.

"Enjoy, my lord!" called the valet and he clicked his tongue, causing the horse to start up.

"Did you know about this?" Dalinda asked.

"I confess I did. It was Anna's idea and I thought it a most excellent one. She said it was where she and Dez came together and wanted the same for us." His lips twitched in amusement. "Although she did have a gleam in her eyes."

She laughed. "Anna guessed that you have already bedded me."

"Oh, that?" he asked playfully, and pulled her to him. "That was my brief affair with Her Grace, a beautiful duchess I used to know. From now on, my only love affair will be with my captivating countess. I plan to make love to her daily for the entire length of our marriage."

Rhys kissed her, stirring desire within Dalinda. She broke away and playfully said, "Daily starts now, my lord."

She lifted her skirts and ran toward the cottage, throwing the door open and hurrying in. Inside, the cottage smelled of the freshly-cut roses sitting on the table.

Rhys arrived, slamming the door and dropping the hamper. He grabbed her by the waist, jerking her toward him for a searing kiss that branded her as his. She entwined her arms about his neck, pressing her body against his hard one, her breasts already full and aching for his touch.

He spun her around, bumping her against the door, his lips dragging along her cheek, his tongue flicking out to tickle the sensitive spot just below her ear. Dalinda sighed, her bones melting, as his lips nibbled their way to her neck. Her head fell to the side, allowing him better access as he nipped and licked her throat. She felt the dampness spring between her legs, now eager for his touch. Her fingers entangled in his thick hair, massaging his scalp.

"I cannot wait," he murmured against her neck.

"Don't," she told him.

Frantically, he unbuttoned his trousers. She helped push them down his hips. He grabbed her gown, bunching it up past her waist. His fingers found her, two slipping inside her.

"You are ready," he growled.

"I am always ready for you, my lord," she said huskily.

He thrust his cock into her and she moaned at the pleasure of having him within her, tightening around him, claiming it for herself. Holding her against the wall, he moved in and out frantically, their joining heated and wild, causing her to call his name loudly over and over, no worries of being overheard. They came at the same time, a high-pitched scream from her, a low groan from him.

Rhys rested his forehead against hers. "I'm sorry. I was like a rutting bull. I just had to have you." He kissed her hungrily. "I don't think I will ever be able to get enough of you, Dalinda. Never."

Her palms cupped his cheeks, the beginning of his stubble chafing them. "I feel the same, Rhys. I never knew it could be like this. I love you so much. It's incredible. And a little bit frightening, the intensity of my feelings toward you."

He kissed her softly. "In truth, it scares me, too, love. My feelings for you are incredibly fierce. Even out of control."

He stepped back and lowered her gown before yanking up his trousers. "Give me a few minutes and I will be randy again."

Sweeping her off her feet, he carried her into the bedchamber and placed her on the bed. Rhys removed her shoes and stockings, kissing her feet and ankles and sinking his teeth softly into her calves, causing desire to rush through her again. She helped him pull the layers over her head and he unlaced her corset. He placed everything neatly in the chair beside the bed and then quickly stripped himself.

Lying down beside her, he wrapped her in his arms. Her ear rested against his beating heart. Dalinda idly stroked his chest, playing with the dark hair there. His body was hard and muscled everywhere, so very different from her soft, pliant one. She felt in every way they were a perfect match.

Slowly, Rhys' hands began stroking her again. He took his time, caressing her breasts. His tongue teased her nipples, his teeth dragging across them, as she arched into him. He took one breast into his mouth, sucking hard, causing bolts of lightning to rocket through her. He kissed his way up and down her body, along every curve, and then came to her core. She shivered in anticipation, knowing the magic he could conjure there. His fingers parted her folds, slipping inside and stroking her deeply. Her breath was ragged as he brought her to her climax.

He didn't stop there. Not giving her any rest, he parted her legs wider and buried his head between them, his tongue delving into her, licking and sucking and causing another wild rush to sling her to the highest heights. Dalinda gradually floated back to earth, weak and spent, barely able to keep her eyes open.

"Oh, no, you don't, Countess," Rhys said, a wicked smile on his lips. "You have more work to do."

He lay down beside her and taking her waist, brought her over him, lifting her high and then placing her next to his cock.

"You'll like this, my love," he promised, easing her onto him, seating himself deep within her.

Dalinda gasped at how much of him she took inside her.

"I want you to ride me as you would Stormy," he ordered.

She grinned. "Yes, Colonel. I am yours to command."

She moved, the friction bringing a sweet sense of pleasure. Placing her hands on his shoulders to help anchor herself, she moved again, taking him in and out.

"Do you love the control?" he asked, his eyes dark with desire. "Setting the pace?"

"Yes!" she cried and she began to move with abandon.

She altered the pace, slowing down and then speeding up, loving his groans and the way she had absolute power over him. Finally, she quickened the pace again and kept it up, riding him as hard and fast as she would Stormy. The beautiful sensations built within her again and she reached her peak as Rhys did his. They both cried out, shouting triumphantly, and Dalinda collapsed atop him.

"I may not be able to move for a while," she told him.

His arms came around her, slowly stroking her bare back. "You are exactly where I want you, sweetheart. Go to sleep. You've worn us both out."

Dalinda closed her eyes, her cheek nestled against the soft fur on his chest. She drifted on a cloud of happiness until she tumbled into sleep.

When she awoke hours later, she was no longer atop him but rather spooned against him. She listened to the sound of his breathing as her thumb stroked his forearm, marveling that this incredible man was all hers. That there was no limit to their happiness.

Rhys awoke and made love to her again, slowly and tenderly. When they finished, he held her close.

"I know not every day can be spent in bed all day," he murmured, kissing her hair, "but I am glad this first one as husband and wife has been."

She glanced over her shoulder. "Perhaps we could dedicate one day a week to bed sport?" she teased.

"You always have the best ideas," her husband told her. "I have chosen wisely in wedding the most brilliant woman of the *ton*."

"Rhys? I must thank you for the lapel pins you gave my boys. You made them a part of our day and this marriage. I will never be able to tell you how much that means to me."

"They are my sons now in every way." He paused, his brows arching. "As for telling me how much it means to you?" A slow smile spread across his handsome face. "I would rather you show me, Countess. And take your time."

Dalinda did exactly that.

CHAPTER TWENTY-FOUR

"WAKE UP, SLEEPYHEAD," Rhys said. "I have our breakfast."

Dalinda stirred and opened her eyes. She saw her new husband carried a tray and pushed herself up, yawning sleepily.

He set down the tray and propped up the pillows. She snuggled against them and he sat on the bed next to her, bringing the tray up.

"Tea? You made tea?" she exclaimed.

"Yes. Dez explained to me what to do before we left yesterday. It seems while he and Anna were here that he learned how to do so."

She lifted a scone from the plate and sank her teeth into it. "I am so glad Cook sent along food for us. I would have hated for you to have to learn how to make scones."

He laughed heartily. "My talent is for eating scones, not baking them."

He plucked a strawberry from the plate and held it to her mouth. She bit into it, a bit of the juice running down her chin. Before she could wipe it away, he licked it.

"You smell like roses. You taste like strawberries." He glided a hand along her arm. "You feel like silk. I may need to make love to you again, Wife."

"Let me finish eating," she protested. "I am starving. Who knew love play could cause me to work up such an appetite?"

They finished their breakfast and then Rhys leisurely made love to her. She had become bolder in their lovemaking and enjoyed exploring his body, thrill shooting through her at the growls and moans he made when she did so. After they washed and dressed, they opened the door and found Coral waiting with the cart.

"Good morning, my lady, my lord," the valet called. "I hope you had an enjoyable time."

"Very much so," Rhys assured the servant. "So much that I am thinking of building a cottage for Lady Sheffington and me to retreat to upon occasion." He grinned shamelessly at her.

Coral drove them back to Torville Manor and Rhys asked him to alert the stables to have their carriages readied for departure. He lifted Dalinda from the bench and they entered the house. Meadows greeted them.

"Lady Torrington is in her sitting room. Lord Torrington is out on the estate with your children and Mr. Selleck," the butler informed them.

"Thank you, Meadows," Rhys said. "I will go and find Callow and Tandy and tell them we are ready to leave." He glanced down. "I'm sure Callow will find the need to retie my cravat for me."

"I'll visit with Anna a few minutes."

Rhys kissed her. As he started away, she pulled him back and kissed him a second time.

"Now, you may go," she said.

He left, chuckling as he did, and she went to see Anna. Her friend was seated at her writing desk and looked up when Dalinda entered.

Rising, Anna said, "How was your wedding night? Do come and sit."

They went to the settee and she said, "I will not be one to kiss and tell—other than to say it was divine."

Anna laughed. "I am so glad to hear that. Dez and I are very fond of Rhys. He seems to be the perfect man for you, Dalinda."

"I am delirious with happiness, Anna. Oh, I know I was lucky to have Gilford for several years but with Rhys? It's as if I have come alive and the world is more vibrant in every way."

Her friend nodded. "It's the same with Dez. Even though we had to wait years to finally be together, I feel each day is a magical adventure." She took Dalinda's hands in hers. "We are so blessed to call each other friend and now family. Our children are cousins and will grow up together. I couldn't ask for a better life."

Anna released Dalinda's hands and added, "I was so impressed with the way Rhys included Arthur and Harry into the ceremony yesterday. What a clever, sweet way to show the boys how much he cares for them."

"He truly does. He hasn't shied away from taking on the responsibility of fatherhood in the least."

"Did you know he was going to give them the tokens?"

She felt tears sting her eyes. "No. It was a surprise to me as much as it was to them. They are so proud of their lapel pins. Arthur even confided that he was happy that I wed Rhys."

"It's good that they have accepted him."

"I think they were lonely for an older male to look up to," she said. "They were close to their father until his heart attacks. Gilford hunted and fished with them. He got down on the floor and moved about toy soldiers in play. After the first one occurred, they still visited him and he read to them and played games with them. Once the second heart attack happened, however, he was confined to his chambers and not in a mood to see them much. They pined for his attention. I know Rhys will spend time with them and they will thrive under his guidance."

Rhys entered the sitting room. "Good morning, Anna. I must thank you and Dez for the loan of your lovely cottage. I only wish Dalinda and I could have spent more time there. I would have enjoyed walking around the lake again."

"Then the next time you visit us, I will make sure that happens," Anna promised.

Dalinda rose and Anna followed suit. "We must also thank you for allowing the boys to stay on."

"We had already planned for them to be at Torville Manor for two weeks. That isn't a problem. And Dez will bring them and Mr. Selleck back to you."

"I don't mind coming for them," Rhys said.

"No, Dez definitely wants to escort them so he can see the improvements you have made at Sheffield Park." Anna chuckled. "I think he wants a day of escape from Charlie exercising his lungs."

Dalinda laughed. "Harry did ask me if all babies were so loud. I happily informed him that he was louder than his brother and cousin at that age."

"Are you ready to go, my love?" Rhys asked.

"Yes."

"I'll walk you out," Anna offered. "I am only sorry that Dez isn't here to say goodbye to you."

"We will see him soon," she said.

They went out the front door and she only saw Rhys' carriage there. Before she could ask, he told her that he'd already sent Callow and Tandy on in her carriage.

Dalinda hugged Anna. "Thank you again for the lovely wedding and breakfast."

"It was my pleasure," her friend said.

"My thanks, as well, Anna." Rhys kissed her cheek. "Tell the boys we'll miss them."

"And give them our love," Dalinda added as Rhys helped her into the carriage.

The vehicle started toward home and he laced his fingers through hers. She watched out the window as Torrington lands passed by. She had spent a wonderful childhood here and was glad that she would be visiting the estate frequently in the future.

She turned to Rhys, who said, "We have a few hours ahead of us with nothing to do. What do you suggest to pass the time, Countess?"

Dalinda pretended to think a moment and then said, "I definitely think kissing should be an activity to consider."

He leaned in and kissed her softly. "Anything else?" he asked huskily.

"Touching. Definitely touching," she concluded.

"Kissing and touching. My, you are a clever woman, Countess."

His mouth seized hers.

Hours later as they pulled up to Sheffield Park, Dalinda said breathlessly, "Perhaps we should consider taking a long carriage ride once a week, my lord."

Rhys roared with laughter.

THE NEXT TWO weeks were busy ones for Dalinda and Rhys. Her husband threw himself into estate business, while she became even more familiar with the household. She liked that they both spent time with the various soldiers each day, as well. Dr. Robinson had proven to be knowledgeable and sympathetic with his patients and yet tolerated no nonsense, pushing them as they worked toward rehabilitating their bodies and minds. Miss Robinson and Mrs. Nathan were caring and patient as they supported the physician's treatments.

Dalinda had composed a list of various occupations in which the men might train to do, such as carpentry, bricklaying, or horse grooming. In some cases, it would simply mean finding a situation to place them in, such as becoming a chandler, a man who ran a neighborhood store.

They met now in Rhys' study before dinner and went over the names of the men who were physically well and in need of a position.

"Mr. Hensley has shown an interest in painting," she told her husband.

"Painting?" he asked, surprise in his voice. "As in landscapes or a still life?"

"No, silly. As in buildings, such as barns and stables. He only has the one arm now but he was left-handed to begin with and that has helped in his transition. He and Morrison repainted our stables over the past two days and Morrison said Hensley did an excellent job."

"Who else?" he asked.

"I think Mr. Davis would make for an excellent gardener. He has been working with ours, planting all those rose bushes that you have insisted must go in."

His sudden, seductive smile took her breath away. "Those rose bushes are for you, my darling girl. I want them to be throughout Sheffield Park as a reminder of you everywhere I go."

Dalinda's cheeks grew hot with his stare. "I see. That is very sweet."

"Not as sweet as tasting you." His eyes now darkened with passion.

She swallowed. "Let me finish first."

"And then?"

"And then you may have your way with me," she said primly.

Rhys chuckled. "Then by all means, go ahead."

She continued, mentioning how Finnerty wanted to be a costermonger and Brown longed to be a groom.

"Brown is blind," he pointed out.

"Yes, but he is very sensitive to the moods of our horses. I have watched him care for a horse. Feed and water it. Wash it. Groom it. Saddle it. I think he should remain with us, Rhys. He is already familiar with the layout of our stables and can make his way to and from there without assistance."

"It's up to you. You're as much a part of this project as I am," he insisted.

"Hayward and I have talked at length. He has a bit of wanderlust in him. He doesn't really want to settle down and stay in one place.

Because of that, he would like to be a packman."

"A traveling peddler? Hmm." Rhys rubbed his chin. "I can see that. Do you think he can focus enough to keep track of his stock? I know that lack of focus has been a recurring problem with Hayward."

"I believe so. We spoke of that at length. He doesn't mind some contact with others, which would certainly be a part of his business, but he prefers being outdoors. I thought we could help supply him with some stock to begin with. Most packmen carry goods women are interested in. Linens. Cottons. Silks, when they can get them."

Her husband nodded. "I believe we can help set Hayward up in this venture."

"Marvelous!" Dalinda declared.

A knock sounded at the door and Rhys bid them to enter.

"Dinner is served, my lord," the butler informed them.

"We'll be there shortly." Rhys rose and came to her, bringing Dalinda to her feet. "I suppose I will have to wait until after we eat to have my way with you, Countess."

"Well, we wouldn't want to keep Dr. Robinson and his daughter waiting, would we?"

He escorted her to the small dining room. The physician and Miss Robinson ate with them every night and had proven to be good company. Twice, though, Rhys had Cook send their dinner straight to his rooms so they could dine privately. The food had barely been touched—and they had feasted upon one another instead.

Their company was already present and Dalinda greeted the pair. Once the soup course arrived, Dr. Robinson said, "I think we are ready to take you up on the offer of a cottage, my lord."

"Are your rooms in the east wing unsatisfactory?" Rhys asked.

"Not at all," Miss Robinson said. "I miss cooking, though. I did most of it before we came to Sheffield Park. It would also give Father and me a place to go home to, to separate work from relaxing a bit."

"I can talk it over with Mr. Simpson and see what is available. I know you would prefer being closer to the main house and yet still maintain a bit of privacy," Rhys told them.

"That would be ideal," Dr. Robinson said. "I also wanted to broach the idea of a trip to London, my lord. With so many amputees returning from the war, there have been a few medical advances. Nothing for arms, of course, but some prosthetics are being made for men missing a leg, as Mr. Pimmel."

"Do you know of anyone we might speak to about these prosthetics?" Dalinda asked.

"I do. A man called James Potts has designed one which fits above the knee. It is composed of a wooden shank and socket, with a steel knee joint and a flexible foot controlled by catgut tendons from knee to ankle. Its articulation is superior to previous prosthetics and is supposedly more aesthetically pleasing."

"That is certainly intriguing, Dr. Robinson," Rhys said. "Write to this Mr. Potts for an appointment. Both Lady Sheffington and I would like to accompany you to it. It's a certainty General Shepherd will continue to send men to us with missing legs. Having knowledge of and purchasing these new prosthetics would be a godsend. The men could learn to walk again and become much more employable."

"I concur," the physician said. "I will write the letter of introduction and inquire when we might be able to visit with Mr. Potts. As for Pimmel, his attitude has been most positive despite my having to remove his limb. And Wharton, the man with the bullet in his thigh, is healing nicely. He'll be able to keep his leg and will soon leave his crutches behind."

"What about Garfield?" Dalinda asked, knowing the ex-soldier had no physical disabilities but was becoming increasing isolated from the other men, despite efforts to keep him involved with the others.

Dr. Robinson shook his head sadly. "Garfield is hard to reach. Physically, there is nothing wrong with him. It is his mind which has been damaged severely by the war. He sits and stares blankly for long periods of time. Chooses not to converse with most of the men. Rarely speaks to me or my daughter or Mrs. Nathan. I am beginning to think him a lost cause. Perhaps our next step might be to place him in a madhouse since he has no family to return to and no one else to care for him."

Dalinda went cold inside, knowing what Anna had suffered at Gollingham Asylum. Yet she didn't know what else could be done with Garfield. She didn't want him to be a danger to himself or anyone else at Sheffield Park.

"Let's try to work with him a bit longer before we take such an extreme measure," Rhys advised. He turned to her. "Has Garfield worked with the horses or in the gardens?"

"He came with us two days ago to the stables but didn't participate," she revealed. "Mr. Morrison did his best to persuade Garfield to take part but he was having none of it. He went and found an empty stall and sat alone in it the entire afternoon."

Rhys sighed. "Let's give him another week before we discuss committing him. I would hate to see it come to that."

Dalinda knew a madhouse wouldn't be the answer for Garfield's demons. Not with their harsh rules and punishments for violators. They were more a holding pen for lost souls than a place for a person to heal.

Still, she didn't have an answer for what to do with the angry, sullen veteran and prayed that, somehow, someone might be able to reach him.

Before it was too late.

CHAPTER TWENTY-FIVE

"M Y LADY, THE carriage has been spotted," Mr. Marsh said. Dalinda rose quickly and thanked the butler. "Where is Lord Sheffington?"

The butler smiled. "He is with Mr. Simpson. I will go inform him now that the little lords are home. I just thought you would wish to be the first to know."

"Has cook baked the biscuits I asked for? And the sticky buns?" she asked eagerly.

Marsh didn't try to hide his smile. "Yes, my lady. All preparations have been made for the boys' return. I will go find his lordship now."

She hurried out the door to wait on the front lawn. Moments later, Rhys joined her, slipping an arm about her waist.

"I don't know why this time is different," she told him. "They have been off longer at school before."

He pressed a kiss to her temple. "It's because this time they are coming home to *us*."

"You do really love them?" she asked.

"I most certainly do. Even when they are irascible or grumpy or naughty. Especially when they are naughty because you won't be pleased with them at all." He squeezed her waist. "It is fine, Dalinda. You have missed them. It is only natural. They have missed you, too."

"They'll be gone in another week back to school," she said glumly.

"But they will be with their friends. The duke and duchess will be in charge of and look out for them. Mr. Selleck and the other tutors, as well."

"They do love school now. And their friends. Edward. Peter. Drake. Samuel." She sighed. "At least we will have them for a few more days. I plan to spoil them some, you know."

"And well you should. We can also stay a day or two at Gillingham to make sure they are settled in once again," Rhys assured her. "The Gilfords won't mind, I'm sure."

"I am so fortunate to have Reid and Ashlyn watching over them."

The carriage pulled up and the footman placed the stairs down. Harry was the first to come racing from the vehicle, with Arthur not far behind. Harry hugged her tightly and she noticed Arthur did the same to Rhys, warming her heart. The boys switched and then they both started talking at the same time. She caught bits and pieces of what they said. Something about frogs and swimming and where they'd ridden and things they'd found while exploring the attics of Torville Manor.

"Slow down," Rhys said, laughing. "We can't take it all in."

Dez approached. "Being around these two has given me a good idea of what to expect when Charlie gets older."

Harry started telling Dalinda everything Charlie was doing and Arthur chimed in with the words they had tried to teach their young cousin.

"Charlie is a little young to be talking," she said.

"But he is sitting up by himself now," Arthur said. "He wasn't when we first arrived."

"And he gets up on all fours and just rocks and rocks," Harry added. "It's like he's a horse and the gate has been opened and he's not quite sure how to move through it yet."

"He'll learn," Rhys said. "And then Dez and Anna will have to watch Charlie like a hawk because he will be crawling and getting into everything."

She saw Mr. Selleck standing to the side and motioned him to join them.

"I trust the boys were well-behaved, Mr. Selleck?"

"Very much so, Lady Sheffington. Your brother even joined in on a few of our lessons."

"I wish I would have had a lively tutor like Mr. Selleck," Dez proclaimed. "Learning would have been far more entertaining if I had."

"Are you eager to return to Gillingham, Mr. Selleck?" Rhys asked. "I know school will be in session next week. I can send you back anytime you choose so you can have some time to yourself."

"I don't want to inconvenience you, my lord. If you don't mind, I think I will return when the boys do."

"Then take a few days off from your duties," Dalinda urged. "Ride when you wish. Go into the village for a pint. I'll make sure these two are occupied so that you might take some time for yourself."

"I think I will do that now," the tutor said. "A cold pint on a hot day sounds just the thing. If you'll excuse me."

"Can we go see the men?" Harry asked. "I want to see how they are doing. Mr. Pimmel, Mr. Brown, and Mr. Garfield, in particular. I'm friends with them."

"We can do that," Dalinda said. She looked to Dez. "Didn't you wish to ride about with Rhys and see what's been taking place at Sheffield Park?"

"I would like to," Dez replied. "Rhys?"

"Yes, I am free to take you around now." He took her hand and brought it to his lips, kissing her fingers. "We'll only be gone a couple of hours. Back in time for tea."

"Very well. I will see you then. Come along, boys."

She held out her hands and was glad when both Arthur and Harry took one. The last year, Arthur had been pulling away from her, claiming to be too old to show affection. It seemed at least for a little while he was back to his old self. They returned inside, both jabbering away at her. It made her realize how giving them the opportunity to spend time with Dez and Anna had been the right thing to do. She hoped it would become a tradition. Perhaps her twin's children would also come to visit their cousins here at Sheffield Park in the future. Hopefully by then, she and Rhys would have added to their family.

They went to the ballroom and Dalinda introduced her sons to Dr. Robinson, his daughter, and Mrs. Nathan, as well as another girl from the village who had been hired to help with the nursing of the men. Four more injured veterans had arrived in the past week and the boys accompanied Dr. Robinson as he went about the room tending to everyone present. The former soldiers seemed happy that Arthur and Harry had returned and they sat in a circle as the boys told them about the different activities they had participated in at Sheffield Park. Pimmel shared his news about the possibility of having a prosthetic made for his missing leg and that Dr. Robinson was going to London to consult someone about the possibility.

"You'll have to learn to walk again without your crutches," Arthur said. "If anyone can do it, it's you, Mr. Pimmel."

She glowed with pride at how well her children had adjusted to having so many wounded men around and how well the boys accepted these men, no matter what their physical appearances.

After an hour, they left the ballroom. Arthur was wanting to see some of the men already working on the estate. They went to the garden first and found Davis weeding. He greeted the boys enthusiastically and they spent a quarter-hour with him, catching up on his news and sharing their own. Next, they located Hensley, who was painting new chicken coops built by another soldier, and they did the same with him.

Finally, they headed toward the stables, where Brown was outside bathing Arthur's pony. The blind man tilted his head as she and the boys drew near.

"Is that Lord Harry and Lord Arthur come home?" he asked.

"How did you know?" Harry asked, a look of delight on his face as if Brown had performed a clever parlor trick.

"I can tell by your gait, Lord Harry. And Lord Arthur cleared his voice. I would know that sound anywhere." Brown paused. "Lady Sheffington is also with you, I suspect. Good morning, my lady."

"How did you know about Mama?" Arthur wanted to know. "She is light on her feet and didn't make a sound."

"Ah, she is, indeed, but your mother always smells of roses. I have learned since becoming blind that all my senses are magnified. I can hear and smell things better than I could before the shell exploded, robbing me of my sight."

"Do you like working in the stables?" Harry asked.

"I am in tune with the horses," Brown replied. "I think this is a good place for me. Lord Arthur's pony is getting his bath. Yours is next, Lord Harry."

"I want to go see him now," Harry said, dashing into the stables, Arthur in close pursuit.

"They are good lads, my lady. I know you are proud of them," Brown said.

"I am, Mr. Brown. I am also proud of you. You have met every challenge with purpose and fortitude. I hope you will remain at Sheffield Park for many years to come."

Dalinda saw Rhys and Dez approaching and waved to them. She waited for them to arrive and they dismounted, leading their horses into the stables. Harry was at his pony's stall. She stopped as Stormy stuck her head out and affectionately petted her horse.

Then she heard Harry cry out, "Mr. Garfield, what are you doing in there all alone?"

She turned and saw Harry begin to step forward. Dalinda knew Garfield had been spending most of his days in an empty stall in the stables, sitting morosely in a corner, sullen and uncommunicative. Fear seized her.

"Harry, come here!" she said sharply.

But her son had already moved inside toward the former soldier.

Dalinda dashed to the stall—and saw Garfield's arm banded about Harry's chest as the man held a knife to her boy's throat.

"Please," she begged, tears blinding her. "Don't hurt him."

"The war will hurt him," Garfield growled. "It hurt me. Better he die now and not have to suffer like I do every day."

Rhys joined her. "Put down the knife, Mr. Garfield. Let Harry go."

The soldier clutched Harry more tightly. The hand holding the knife shook. Harry's eyes were wide with fear.

"Why? I'm doing the little man a favor. He won't have to know pain and fear. War and blood and death. He can die now, happy, never having seen how ugly life is."

"This war won't last forever," Rhys said firmly. "It could be over tomorrow. And then what? You will have killed a child—a boy who has befriended you during your pain and loneliness. Harry is a sweet soul. He wants to captain a ship someday. Who is to say that he won't do this? You could join him, Mr. Garfield. Be one of his crew. Sail the Seven Seas and find adventure together.

"But none of that can happen if you don't release the boy. Now. Give Harry a chance to grow to manhood. Let him become who he is meant to be. Give yourself a chance, Garfield. To put the war behind you and live the life you were meant to live."

Garfield's jaw fell open. He dropped the knife. His hold relaxed and he collapsed to the ground, sobbing. Instead of running away, Harry patted the man's shoulder.

"It's all right, Mr. Garfield. You didn't mean it. You'll be fine."

Harry looked up at his mother and quickly closed the distance between them. Dalinda threw her arms about her son, tears streaming down her face. Arthur joined them, hugging them both. Rhys protectively wrapped his arms about the three of them as Dez and a groom rushed into the stall.

"You saved my son. *Our* son. Your words made the difference. You convinced him, Rhys. Harry wouldn't be alive if not for you."

He kissed her brow. "You have raised two wonderful boys, my love."

"What do you want done with him, Rhys?" Dez asked, his face dark with anger.

Harry pulled away as Dez and the groom lifted a weeping Garfield to his feet. "You have to help him!" he exclaimed. "He didn't really want to hurt me. Mr. Garfield is hurt, just like Mr. Pimmel and Mr. Brown. He's hurt inside where we can't see it. We need to help him, Rhys. Please."

Rhys looked at her. "You have raised two remarkable boys, my love. I don't know any man who would have the empathy to fight for someone who had just tried to take his life."

Harry ran to Garfield. "It's all right. I won't let them harm you, Sir. You're sick, that's all. We're going to help you get better. Aren't we, Mama?" he asked, pleading with her.

She wanted to claw the man's eyes out. See him strung up for even touching her baby. But she also knew if Garfield were arrested and punished, something inside Harry would die. Something good and true and wonderful that made her boy so unique.

Dalinda uttered the hardest words that had ever come from her. "Yes, Harry. We will help Mr. Garfield become whole again." She met Rhys' gaze and he nodded.

Harry nudged Dez aside. "I will help Mr. Garfield return to the house."

Her lovely boy placed an arm about the soldier's waist. "Come on, Mr. Garfield. Let's go talk to Dr. Robinson. He's a very good man. He's going to help you. And we'll keep on helping you. Me. Arthur. Mama and Rhys. All of the men who have come to Sheffield Park."

Arthur rushed over and went to Garfield's other side, also putting his arm about the man, and the boys led him from the stall and out of the stables. Dalinda marveled at the compassion and bravery her youngest child had shown and how her older one had also joined in.

"I may never be prouder of them than I am at this moment," she told Rhys.

He slipped an arm about her. "They are good boys who just took a giant leap toward manhood." He pressed a kiss to her brow. "Come. Let's go help Mr. Garfield."

Gratitude filled Dalinda. For this man who stood by her side and the sons she had birthed. She hoped the children she would have with Rhys would be just as kind and full of courage as Harry and Arthur were.

EPILOGUE

Three years later . . .

"THANK YOU AGAIN for taking the boys off our hands, Dez," Rhys said, juggling the twins in his arms. "They look forward to coming to Torville Manor each summer."

"Anna and I love having them. I only wish the two of you could accompany us this time."

Dalinda placed her hands on her swollen belly and rubbed it. She felt a kick as she did so, one stronger than ever before.

"As you can see, Brother, I am slightly tied up." She stroked her belly again. "Hopefully, early next week this will all be over."

The carriage pulled up. "I suppose this is goodbye. Send word once the baby comes." Dez kissed her cheek.

"Thank you again for coming to escort the boys," Rhys said. "I did not wish to leave Dalinda when she is so close to delivering."

She watched as Garfield shook hands with first Arthur and then Harry. The man had remained at Sheffield Park and, with time and patience, he had slowly acclimated back into life. He worked as a groom in their ever-growing stables, the horse breeding farm a large part of life at their country estate. Garfield proved immensely loyal to Harry and Dalinda knew if danger ever threatened Harry, Garfield would lay down his life for his young friend.

Arthur and Harry told Garfield goodbye and then came toward her. Harry ran over and patted her belly.

"Let's hope you're a boy," he whispered. "We've put up with girls for almost two years."

Arthur leaned down and nestled his cheek against her stomach. His eyes lit up. "Did you feel that, Mama?"

"I did," she assured him. She hugged them both and said, "Be good for your aunt and uncle."

"We will," Arthur promised as he climbed into the carriage, Harry following. Dez gave them a final wave and entered the vehicle and it started up.

She waved and urged the girls to tell their brothers goodbye. One twin did as she asked, waving with one chubby arm and sucking the thumb on her free hand. The other buried her head against Rhys' chest.

They slowly walked back toward the house, her husband matching her snail's pace. She turned a final time, watching the carriage as it drove away, down the lane lined with rose bushes that Rhys had planted in her honor. She entered the house behind her husband. Rhys set the girls down and they toddled toward Nanny.

"It's time for your naps, my little ladies," Nanny said, taking each girl by the hand and leading them up the stairs.

Rhys slipped an arm about Dalinda. "Is it time for your nap, my love?"

She had been very tired the last two weeks as the time for the birth of their child approached. Rhys had encouraged her to lie down each afternoon when the twins did. The thought of climbing so many stairs, though, seemed beyond her as a weariness settled over her. Suddenly, she felt the warm, familiar trickle.

"Rhys?"

He kissed her temple. "Yes, sweetheart."

"My water. It's—"

A huge swoosh sounded and water covered her skirts and the foyer.

"Marsh!" Rhys roared.

The butler appeared at once. "I'll summon the midwife and let Mrs. Marsh know to put on the water to boil." He hurried away.

Her husband swept her off her feet, despite her protests, and raced up the stairs with her. Her previous labor had been much longer, most likely because she had delivered twins. She wasn't nearly so large this time and hoped it would only be one baby coming instead of two.

Rhys carried her to her bedchamber. The last time she had been in this bed was to deliver her girls. The rest of her nights had been spent with her handsome husband.

The midwife entered the room. Rhys had insisted the woman stay in a bedchamber down the hall for the past week so that she would be nearby when Dalinda's labor began.

"I'll see to the countess, my lord," the midwife said. "Come back in a few minutes."

Rhys had remained with her throughout her labor and delivery two years ago. Though that had been unusual, he had insisted and refused to leave her. He'd butted heads with the midwife over this— and won.

Mrs. Marsh came into the room and she helped remove Dalinda's shoes and stockings and then her clothing, which was soaked. Once she had a clean chemise slipped over her head, the women led her to the bed. Mrs. Marsh turned the bedclothes back and Dalinda eased onto the bed.

After the midwife checked her progress, she told Mrs. Marsh that his lordship could be summoned. Rhys flew to her side, kneeling beside her.

"How do you feel?"

"The pains are beginning," she told him. "They aren't terrible just yet."

He slipped into the bed beside her, putting his arm around her and taking her hand. "I will not leave you. We are in this together."

"Do you hope it is a boy this time?" she asked softly, knowing he needed an heir from her.

Her husband kissed her brow tenderly. "We have two girls and two boys. I merely want a healthy baby. Son or daughter, this child will be loved. As will the one following it and however many we are blessed with."

Dalinda blinked back her tears, loving how Rhys thought of Arthur and Harry as his. As theirs. The bond between them had grown strong over time. She knew her sons would never forget their father but they had asked Rhys and Dalinda if it was all right to call him *Papa*. Rhys admitted to her later that it was one of the happiest moments of his life.

A pain struck her, hard and strong, and she gasped. Soon, her entire body was drenched in sweat. Her husband bathed her face with a cool, wet cloth, murmuring soothing words, encouraging her.

The midwife checked again. "I see the crown, my lady. It's time to push."

"Good," she said through gritted teeth. The urge had been strong for the last several minutes and she had fought against it until now.

"Bear down hard, my lady," the midwife said.

Dalinda locked her jaw and pushed as hard as she could.

"That's right. Keep it up. Wait. Wait. All right. Again!"

After several minutes of effort, she heard, "The head is through. Wait a moment." The midwife bent and then rose. "I've helped the shoulders come through. Push again. Keep doing what you're doing, my lady."

Rhys kissed her hair. "You are a true champion, my love. Just a little more."

She groaned and bore down again, a scream erupting from her. She felt the pressure build and build and then her body shudder, the babe passing from her into the world.

"Ah, it's a boy," the midwife said, cutting the cord and then thumping the baby's back.

A loud wail erupted.

Dalinda fell back against the pillows, breathing heavily. Rhys kissed her fingers.

"You did it, my love. We have another boy. Viscount Raleigh."

Mrs. Marsh took the infant. "I'll see him cleaned up."

"Give us a few minutes, my lord," the midwife said.

Rhys knew that Dalinda still needed to expel the afterbirth. He kissed her gently and said, "I will go and tell the girls they have a brother. I'll be back soon."

He kissed her fingers again and she brushed her lips against his hand. "I love you."

"I love you even more," he replied.

He left her bedchamber and wandered up to the nursery. Nanny was rocking in her chair while the girls sat on the floor, playing with blocks. He sat with them and began adding to the tower they built.

"You have a baby brother," he told them, knowing they didn't quite understand what had gone on during the last few months, with Dalinda not being able to lift or carry them. "Your mama is fine and you can see her and your baby brother tomorrow."

Rhys stayed a few more minutes and then rose.

"Congratulations, my lord," Nanny said.

"We'll have to get you some help," he told the servant. "The girls are already active. Throw a baby into the mix and you'll definitely need someone else on duty with you."

"Lady Sheffington has already hired someone, my lord," Nanny said.

He chuckled. "Of course, she has."

Leaving, he took a last look at the twins, love bursting within him. Having had no family for so many years and then seeing his grow in such a short time was like a dream come true. Not only did he now have five children, but Rhys had many friends beyond Dez and Anna.

He and Dalinda had grown very close to Reid and Ashlyn, who in turn had introduced them to their friends, Burke and Gemma, the Earl and Countess of Weston, and Gray and Charlotte, the Earl and Countess of Crampton. Both earls had also been officers in the Peninsular War, giving him something in common with them.

What all five of the men shared most of all was an unmatched love for their strong, spirited wives, as well as for the children resulting from their marriages. Rhys felt blessed a thousandfold having Dalinda as his countess, his lover, his best friend and confidante, as well as their children and all these new friends.

He returned to her rooms and found her wearing a sedate night rail, her luxurious brown hair now brushed to a sheen and falling about her shoulders. In her arms, she held their baby.

Rhys nodded and the midwife and Mrs. Marsh slipped from the room. He went to the bed and climbed in next to his beloved wife and newborn son, placing his hand on the baby's head, his thumb gently rubbing the soft skin.

"Isn't he perfect?" Dalinda asked, glancing up at him, her eyes shining with love.

"He is—and you are, too, my love." Rhys kissed her, love for this woman filling him.

"I am the luckiest man in the world, Dalinda. I am a soldier who found his soulmate. My life is complete."

Dalinda's palm cupped his cheek. "I think the best is yet to come."

THE END

About the Author

Award-winning and international bestselling author Alexa Aston's historical romances use history as a backdrop to place her characters in extraordinary circumstances, where their intense desire for one another grows into the treasured gift of love.

She is the author of Medieval and Regency romance, including *The Knights of Honor*, *The King's Cousins*, *The St Clairs*, and *The de Wolfes of Esterley Castle*.

A native Texan, Alexa lives with her husband in a Dallas suburb, where she eats her fair share of dark chocolate and plots out stories while she walks every morning. She enjoys reading, Netflix binge-watching, and can't get enough of *Survivor*, *The Crown*, or *Game of Thrones*.

Made in the USA
Middletown, DE
15 October 2021